Everything Love Is

Claire King

BLOOMSBURY

LONDON · OXFORD · NEW YORK · NEW DELHI · SYDNEY

Bloomsbury Paperbacks
An imprint of Bloomsbury Publishing Plc

50 Bedford Square
London
WC1B 3DP
UK

1385 Broadway
New York
NY 10018
USA

www.bloomsbury.com

BLOOMSBURY and the Diana logo are trademarks of Bloomsbury Publishing Plc

First published in Great Britain 2016
This paperback edition first published in 2017

© by Claire King, 2016

Illustrations by James McCallum, www.jamesmccallum.co.uk

Claire King has asserted her right under the Copyright, Designs and
Patents Act, 1988, to be identified as Author of this work.

British Library Cataloguing-in-Publication Data
A catalogue record for this book is available from the British Library.

ISBN: HB: 978-1-4088-6842-3
TPB: 978-1-4088-6843-0
PB: 978-1-4088-6845-4
ePub: 978-1-4088-6844-7

2 4 6 8 10 9 7 5 3 1

Typeset by Integra Software Services Pvt. Ltd.
Printed and bound in Great Britain by CPI Group (UK) Ltd, Croydon CR0 4YY

To find out more about our authors and books visit www.bloomsbury.com.
Here you will find extracts, author interviews, details of forthcoming
events and the option to sign up for our newsletters.

For Charlie,
for everything.

It was May, 1968 and there was a woman on a train. She was slight, seated by the window and wearing black, her feet bare against the dirt of the carriage floor. Above her on the rack was a violin case and a green woollen coat, although the weather was scorching. The windows of the train were open, a pale wind gusting into the carriage and through the dark hair that fell loose around her shoulders. The woman's belly filled the hot damp air between herself and the seat in front of her and she had to lean back, her legs parted, her hips forward in the seat, in order to accommodate her body in the space. She pressed her sweat-beaded forehead against the window and stared out across the springtime fields, fecund with sunflowers and barley.

The pink city walls ought to have been close by now, and yet the countryside was unrelenting. The vast blue skies softened down to a distant apricot horizon. She should have arrived in

Toulouse mid-afternoon, but already the sun was setting. The conductor had passed through the carriage several times, and each time the news had not been good. She hadn't understood the exchanges, but other passengers had shaken their heads, looked at wristwatches, thrown up their hands. What would she do if she was too late? Would there still be someone there to meet her? Would she even get there at all? We have always assumed she was expected, although no one ever reported her as missing.

The train slowed, and the man next to her rose to his feet and began to gather his belongings. Her eyes scanned the platform running up alongside them, the single, small stone building surrounded by scrub grass. 'Toulouse?' she asked him, pointing at her forearm, where the word was spelled out in blue ink.

Later the police would ask passengers to place her accent and they would recall only the sibilance of her 'S's, the way her words seemed round and throaty, but nothing of more use than that. Her voice would already have receded too far.

In my experience it doesn't matter how long you've known someone or how intimate the things they've whispered in your ear, no matter what memories you are left with, when they leave their voice goes with them. Even in dreams their words have no form. Now I don't recall if there was anything extraordinary about how she spoke, only the coastal sound of her breathing when she slept.

I can still usually place a face, describe what makes it unique, but for most of us catching the timbre of a voice is like trying to catch rain in a cup. Still, people were keen to offer other useless details, like the sour smell in the carriage as they waited for hours in the thick air between stations, or the way they had to lift their feet from the pooling blood.

The man shook his head. 'Another twenty minutes,' he replied. But the woman's face was blank. He held up his fists to her, flashed out his fingers, made fists again, then spread them once more. 'Twenty,' he said again. Louder this time. People turned to stare.

'Twenty,' the woman repeated. She couldn't have been sure she'd make it. A storm was rising deep within her; clouds like knuckles, twisting and tightening. The pressure of her own body bearing in on itself. The baby was coming. Twenty minutes. She braced herself against the back of the empty seat before her and closed her eyes.

'Are you alone?'

She opened her eyes to find the man was gone. An older woman from across the carriage had moved over to the vacant seat, and was asking a question. The train was pulling out of the station. The younger woman stared back at her through dark, feral eyes as a cool hand was pressed to her head. As the train picked up speed she slid one protective hand back on to her belly.

'How many months?' the older one asked.

The young woman shook her head. Tears cascaded over her flushed cheeks. The older woman wiped them away with the backs of her fingers then held up her two hands, less one thumb. Nine fingers. She pointed to her belly. The young woman brushed dark fringes from her eyes. There seemed to be a battle going on inside her, but it looked as though she'd understood. Reluctantly she lifted her hand from the seat back and showed her three fingers.

The older woman waited an instant, then shook her head, no. That wasn't right. She mimed the roundness of her belly, imitated rocking an infant in her arms. The young woman watched her, then looked down again at her own pregnant body. She pinched the bridge of her nose and screwed up her face as if trying to concentrate all her effort on that one part of her body, then held up her hand once more. All five fingers. She closed it again. Then showed three fingers, plus one more, bent at the knuckle. The older woman grasped the hand and pressed her fingertips into the pulse. Her lips twitched. Then the younger woman twisted away and grabbed the woman's hand back, wrenching the bones together.

The older woman didn't flinch. 'I can help you,' she said, enunciating carefully. 'I'm a midwife.' The other woman looked up with obscured eyes and lowered brows, and then, slowly, she nodded, removed her right hand from her belly and held it palm upwards, outstretched.

The midwife looked at her. The woman didn't look like a beggar. She was well dressed, clean. She shook her head. 'I mean I can help you with—'

'Say me!' the woman urged. Her index finger trembled along the groove on the palm of her hand, right to left, tracing her life line, dark with dust blown in through the carriage window.

Instead the midwife took her hand again, firmly. She shook her head. 'I help women deliver their babies.' She spoke slowly and clearly, but there was no recognition in the young woman's eyes, only panic. '*Children*,' the midwife tried, '*niños.*' But it was too late for translations. Suddenly, in a single, brutal cry, the young woman's breath was carried out of her. Her chin extended, her neck thrust forwards as though someone were ripping strings of vowels from her throat.

She gripped the older woman's hand once more. 'What happens?' she gasped.

The midwife was still talking, softly, urgently, but the younger woman did not answer, could not answer because the carriage full of people was blurring away. She was already in a tunnel, the clickety-clack of the train carrying her through. She was waiting for the light. There were voices, they were getting louder and yet more and more distant. Then there were hands at her knees, pulling them apart, and fingers inside her. The fingers were pushing hard, but the woman could not open her eyes, she was given over to the agony. She felt hands lifting her, many hands. She was being moved, shifted, but the pain, the pain. And then she couldn't bear it any longer and she began to bear down, her face contorted with effort. She leant on herself, pushing and straining. Outside her a voice was shouting, '*Non! Non!*' But she was in a tunnel and the train was rocking and the hands were pressing and pulling and the voices only bellowed meaningless words in her ear. Then the wind found her. They said you could see it pass over her, from her feet up over her body until her face finally stilled and she became nothing but a memory.

It was May, 1968. On a train half way between stations, a woman in a black dress lay on the carriage floor in an animal slick of blood and fluid and the silence of the moment was broken by the first cry of an orphan, held in the arms of a stranger and wrapped in a green springtime coat.

The midwife, the stranger who was holding this baby, who was sucking out fluid from his nose and spitting it to the floor, would soon become his new mother. She had delivered many babies, but never her own. She had prayed for it since the day she married, but in twenty-three years God had not granted her a child. The doctors had told her it was impossible, that for her it was not meant to be. But now, as she held this baby boy, still bound to a dead woman by a thick blue cord, she saw it all as clear as day. She felt jubilation wash over her, the presence of her God, and she whispered, 'Thank you.' Words that she would look back on with shame in the years to come. Not the gratitude itself, but how it rose from her heart before the poor mother was even gone cold.

Amandine Rousseau's shoes were as green as a springtime coat. I told myself it meant nothing, but how many people do you know that wear green shoes?

It was early September. The sun sloped hot over the planes and cypresses along the left bank. There was barely a breeze, but what little there was bore with it the first tumbling of yellow-edged leaves. I heard them settling softly upon the boat as I woke. We hadn't had a cold day since May, so I should have realised then that change was in the air. The trees always have their reasons. They knew the wind was coming. I can still picture the distinctive yellow light that spilled across my pillow that morning and how, lying in its warmth, it took me a while to surface from the tugging tide of sleep where Candice rose and fell with the swell. I have dreamed of the sea for as long as I can remember, long before Candice. Perhaps it's an echo, I will never know.

I was playing the piano when she arrived. As soon as I heard the footsteps through the open windows, I knew it must be her. Most people walking on the towpath move with purpose and rhythm, even if they are just out walking a dog. But my clients' footsteps were always hesitant the first time, and Amandine was no exception, despite the impression she tried to give. It takes courage to expose the most vulnerable part of yourself to someone. I always tried to make that first meeting as easy as I could.

She came to a stop a few metres from Candice. I stood, closed the piano lid and put away my music. Then the bell chimed out and I climbed up into the wheelhouse to greet her. She was far enough back from the door that I could see all of her through the glass pane, head to toe, straight-backed and impeccably dressed. Her shoes were bright green. As I opened the door she stepped forward, offering me a slender hand and a broad smile.

'Amandine Rousseau,' she said.

She wore a silver ring on her thumb, and none on her long fingers. Her eyes were wide and her face looked younger than her pale hair suggested. Something about her made me think of the unbroken surface of a lake. Her hand fit within mine like a child's.

Once invited in she moved through the wheelhouse as though through water, glancing around as she went. Her eyes fell first upon my dining table, big enough for four but laid for one. Then on to Candice's golden wood and rounded edges, the pilot's wheel like a web strung out below the window, the varnish worn from its handles a reminder that she has been on adventures I will never know. Candice and I had never travelled together, but I would often stand at the wheel, looking downstream and wondering. It can be enough to know that you could slip your moorings should you wish.

I led the way, backwards down the steps into the sitting room, motioning for her to take a seat, and following her eyes as she considered the options: the Voltaire in velvet stripes, the worn couch in leather the colour of dark chocolate, the gilt-edged Louis XV chair in faded violet plush, with books piled up precariously on either side. The folding wooden chair by my writing desk and then the piano stool, pushed under the upright. She chose the Louis XV, sitting neatly with crossed legs, straightening her skirt and regarding me directly. Her skin was pale, almost translucent, but her cheeks were bright with colour. I was convinced that I had met this woman before. Something in the cheekbones? Her mouth? A thrill of anticipation washed over me, like the excitement that comes with the first ink on a fresh score sheet, the beginnings of a new composition. What was it that she stirred in me? I grasped at a memory just beyond reach, but there is only so long that you can look at someone's face without appearing to stare and after a few seconds I was forced to look away without an answer. I should have looked harder.

My clients usually chose the shabby comfort of the leather couch on the starboard side, its back against the towpath giving whoever sat there a view out over the water. Unhappy people in particular seem drawn to the water. Typically I would take the Voltaire opposite but now it was too close to where Amandine was sitting, so I tried to arrange myself as professionally as possible on the couch. The problem was my height. The low couch is fine for stretching out on at night but if I sit normally it collapses me down, folds me in three.

I settled on a compromise, sitting sideways, leaning against the armrest, with my legs stretched out into the room. She must have sensed my discomfort but Amandine said nothing. Instead she dropped her eyes to the knotted floorboards, where that same yellow light fell across the dark varnish, and over my bare feet which rested a short distance from her own, small, neat and still wearing the vibrant green shoes so discordant with her otherwise neutral appearance.

I tried not to think of violins. Of a train between stations. Of a woman … Amandine glanced up and caught my eye. 'I'm sorry,' her voice was as fine as mist, 'should I take my shoes off?'

'However you'd be most comfortable,' I told her.

She brought her hands together in her lap, lifted her chin and regarded me with calm, appraising eyes the colour of lichen. With the sun reflecting off the water behind her, making her hair glow like pearl, the first silence bloomed in the space between our bodies. I waited as always for my client to break it, but Amandine seemed perfectly at ease, letting the silence settle until the absence of our voices was less noticeable than the creak of Candice on her mooring and the distant bark of dogs. She relaxed back against the violet chair-back, re-crossing her legs and folding her fingers together.

'It's very quiet here,' she said.

'Yes.'

'Doesn't it drive you mad?' I smiled at the question, and after a moment so did she. 'No, well,' she said, 'I guess you prefer it that way. I have to say I'm more of a city person, but I didn't mean to be rude.'

'Not at all. Newcomers often find Candice unsettling to begin with, but most grow to love her in the end. What are your first impressions?'

'I've never been on a houseboat before. Strange, really, after so many years in Toulouse.' Amandine looked out along the towpath thoughtfully. In the galley, the cafetière hissed on the stove. I had forgotten to offer her coffee.

I rose awkwardly. 'So,' I said.

'Yes,' she said, 'indeed.' Amandine looked up at me warily. 'So. Well, I can see why you're so fond of her.'

That was quite an assumption. 'Is that so obvious?'

She ran a fingertip along the curve of her lower lip. 'You're kindred spirits,' she said.

Taken aback by her assertion, I just stood there for a moment, caught in her gaze. Had she answered my question, or avoided it completely? Amandine leaned forward slightly and closed her eyes in concentration. 'I'm surprised you can't feel the movement of the water more.' Two more breaths, as if to confirm the stillness of the boat, and she looked up again, scanning the cabin, the small galley kitchen, the piano, my various belongings, the corridor down to the bedrooms and bathrooms. 'And I hadn't imagined a boat would have so much room,' she said.

'That all depends on the size of the boat,' I told her, placing the coffees between us. 'And of course what you want to keep on it.'

Amandine looked at her watch. 'I'm afraid I have to leave in about half an hour.'

'We can work with that,' I said.

She looked at me oddly. Again I felt the curious familiarity. 'Well then,' she said. 'I'm told you make people happy? That's quite a claim.'

'That's not really how it works,' I said. 'As I tell all my clients, I don't believe anyone else can make you happy. But sometimes you can be helped to find your own way there.'

She nodded. 'So to help others presumably you must already be happy yourself? What's your secret?'

Amandine was steering the conversation. I shifted on the couch, trying to raise myself to her eye level. 'It's important I keep my personal feelings distinct from my work,' I said.

'I can see why. I imagine misery could be contagious if you let it.'

Misery? 'Well, not everyone is so unhappy. There are plenty of people who are just fine, but they're looking for better than that. They don't think "fine" is enough.' I caught her eye, hoping to see a flicker of recognition, and followed a hunch. 'What do you think?'

Amandine gave a slow, crooked smile and took a sip of her coffee. 'Oh, I think fine can be more than enough, considering the alternatives.' Her eyes held mine. 'But happy is better. So are you happy, or not?'

I had everything I needed back then. The peace of the water, Candice, work I loved. Blessings spilling over. At the time I was wary of her question but now I'm glad she asked it. It is a folded corner on a page, a reminder of who I was. 'I am happy,' I said, and it was true. Amandine looked satisfied with my answer. 'And what about you?' I said.

She looked at me then for a long while, her expression inscrutable. When finally she replied, she spoke quietly, as though she expected the wind to carry her words. 'I'm fine,' she said.

Despite what I told her, by the time most people came to me they were already in despair. People leave this kind of thing so late, until it has got out of hand and become overwhelming. Amandine was different. She didn't look lost. She didn't look like someone searching for something. Why, then, had she come? It was altogether puzzling. 'And are you hoping to improve on fine?' I said.

Amandine looked amused. 'Are you going to try and cure me?'

I took a deep breath. 'We're just talking,' I said.

'Hmm.' She looked down at the ball of her thumb then raised it to her mouth, the sun flashing on the silver ring as she bit gently into the skin. 'So how long have you been a therapist?'

'Years. It's all I've ever done.'

'Don't you find it hard, spending your whole life thinking about other people's happiness?' she said. 'I don't think I could do that.'

'Plenty of people do it and don't get paid for it. At least I can expect to be paid at the end, assuming my clients are satisfied.'

'That's quite a guarantee. Has anyone ever refused to pay?'

I shook my head. 'We all want to be happy, whether we do anything about it or not. To be here means you have already taken a first step. After that it's just a matter of time.' Amandine was still distracted, frowning down at her thumb, worrying it with the nail of her ring finger. 'What is it?' I asked.

'Sorry, it's just a splinter. It's only tiny, but I'm left-handed and I can't get the thing out.'

'Here, let me?'

'With pleasure.' Amandine smiled and held her left hand forwards, her palm open. Life line, I thought, love line, heart line, head line. Something jumped in my chest. I blinked. 'Let me get the tweezers.'

I pinched the skin below the dark speck, my fingers too large and fumbling. The splinter was deeply embedded. 'Tell me if it hurts.'

'I'm a doctor,' she said. 'I'm not squeamish.'

'And you say my job is hard?' I looked up at her again, changed in my eyes already, the way people do as we come to know more about them. 'What kind of doctor?'

'A generalist.'

I reached for my glasses. 'It's tiny.'

'It still hurts.'

'I'm sure,' I said. 'The tiniest splinters can be the worst.' At last I had found purchase on the sliver of wood and eased it out. 'There.' I rubbed the ball of my thumb gently over the place where it had been. 'Is it all gone?'

'Thank you.' Amandine sat back and pushed away the hair that had fallen in front of her eyes, tucking it behind her ears. 'I'm sorry,' she said. 'I must come across as quite cynical about what you do, and I'm not, honestly. It's just that the world these days is greedy for happiness, yet people only make themselves miserable by chasing it. And we say that all we really want is for our children to be happy, which is true enough' – she threw open her hands – 'but how can a parent show their child the way if they're lost themselves?' I watched as she scanned the cabin again, the patchwork of furniture, the scant belongings. 'You don't have children,' she said.

'No.'

'Never wanted them, or never met the right person?'

'Amandine,' I said, ready to turn back the conversation, to insist we kept the focus on her, but then I realised the question was probably more about her than me. 'It's not something I've gone looking for, and it's never found me,' I said. 'How about you?'

Amandine nodded and drank the remains of her coffee. 'You're not one to do the chasing. You'd rather wait for things to come to you?'

'As you said, we only make ourselves miserable when we're too greedy.' I took my place back on the couch, moving the notebook and pencil I had left there on to the old chest between us, which doubled as a coffee table. The pencil rolled slowly towards her. Before it reached the edge she stopped it with a finger and picked it up. 'So I don't listen to what others tell me would make me happy, I trust myself to know. But what about you, Amandine? What are you looking for?'

Her eyes dropped as she turned the pencil in her hands. I let my gaze drift out to the sunlit canal, where a flotilla of young mallards glided by. Who had sent this woman to me, I wondered. Candice gave the slightest of shrugs, just the wash of a boat but perfectly timed. I smiled and looked up again to find myself meeting Amandine's eyes directly. Cool and considered, her face tilted, her gaze intense. 'Well, Baptiste, what I want is something that makes me feel alive. Joy, passion, despair, something to remember or something to regret. I want to have my breath taken away, or knocked out of me altogether. Perhaps after all this time what I really want,' she said, 'is to fall in love.'

I kept my expression neutral, but it belied my disappointment in her. She had seemed so much more considered than that. 'Do you think love will make you happy?' I asked.

Amandine gave a wry smile. 'What's that got to do with anything?'

After she left I took my notebook and placed it beside me at the piano. The perfect, altered state of consciousness that comes when playing music I know by heart would always leave my mind clear to reflect on a session. A space for ideas to grow. Beethoven, Satie, Bach. As I played I would let the thoughts come, let them form and spin and settle until eventually I would know what was important and stop playing to make notes that roamed untamed across the page, blossoming into doodles and back again to words. But that morning I played on and on. Bach. Only Bach. You can't argue with the logic of Bach, the musical antidote to the perplexing thirty minutes I had just spent with Amandine Rousseau, a woman who had come to me looking for happiness yet was reticent to discuss why, and who had left declaring she was looking for love. What clues had she given me? What was I missing? Nothing was coming to me. And this is how it started.

Nobody ever starts at the beginning. It wouldn't make sense. Instead we start with what matters most to us at the time, or what we think matters to whoever is listening.

You walked up and down the room as you spoke, the boards creaking under your feet. You trailed your long fingers over the piano lid and over the contrasting fabrics of each of the chairs. When you reached the end of your story you paused for a moment and then turned down the corridor, opening and closing doors to bedrooms and bathrooms as you went, as though you were looking for something misplaced. I waited for you by the galley.

'Come outside,' you said when you returned, reaching for my hand. I let you lead me up and out into the chill morning air, over the icy gangplank and along the frosted towpath to the water's edge. 'Here,' you said.

I crouched beside you on the bank, my heart pounding as we stared down at the water, terrified that you would lose your balance and not know how to swim. Or worse, that you would see something in the water that shocked you. But you were calm, seemingly reassured by what you saw there.

'Baptiste?'

'Just checking,' you said with a smile.

The winter waters were so clear that our likeness was almost without distortion. When was the last time I had seen us together this way? Then, as I looked closer at the mirror of your eyes I saw how their focus went deeper. You weren't looking at our faces at all, but at the crisp reflection of the banks, the naked branches of the vertiginous plane trees that reached down into the cold flow like roots below the surface.

Was the way you recounted that first meeting with Amandine how it always seemed to you, I wondered, or have you reshaped this piece of the jigsaw to make it fit? Either way, this is your story and that is how it must be told. Whatever the truth, you must recognise these memories as your own. If I were to change your words you would lose your trust in all of it.

My parents were either side of sixty by the time I learned the truth. I was twelve. My mother came into my room without knocking and found me sitting on the edge of the bed by the window. I sat there often. My room had flimsy curtains the colour of persimmons and on bright days I liked to close my eyes against the soft light that filtered through them, letting it bathe my face. There was something in the quality of that light that felt like home. But that day, as I had been sitting there, thick cloud had swept north from the mountains and there had been a sudden downpour. Dark shadows had flooded the room and I'd become distracted by my reflection in the long mirror on the far wall. It was telling me something I should already know. I was staring at it trying to work out what it was when my mother burst in, her arms full of rain-spattered clothes from the washing line, raindrops glistening on her cheeks. When she saw me she laid the laundry down on the bed without folding it and came to sit beside me. 'Baptiste, what is it?' she said.

Her reflection joined my own in the mirror, and it clicked. Realisation swelled in my stomach, sour-tasting and dense. 'We're not the same at all,' I said, 'are we?'

She didn't need to answer. Our reflection was almost comical. A soft, round, fair-skinned mother and her darker, bony, crane-legged son, so ungainly even when sitting that my spine curled in embarrassment. On the school fields when obliged by the masters to run they said I looked like a deckchair being blown along a beach. My father was cut from the same mould as my mother; just as short and born fair, although he was lithe and tanned from working out in the fields. They were both shrinking under the weight of their years whereas I was at the age where it seemed as though I would never stop growing. Not even a teenager, and I towered over them like a cuckoo in the nest.

My mother put a trembling hand on my knee with a sigh. 'Son,' she said, 'there's something I need to tell you.' I turned away from the mirror, looked down into her eyes. 'A long time ago, when I wasn't much older than you ...' she began.

Her anxiety was palpable. I put my arm around her, tried to reassure her that whatever she had to say, it would be all right, but she remained tense within my tentative embrace. She was afraid. This kind of news can change everything, it can break families. I have often wondered, how did it change me? Would my life have been different if I had never known? You can never predict the effect such a revelation will have on a person.

My mother had nothing to fear. By that point I was already hers. A birth mother doesn't have the power to erase the one that raised you from an infant. And I wasn't angry at her for keeping it secret so long. We all do our best. Above all I remember being excited to discover that I wasn't who I thought I was, because I hadn't completely decided anyway. As the rain hammered against the window I had the thrilling sensation that we had taken to an ark, leaving behind dry land and striking out until the storm had passed. We sat together on my bed in the dark room for what seemed like hours, tossed on the waves of her justifications.

My mother told me first about herself as a young woman, and of the illness that had left her chances of conceiving slim at best. It was hard to picture her so young. 'I was beautiful back then,' she said. She hadn't thought much of having children before the illness took the possibility from her. It had been taken for granted that one day she would, and in any case there was a war on. What kind of world would it be to bring a child into? But the idea of never having children buried itself into her like a seed and grew and grew until it was all she could think about. Pregnant women seemed to be everywhere, and mothers with wide-eyed babies and chubby-legged toddlers were now transformed from a normal part of life into members of a club that denied my mother entry. She became resentful of them, and the resentment bred anger and the anger bred a black despair. When she sought counsel from the priest one Sunday at confession, he told her to find a way to engage with them, to understand and empathise, so my mother who had never been one to do things in half measures trained as a midwife. 'The priest was right, you know,' she said. 'Every time I delivered a baby I just knew this was what God had always meant me to be.'

She had known my father since they were children, but fell in love with him only when he returned transformed from the war. He'd always been the best-looking boy in the village, she told me, but he knew it well and had been a strutting cock before he went away. But the young soldier who returned was more interested in talking about other people than himself. He had hidden the war away, pinned it to his heart, the real heart that beat under his ribs, the pin sinking deeper with every contraction. Yet the pain had changed him in the strangest of ways, for on the outside he had become the kindest man she had ever met, always cheerful, always putting others before himself. He showed no interest in starting a family, indeed her barrenness had seemed to encourage him, but she ached to bear his child. Creating new life with him might bring light to the darkness in his soul and, despite the odds, she thought that perhaps God would grant this to her, to them. A small miracle was all she prayed for. Her desires were not selfish, but pure.

'But God sees far beyond our horizon,' she told me. (She knew already by then that I didn't really believe, but she blamed my age and was sure that eventually I would see sense again.) After they married they tried to conceive for years. Every month the coming of her blood was an immutable tide, eroding her hopes and revealing her deepening despair until one day a sadness settled upon her which could not be lifted. 'I wasn't strong enough for the cross God asked me to bear, you see?' This cross grew heavier every day and with every child she delivered until she came to the conclusion that her lot was not to ease her husband's suffering, but to know it for herself. And so she accepted her burden as my father did his, with a smile. Years passed.

My mother paused. She took my hands in hers, turned me towards her. 'So you see, son, I waited for you for so long. I wanted you so much. And I love you more than anything in this world,' she said. 'But it's time you knew how you came to be. As much as we know.' And then at last she told me about my mother. My other mother. In remembering, her face became radiant, her breathing more rapid, and we were joined in my room by the dark-haired woman, the rattle of the tracks, the slick of blood on the floor of the train and the green springtime coat.

That story was alive like no other. It grew and transformed year by year. Every spring the urge would rise in my mother to tell me once again how it happened, and every year she embellished it a little more. With each new recollection her account became more spiritual. It began with a faint glow around the woman in the carriage, her expressions during labour becoming more and more beatific until finally you would think it was Mary herself who bore me. I myself became rosier and more angelic in every iteration and any presence of blood became the slightest stain. But no matter how much that story evolved, I have never forgotten how in that first telling of my birth the blood poured from that woman just as the story spilled from my mother's lips, like an absolution.

Back home my parents had a drawer stuffed with old photographs. This was before everyone had digital cameras, when you would get back a paper envelope of twenty-four photos from the printers. My parents took plenty of snaps, but they never put them in albums and over the years the envelopes split and spilled and the photos jumbled together. In amongst them were hundreds so blurred or overexposed that the content was barely recognisable, but my mother couldn't bear to throw them away. There was a memory in there somewhere, she said, a sliver of our lives. Sometimes, when my mother felt melancholic, she would have us sit cross-legged on the floor by the drawer and pull out a handful.

'Oh,' she would say, 'we took that in the Aquitaine. You were about six I suppose. Do you remember that holiday?'

I did recall going there, but my memories of it were different: the taste of an apricot tart, a thunderstorm over sand dunes. Encouraged, my mother would show me houses, churches, and markets, photos of me with a friend I had apparently made on that trip. 'You remember her, don't you? You wrote to each other for months afterwards.' I didn't. But the next time we came across those photos I would remember more, the holiday, the penfriend, the lashing waves. The sweet tang of apricots faded into the shadow of those memories that had their authority stamped on to glossy three-inch squares.

This is how I came to know my mother's version of our shared past, and later, this is how I came to know you too, glimpsing your snapshot stories as they rose to the surface, rifling through fading pictures out of context. I have been glad of them. For many these days, if a moment is not recorded and shared it doesn't truly exist. Our tiny experiences are captured, passed about and approved of, a trail of breadcrumbs we leave as we go, permanent in their record. I never liked that way, it was never my style, I always preferred living to talking about having lived, and so did you. But now I am thirsty for those details. If only there were more. And so I tug at any slight thread of the past, teasing it from you to see if we could fill in the gaps before it's too late.

My mother is always happy to remind me about the childhood memories I fail to recall. Every minute seems fresh in her mind, aided by the hundreds of photographs fluttering in unmatched frames around the cottage walls like fading butterflies, each one with its own story that she will tell and retell to anyone who'll listen.

There is one at the foot of the stairs where I am tiny, perhaps two years old, standing precariously on the lid of the old upright piano in the front room, looking down into the open box. I am on the tips of my toes, one hand pulling at the strings inside, the other splayed against the garish, floral wallpaper behind me for balance, a small brown bird on a giant scarlet tulip. 'I look like I'm about to fall,' I said to my mother once. 'Why didn't you stop me? Why take the time to go and find the camera and take a photograph?'

'I know, I'm sorry,' she said. 'It's foolish with hindsight. It was just so typical of you, it was a moment I didn't want to forget. I wanted to show it to you when you were older. As it turns out I never forgot, of course.'

'You weren't afraid?'

She shrugged. 'I was always afraid, but we couldn't guarantee we'd always be there to catch you. We tried to let you learn your own lessons. And you've survived, haven't you, more or less in one piece?' She smiled at the photograph. 'That's your character right there, Baptiste. Always so curious.'

'Really?'

'Constantly. You had to break everything down until you'd figured out how it worked. You took your father's radio to pieces once. The older you got the messier your bedroom floor became, always covered in dissected objects, and it all made sense to you. I wasn't allowed to disturb them to clean. One day your father misplaced his slippers and went in to wake you in his bare feet. That was the only time I ever heard him swear.' I tried to bring that stormy afternoon back into focus, my mother and I sitting on my bed, adrift in her stories. How had the floor looked that day? Was it messy? When she walked in with the laundry, how had she moved through the room? But the floor hadn't seemed important at the time and all I could picture in the memory was the swept-clean, sand-coloured tiles that are still there to this day, a half-formed image completed from what I know is true.

'But I'm so tidy,' I said. 'That seems so unlike me.'

A shadow passed across my mother's smile. 'It all changed the day you discovered you were adopted,' she said, the creases in her brow deepening. 'After that it was just questions, questions, questions. You put away your screwdriver. You lost interest in things. You had decided that understanding how people worked was far more interesting.'

'Just like that?'

'Just like that. When you were little your father was convinced you'd make an excellent engineer. That's why he didn't mind so much about the radio. But after that day it was different. You still spent hours alone in your room, but no one knew what you were doing in there any more.'

My father had put it down to adolescence. All boys went through that kind of phase, he said, but my mother was worried. At least the mess of objects had been easy to understand. But perhaps that's exactly why I lost interest in it. Objects can be complicated but people are another story altogether. The day my parents told me the truth, a light came on. Behaviours that until then had seemed inexplicable made sense at last. My father's single-minded pact with God that put so much distance between us. The way my mother changed around strangers, her body closing up like a lock, the warmth draining out of her. How she would startle when an unexpected knock came at the door, and the way she would alternate between clinging to me and keeping me at arm's length. They had never been sure they would get to keep me. How long does it take until you stop looking for a loved one you have lost? The prospect of my family one day coming to claim me hung heavy upon them and its repercussions rippled through everything.

My parents were one mystery to solve and I was another. At school I'd learned that there are approximately seven billion, billion, billion atoms in a human body. Hydrogen, oxygen and carbon mainly, with a few other elements thrown in for good measure. And yet you could take me entirely to pieces and not find the person I believed I was. If you dismantled me right there on my bedroom floor, where would you find my character? Somewhere in me was a part of my other father, my other mother, a woman I had grown inside who I now sensed inside me, buried treasure without a map. I was convinced that one day I would find her, or that she would find me.

I know what I was doing in those long teenage years in my room. I remember it clear as day. I was bringing her to life. I didn't give her a name but I gave her everything else, and in my own way I came to love her, or my idea of her. I took to laying her few possessions before me on the bed like a puzzle. They had kept them for me all this time, fusty-smelling from the cellar: the violin case, and the green springtime coat still stained with her blood. She had carried no other luggage and no identification. In the violin case, as well as a violin, was her train ticket (she had left from Barcelona) and a small piece of sun-bleached driftwood, roughly carved into the shape of a horse. I kept that little horse safe for years like some kind of totem, a clue in a murder mystery. Perhaps more mysterious still, one day it disappeared from the violin case and I never saw it again.

When you have such sparse information, too much weight is given to the little you have. Was green her favourite colour? Was her personality as luminous as the coat? Or was it a hand-me down that she didn't even like? A mark of frugality rather than flamboyance? Why did she carry nothing but a violin? Was it her most beloved possession or was that how she made money? Why was she coming to Toulouse and who had written her destination on her arm like an unaccompanied child? Was she running away from something bad, or towards something good? To help me I had nothing but my mother's recollections, my imagination and a clipped-out image of her corpse in a newspaper.

Ah yes, the photo. I found it tucked inside the violin case like a stain. Under a small column headline asking for help identifying her, she was laid out in grey ink, her hair smoothed against her cheeks and over her shoulders. Her eyes were closed. The coldness of her skin flooded over me. My dead mother. Not a mother, I told myself, just an abstraction. Only memories can make a mother: the scent of her, the softness of her, her words and expressions. All of these things were already deeply imprinted on me by the woman in the kitchen. The woman who nursed me when I was sick, who taught me to read, whose hands had pulled me into this world.

But the woman on the train was someone to me too. She was important now. I had already started to form an impression of her from my mother's story, an impression that was nothing like the woman in the newspaper clipping. Yet the more we look at a photograph the more time condenses into that one single moment. I had barely glanced at the photo before tearing it to shreds, but it was too late. For weeks my nightmares reeled with the image of her corpse until I could bear it no longer. I began work overwriting that memory of her with new, imagined ones. I told myself stories at night, picturing her boarding a train, walking on the beach at Barcelona, playing her violin. I repeated them over and over until the stories had sharp edges and vivid colours. Whilst my real mother was already closing in on her pension, soft and round and covered in flour, with earthy fingernails and thinning hair, I painted this other woman with bright skin, wild hair and lithe limbs. These images seem real to me even now, although I know they are not, nor the dancing violin music that insists on accompanying them. Strange, the tricks we can play on ourselves.

After weeks of my introspection, my mother decided I needed a new pastime or project. Something to take my mind off things. I had played the piano from the age of three or four and was already quite accomplished, so one day when she found me staring at the violin case she suggested I could learn to play it. Maybe it was in my blood, she said. But from the first time I opened the case and looked at the instrument I knew that I could not. Just the thought of touching those strings invoked something deep within me that felt like shame.

Six months ago you woke in the pitch black with a jolt. You had been curled around my back as usual, your knees crooked into mine, your skin against mine along the length of me, your arm wrapped over my waist and under my own, with your hand flat on my chest, pressed against my heart. As you woke I felt your whole body tense. Just a bad dream, I thought, in a fog of sleep, pulling your arms closer around me. But you resisted and after a few seconds you were still frozen, your breath coming in short, agitated gasps. My heart, drenched in adrenaline, quickened against your fingertips as I tried to gather my thoughts. I had never imagined it coming in the night like that. I had no plan, no explanation as to why I was there in your bed when you had no idea who I was. I thought about whispering your name, but was worried I'd scare you. You're more than twice my size. I've learnt from bitter experience that when you are disoriented or confused you become angry and unreasonable.

What might you do now in the panic of darkness? For long moments we lay still, our breathing out of beat and fractured, both as scared as the other, then suddenly I felt your tension dissipate.

'Ah, it's you, my little *chouette*,' you whispered, the tips of your fingers caressing the skin between my breasts. 'You came back.' I didn't say a word, but I relaxed a little. You must still be asleep after all, I told myself. Still dreaming. I felt your head settle back into the pillow, your breathing calm again in my hair. Your chest rose up in a long yawn and your body sank back down against mine as tight and as close as ever, except for your right hand, which now rested softly, lightly against my bird-heart.

We were still that way the next morning when we woke. I turned to you as you stirred, my face waiting for you. A question. When you opened your eyes you smiled your familiar crinkled, stubbly morning smile.

'Good morning, Baptiste,' I whispered.

Your eyes flickered briefly and then you said, 'Good morning, Chouette.'

You lost me that day, and yet by some miracle you found a way to love me still.

It was a warm, light evening in the ripeness of spring. I had been at the piano, lost in a piece of music whose tempo was so close to that of a resting pulse it had almost become a meditation. The noise, when it came, startled me. It was hardly an explosion, just a soft thud on the deck above, but I've been jumpy ever since I came to Candice. In a way the quiet makes it worse. In the evenings there is so little to hear, an occasional boat approaching perhaps, but otherwise nothing but the lap of water, the chatter of birds and the churr of cicadas. When that sound came from the deck above me the adrenaline rushed through my blood as fast as if the sky were falling down.

Up on deck at first I saw nothing out of the ordinary. No plants were overturned and the towpath was empty. I wondered if it might have been a curious cat, bounding aboard and leaving just as quickly, which happened regularly, but whatever had just landed on Candice had been heavier on its feet. A duck? I looked down into the water. Not a ripple. Not a mallard in sight. Nothing. Only when I turned to go back inside did I spot her, a newly fledged barn owl, still a little downy, but with a perfect white face, squatting gnome-like between the geranium blossoms and the lemon tree in the blue mosaic pot.

I approached slowly. Was she hurt? She didn't move a muscle, just hooked me in with her wide black eyes, clicking her tongue. I crouched down beside her. 'Hey, little *chouette*, what are you doing here?' I extended a finger. She ignored it and I withdrew it again. I had heard a human scent on a baby bird could cause its parents to abandon it. Could I touch her without hurting her? I wasn't sure. I knew nothing about owls. I wondered if her parents might arrive shortly to retrieve her, but the air around was still. I waited, thinking that perhaps they would come, or that she would fly away, but either she couldn't or wouldn't. She simply stood there trembling and calling out, until eventually my ignorance and nerves were overcome by my desire to comfort her.

She was soft and passive in my hands as I carried her on to the towpath, to the base of the tree I thought she had fallen from. I climbed up the tree as far as I could, but there was no nest in sight and no obvious hollows. I watched her for hours, waiting for an adult to join her, to coax her back to where she came from, but none did, and as darkness fell I became worried. She was vulnerable there. If she didn't return to the nest she'd become prey for the canal-side foxes that seemed to thrive on this borderline between the urban and the wild.

Eventually I carried the owl back on to Candice, made a nest in a box, and offered her some scraps of steak I'd bought to grill with the neighbours the next day. She ate them with little fuss and apparent satisfaction.

I didn't want to bring her inside for fear of disorienting her, so that night, which was clear but cold, I stayed out on the deck, resting my fingers on her lightly, trying to protect her without preventing her from leaving. I hardly slept for fear of crushing her in my sleep with the weight of my hand. Instead I whispered to her, 'Hush, little *chouette*. Hush, my little *chouette*,' and tracked the stars across the sky in order to stay awake.

In the morning I tried again, putting her back by the tree and backing away, but she just sat there watching me as I ate my breakfast at a distance. Still no parent came for her and, back on the boat once more, she showed no intention of leaving. I kept watch on her as I went about my business, and she in turn tracked my movements, slowly turning her head this way and that. If you were so inclined you could have read so much into that face: calm, wide-eyed, the shape of love.

So often we humans mistake other things for love in ourselves and in others – gratitude, servitude, lust – that we have forgotten how to recognise love for what it is. I felt something real for that little owl. Compassion, maybe, and a desire to keep her with me, but what kind of life would a creature like that have with a man on a boat? She was hungry, she was curious and she was not at all afraid of me, but it would have been cruel to encourage her to stay where she didn't belong.

That night we slept together again, and the next day the same thing. On the third night, when my body ached with the weight of itself and my thoughts were muddied with fatigue I finally gave in to sleep, telling myself that in the morning I would take expert advice. But in the morning my little Chouette had gone and I never saw her again.

You told me that story as we stood together at the helm. I had asked you to tell me as much as you could remember, ablaze with the desire to discover all of you in the short time we had. You didn't look at me as you spoke, but cast your eyes ahead towards the next bend in the sunlit canal. I glanced at you from time to time, still with an uncertain restraint. On either side of us the poplars marked rhythmic breaks between fields the colour of ripening lemons. Your hands rested lightly on the wheel's handles. I was to your left, with my right hand on its spokes, low enough that although our arms crossed they were not touching.

You had always been more of a listener than a talker, but standing there like that something in the combination of the water and the shift that had come between us brought words to your lips. I had been waiting a long time for these stories and the wheel of Candice was where they finally found you.

Even after we moored for the last time it became our custom to stand side by side in the wheelhouse, looking out into the distance and waiting to see what memories would emerge from the water.

I knew what you wanted to say when you told me about that owl. You were telling me what you were afraid of. You always had such a knack of giving me whatever was important at the time, your stories perfect for the moment you told them. I wish it were still that way but you tell me very little these days, mostly either new versions of the same story, or stories that I know cannot be true. You prefer to hear a story than to recount one and I often read your own words back to you.

I have done my best to make sense of the things you have told me. Some elements are crystal clear and others out of focus, but there's a story in here somewhere. Some days you recognise yourself in these words, and other days they don't reach you at all but you are happy enough with their fiction and we go with the flow. Even I am no longer sure what I believe to be true. Your mind is so watery now we could all sink within it.

I didn't tell Sophie about Amandine for a long time. That first night I already felt hesitant and as my feelings changed it became harder with time. But Sophie could read me well and if she only looked hard enough the secret was there in plain sight.

Jordi's bar was only five minutes from the canal but the apartment blocks and offices separated it so completely that it had no feel of the waterside. Outside it was stuccoed and plain, with a blue neon sign above the doorway, but inside the walls were exposed red brick, hung with paintings from local artists. The art was Pascale's thing. In principle she ran the place together with her husband, but since Sophie had started work there a couple of years before she rarely made an appearance. When she did it was a brief affair, time enough to nudge her pictures straight and drink an aperitif at the bar. Since Jordi never came out of his kitchen, this meant Sophie usually ran the bar single-handed.

My mind has become myopic, I have to hold so much at a distance to see it clearly, but I can still tell you everything about that place. It was my home from home for years. Since moving on to Candice I ate from Jordi's menu almost every night. You'd think they'd be wondering what had happened to me now, wouldn't you? You'd think they'd pop by.

There were tables along the walls but the bar itself dominated the place, set in the middle of the room, a horseshoe-shaped counter forming a central island with stools set along its longest edges. Above it there was a shelf jostling with spirits that people hardly ever drank: rum, gin, crème de cassis. Only the pastis was kept handy by the bar, along with a crowd of wine bottles, open and corked. There were two taps, two choices of beer, and then there were the syrups – liquorice, almond, peach, mint, grenadine, violet and lemon.

At the low curve of the horseshoe, the cash register sat facing the door. It was a squat grey monster of a thing, with levers and buttons bigger than even my fingers. The clunk and rattle of it was so noisy that Sophie used it as little as possible, preferring to keep tabs on scraps of paper pushed under wine glasses or scribbled on paper place mats, and having customers pay up as they left. Jordi trusted Sophie and Sophie trusted us.

On one side of the room the run of bricks and tables was broken by a massive fireplace. In winter the glow from its crackling logs drew wind-nipped fingers in from their walk home. That night it was still laid with dry wood, as it had been all summer, waiting for the cold to arrive. The bar was half empty and Sophie looked up from serving at a table as I walked in through the propped-open door. We immortalise people in ways they would never choose and this is how I remember Sophie: framed by the doorway, short skirt, long apron, eyes the colour of wet sand watching the red wine rise in the glass, the tangles of her hair in a careless knot at the nape of her neck. Too young to realise how captivating she could be and too nonchalant to care.

The couple she was serving were already eating their meal. There was a thick-set man I didn't recognise sitting at the counter on the other side of the room watching the television, and Rémy was at his usual table in the corner by the kitchen, tapping at his phone and nursing a Calvados. Yes, I know, Calvados in Toulouse, but that was Rémy. If it wasn't coffee it was Calvados, depending on his shift. He must have been on days. Not his favourite. Rémy preferred to be alone, perhaps not the ideal profile for a taxi driver. He explained to me once that his job was worth it because it gave him an excuse to drive around Toulouse at night. Darkness transformed the city, he said. People became shadows against the pink bricks and shuttered shop fronts, and the inky Garonne curved and sparkled under moonlit bridges. His eyes flickered up as I approached the bar. I nodded a hello and took a stool at the counter. Sophie soon joined me, wiping her hands on her apron.

'Baptiste, at last,' she said, leaning in for a kiss. 'Where've you been?'

'It was Sunday yesterday,' I said, taking her by the shoulder and leaning to drop a kiss on each cheek. 'I ate at my parents' like a good son. Did you miss me?'

'Oh, of course.' Sophie folded her arms. 'How was it?'

'Very agreeable. Good food, couldn't fault the company –' I paused – 'which makes a nice change.' Sophie flicked her dishcloth at me. 'Have you no respect for your customers?' I said with a grin.

'You're not so much a customer as a responsibility.'

'Well, it's nice to know you take your responsibilities seriously.'

Sophie narrowed her eyes and set her hands on her hips. Dear Sophie, the daily antidote to my work. Exhausting though she could be, after hours of dealing with doubt and hesitation her unshakeable self-assurance was like a cold shower at the end of a hot day. When she first took the job at Jordi's I found her prickly and stand-offish, and she tells me I asked her far too many questions. It's a hard habit to break. But we soon recognised something in the other that fit. Like salt on butter or lemon on fish. I sometimes thought that had I been half my age our story might have been quite different.

There was a copy of the *Midi-Toulousaine* lying discarded on the bar. I picked it up and feigned interest. On the front page, men holding banners marched through the cobbled city streets. 'Hey,' said Sophie, poking a finger at the newspaper, 'not so much with the reading. I'm counting on you to keep me amused tonight. I want all the gossip from the canal side.' This was her idea of a joke, a poke at my quiet life. She took out her notepad. 'But first let's give Jordi some work to do. If it's dull out here it must be desperate in the kitchen. What do you want for dinner? He's gone mad and made a cassoulet if that tempts you?'

Jordi had felt the shift in the air as well, I thought. Why else would he have made such a heavy dish on such a warm day? 'That's just what the doctor ordered,' I told her. 'And some of your cheapest red to wash it down with.'

'It's cheap but decent,' she said, turning for the kitchen. 'Fancy isn't everything. Stay right there.'

I knew she was expecting me to sit at the counter so she could antagonise me while she polished the glasses, but I felt unsettled that evening. Something was bothering me about Amandine Rousseau and, until I had figured out what, I'd be bad company. 'You know, if you wouldn't mind I might just take a table tonight,' I said. Sophie looked back at me over her shoulder and said, 'Nonsense. Stay put.'

I decided to let the will of Sophie wash over me. There would be time later for reflection. Abandoning the idea of moving to a quiet corner, I settled myself at the counter, taking up the paper again while I waited. It wasn't like me, newspapers sicken my spirits, but there was something about the headline that day which caught my eye. *Boiling Point.* At first glance it looked like the same old story. Unions and strikes. Politics and protests. Elected three years earlier on the back of promises of economic growth and greater equality, the government had been unable to deliver and was floundering. Forced to push through benefits and pension cuts that meant a tightening belt for most working French people, they faced mounting anger. The unions were going to make them pay. But inset into the main picture were smaller photos. Student protests over unemployment levels were also flaring up and racial tensions were rising in immigrant communities too. Everyone was angry, at the government and each other, and a critical mass was building. I stared at the article, at the grainy photographs of angry faces. There was something wrong. A blemish that suddenly seemed just a little larger, just a little darker than usual. I felt a pang of unease and berated myself. This was why I never read the news. Twisting on my stool I offered the paper to Rémy with a wave. He nodded his acceptance and Sophie intercepted before I had time to stand, making the pass.

She laid the usual place setting in front of me: a square of thin red paper, a knife and fork wrapped in a paper napkin, and a small plate of toasts and slices of cured sausage. She leaned close enough that I could smell her perfume – it reminded me of the coast, at once earthy and salty – and on the paper square in soft dark pencil she began to sketch a little kingfisher in the top right-hand corner. She was fast but good. If you sat at the counter at Jordi's bar you would always get one of Sophie's doodles on your place mat. It was how she marked you out, and it had made her indispensable to Jordi. Word had got around about her portraits and customers would travel out here from town just to get one. I've seen many try to fix it, especially young men, hoping for something that reflected the way they saw themselves, but she always ignored their posturing and followed her instincts. The results were often amusing and almost always uncanny. Mine was always a kingfisher. In the early days I'd assumed it represented my life at the water's edge. But when I mentioned this once she had taken offence. 'Baptiste,' she'd said, 'you should give me more credit. The kingfisher is not because of where you live, it's who you are.'

'Explain?'

'When most creatures look down at the canal, they see themselves reflected within it. But not the kingfisher. He sees straight through the surface to everything that lies beneath. That's what you do with people. Most of us only ever see the surface of others, or else our own reflection. But for you it's as though the surface isn't there. That's how you help people.' I had never thought about it that way before, but the idea made me smile. 'Yes,' I told her, 'you're right.'

'I know that,' she'd said with a wink, 'because we're the same.'

That day, though, I didn't feel like the kingfisher. I could sense that Amandine Rousseau was like no client I'd ever had. The light reflected off her and I hadn't so much as glimpsed below the surface. Sophie finished her drawing, leaned on the bar at my side and elbowed me in the ribs. 'Hey, dreamer!' she said. 'Penny for your thoughts. How did today go? Meet anyone nice?'

I looked into her waiting eyes. It was as though she could read my mind. I ran my finger over the kingfisher's small bright eye. 'I've been on Candice all day,' I told her. 'You know I can't talk about my clients.'

Sophie arched a dark eyebrow. 'You're a tease, Baptiste. I want to know what happens out there on your boat.'

'You should come and visit me one day,' I said. 'Come and meet Candice. You'd like her if you got to know her.'

'I get sea sick.'

'We won't take her on the sea then. It's pretty far from here anyway.'

'Where would you take me?' she asked, those provocative hazel eyes challenging me from under black lashes. But at least we had changed the subject.

'Excuse me!' A customer's voice from the other side of the room.

'Damn,' she said, turning away. 'Don't think you're getting away that lightly. I'll be back.'

It's rarely the meals you expect to be memorable that stick in your mind. It's usually unexpected ones, like a perfect soup on a cold day, or the first time you try an oyster and taste the sea in it, or the sandwich you make with someone you've just spent all morning having sex with, hurrying it together so you can eat and get back to bed. I remember Jordi's cassoulet that evening as though I ate it yesterday. The flat terracotta dish was heaped with beans, with chunks of pork belly, sausage and duck poking through the crust on top. I made the first crack in the crust, sliding my fork through, and watched the steam billow out. Sitting there in short sleeves, with the warm evening breeze drifting in through the open door, I breathed in the rich scents of winter, starchy and well oiled with grease. The beans were soft in my mouth, the meat salty, the sausage was seasoned with herbs – parsley and sage perhaps – and the dark duck flesh fell into soft tender strings. The wine was unremarkable but I drank it, and when I had finished Sophie was there across the counter, topping up my glass.

'Not too much,' I told her.

'I don't want you rushing off back to your Candice just yet. Not when we have so much to talk about.' She pushed the bottle back below the counter and made to clear my place.

'Not so fast,' I said, stopping her fingers with my own. She tried to pull her fingers away but I held them just long enough to wipe a piece of bread around the bowl, catching the last crumbs and remnants of sauce. 'You can tell the autumn is coming,' I said. 'Have you noticed? Even this morning I—'

'Baptiste!' Sophie shook her fingers free and snatched away the bowl. 'Stop stalling. We have better things to talk about than the weather.'

'But, *cherie*,' I said, 'we have been together for so long now, it's possible I've run out of things to say. Of course I should have married you years ago, before you had a chance to get bored with me.'

'Great. Trapped in a marriage without the perks. Doomed to make small talk in a bar with the same man for the rest of my life.' She shook her head. 'How do people do that though, seriously?' I shrugged in resignation. It was an old conversation, but one that still amused her. 'Oh that's right,' she said, 'you wouldn't know. Yet.' Sophie had never understood why I was happy as a bachelor. Despite the trend amongst the young to dismiss marriage as old-fashioned and constraining, I think she was traditional at heart. I wouldn't be surprised to hear she was married by now.

'In my experience,' I told her, 'which is admittedly not first hand, the challenge of marriage isn't to stay interested in the same person for the rest of your life but to keep up with how they change. If you don't stay on your toes you can end up living with a complete stranger who you haven't learned to love. I think the couples who make it talk about the weather to buy time while they catch up with how they feel about the person they are now married to.'

'You're wrong, Baptiste. People don't change. We're born raw and by the time we hit thirty we're as set as if we'd been cooked. Just look at you.' I caught a glance of myself in the mirrored shelf behind the bar. My hair was getting long, I thought. I should get it cut. 'The older you get, the more fixed you become in your views,' Sophie washed beer glasses as she spoke, twisting them carefully over the brushes set into the sink, 'and the more resistant to change.'

'Maybe a little, but—'

'There's no denying it. At some point people just lose momentum, you become the establishment and it's left up to the next generation to progress. We challenge the status quo because our parents have become it.' She pointed over at the muted television in the corner where young men and women with hand-painted placards crowded across the screen, the students from the Midi. 'And then this kind of thing happens.'

I shook my head. 'Those students don't want change, Sophie, they want to prevent change. They want to live in the same world as their parents' generation.'

Sophie scowled. 'Don't be pedantic. They're standing up for their basic rights against people who have already feathered their own nests. Anyway, we're digressing. So, you're afraid of how a woman might change, is that your excuse?'

'I'm not afraid. I just …'

'Haven't met the right woman yet?' She grinned. 'Or have you?'

I put my elbow on the bar and rested my chin on my fist. 'Women find me intimidating because of my devastating good looks.'

Sophie blew air through the corner of her mouth. 'Pah,' she said. 'You're not as attractive as all that, you get fatter every day with more grey hairs. I'd get a move on if I were you.'

'Would you now?'

She held my gaze. I could see she was set to labour this one yet again, but then her phone buzzed in her pocket. She looked briefly at a message on the screen, then back at me with a broad grin. And then just like that she dropped it and asked instead after my work. 'Come on,' she said, 'seriously. Whatever happened today has definitely left you preoccupied. Is that a good thing? Are you sure you don't want to bend my ear, womanly advice and all that?'

Amandine came back to me in a flash. My heart quickened. I shook my head. 'I often get like this with a new client,' I said. Sophie waited for me to elaborate, but her question had opened floodgates within me and thoughts of Amandine began to eclipse everything else. The way she sat poised in the Louis XV, the green of her shoes against the boards of the boat, the way she had scrutinised me as though she were the therapist and I were the client. My mind shuffled the images, trying to fit the first pieces of the puzzle.

Sophie gave an exasperated sigh, her patience wearing thin. She could tell I was hiding something, even if she didn't know what, and it had already begun to drive a wedge between us. 'OK, whatever,' she said. 'If that's all you can think about tonight, why don't you go home and think about him there?'

'Her,' I said. But she had already turned away, summoned by Jordi, who was standing at the limits of his world, looking out at her across the room. He filled the doorframe in his faded chef's whites, his apron-wrapped belly and his profuse red beard both proud of the threshold, one hand raised in greeting. He was the captain of his kitchen, the floor of the bar a fathomless sea.

The night is full of ideas. In the slow drift into sleep when the mind softens and unravels, intuition speaks. There is no point then in trying to focus or to follow the threads, all I can do is accept them, write them down without question. Dawn will decide if they make sense. Some mornings I wake to rambling pages of my own scrawl – sometimes brilliant but often complete nonsense. During the night following Amandine's first visit I had written one single, cryptic line: *It's not what you think.*

When I read those words back the next morning I felt a tightening in my stomach. *It's not what you think.* What did it mean? I didn't remember writing it. Was it about Amandine at all? Did I suspect she was lying? About what?

I had a headache, not helped by the ducks battering their bills against the hull behind my head. I craned to look out of the porthole, where the mallards were breakfasting on algae along the waterline. A small brown face peered up at me, and then turned tail as I stretched and swung myself out of bed. I needed some fresh air to think straight.

Barefoot as usual, I took my coffee, my bread and my notebook out to the old fig tree that grew slightly downstream from the mooring, my favourite breakfast spot, where I could press the soles of my feet against the roughness of the roots that reached like arteries over the earth and down into the water. I often feel unstable on land, but the banks are different. For me, the roots are part of the fabric of the canal, holding things together, forming the cradle in which we rock.

I looked back over at Candice, her bottle greens and inky blues, her name in wine-red script along her starboard flank and the scattering of yellow-green leaves as big as my hands that lay discarded on her decks. There was no new fall at my feet yet, only the older, desiccated leaves from last year, or perhaps the year before, caught in the grasses at the water's edge. There's something melancholy about the way trees stand amongst their fallen leaves, like old men in dusty houses, indifferent to the skin they shed.

My mother refused to tolerate dust, but many of my friends' houses were thick with it all summer. When we were forced indoors on an odd rainy day, or to eat at the table, it was clear that summer had made dusting irrelevant. You could write your name in it, although we soon learned not to. I ran my fingers through the grass. With the children now back at school, mothers across France would be setting their houses in order. The same routine as every year. Summer dust would be wiped away, memories of seaside afternoons whisked from sandy corners and windows thrown open to let the early autumn winds sweep through rooms left shuttered all summer against the heat.

I could never bear shutters. The ones in my bedroom back home were the colour of irises. They would creak as they folded into place, shutting me in and the air out. To quell the claustrophobia I would imagine they were not shutters but a window looking across the ocean. But my imagination was thin and I couldn't convince myself for long. One spring as a boy, when the light evenings continued beyond my bedtime, I decided I couldn't stand it any longer. I waited until my parents had said goodnight to me, then slipped out from under the covers, opened the shutters wide and returned to bed. Only a few moments later though, the wind caught against them and they banged closed. I would have to fasten them back against the wall. Even though I was a tall child, I couldn't reach, even standing on my toes. I had to lift myself higher. I remember the hard line of the windowsill under my hips, the unfamiliar horizontal perspective as I leaned out of my room and over the twilight garden in order to reach the clasps. The tulips below. I don't recall the sensation of falling at all.

Although I landed in the soft flower beds I broke my right leg so badly that I still have the scar. The upside was that from then on the shutters remained permanently hooked back against the cottage wall. My parents put bars up and hung a thin pair of curtains the colour of the fat ripe persimmons that shone like baubles on the tree in the garden every winter. By the time I was a teenager the shutters had remained unmoved for so long that a family of bats had nested behind one of them, and occasionally on summer nights a dark little creature would flit into my room, circle for the duration of a held breath and leave.

I put my coffee cup down in the grass and stretched out my legs into the sunlight, traced the jagged line across my shin, pearly pink against the summer-darkened skin. They say you heal more efficiently as a child and the scars are all but invisible later in life, but that scar never faded. It has always been there to remind me. We imagine our memories to be ephemeral, yet in reality they're as physical as the knitting of bone and the scarring of skin.

The towpath was empty, and still but for the forward movement of the water at the edge of my vision, the canal lucid again after the agitation of the August tourists. It was always the marker that I would soon be busy again after the empty summer months. The spring sun steals the first of my clients, a hopeful balm for weary hearts. It's hard to be introspective with so much light, when the blue skies are beckoning you to the pavement cafés, the riverbanks and lidos. Then, at the height of summer,

Toulouse empties out into the countryside, down to the fresh air of the Pyrenees and the coastal towns of Languedoc-Roussillon, west to the vineyards of Bordeaux or up into the cool gorges of the Auvergne. In place of the locals come tourists who abandon their cars and take to their feet in the city searching out the culture and gastronomy of *La Ville Rose*, or to barges and boats churning up the green waters of the Garonne and the Canal du Midi. My quiet corner of the canal becomes the backdrop to their holiday, some simply clicking my photo as they glide past, others waving hello, sensing how the water can be a conduit to immediate kinship. I always smile and wave back, it's the easiest way in the world to share a little happiness.

But this was September and the tourists had already returned to a different reality, taking their memories with them. I sat on the bank, looking out at the space they had left behind, and watching occasional leaves falling like words on deaf ears until my own words brought me back to my senses. *It's not what you think.* What did my subconscious know that I didn't? I opened my notebook and got to work.

What is Amandine feeling? I wrote. Then I sat and stared at the words, thinking back on her visit, what she had said, what she had not, how she had looked me right in the eye, apparently fearless. Regret, perhaps? Scepticism? Loneliness? I tried them all on for size. Feelings still made sense to me back then, I could work with them like clay. But that morning nothing fit. Amandine Rousseau had sat with me for thirty minutes and had left me confused. I needed to see her again, and soon. Until then all I had were questions and cold coffee.

A paperback book, a little nest of hand-painted pottery dishes, a seashell, a photo-frame made of fine, sun-bleached driftwood. You paced the room, picking up objects, turning them in your hands and then replacing them. Two faces smiled out at you from the photograph, a man and a woman, as they were in that moment. Or as they seemed. Their smiles now looked fragile in your hand.

I realised you had been staring at the photograph for a long while, perhaps you could hear its echoes, your brow bearing its increasingly familiar furrows. These lines are new. They sit strangely on a face already weathered with sunbeam crow's feet and the deeply etched valleys of long gone smiles. For now, they pass like ripples on water, the depth of your past defeating the torment of today. But how long will it be before the very essence of you is transformed before my eyes? What was it you saw? Were you remembering, or were you confused?

I tried to bring you back gently. 'It sounds as though you felt something from the day you met her,' I said.

You looked at me in surprise and put the photograph down. 'It was impossible not to,' you said, your hand lingering on the edge of the shelf. 'She told me she wanted to feel alive. Sometimes we don't realise what we are wishing for.'

When we talk, these small, perfect truths swim up to the surface no matter how cloudy your memory. I thought of the flow of water in the canal, how eventually it all goes down to the sea. The waves and the tides and the pull of the moon. I raised my eyes to you and tried for a smile through long-spun breaths. You saw me then, saw everything I struggle to conceal. You knew what I needed even if you didn't know why. Within moments you had pulled me to my feet and wrapped me in your embrace. I became tiny within the magnitude of you. I breathed you in as you lowered your face to mine. 'Don't be jealous, Chouette,' you whispered. 'I don't want to hurt you.'

Rather than offer reassurances I said nothing. If I wait it out you often move on. You continued to gaze down at me, your frown deepening. I stiffened under your scrutiny, knowing I had to tread carefully. Your reaction to me wavers from day to day and minute to minute, hingeing on the tiniest details. I adjusted my body language – my face, the set of my hips, the fold of my arms – but whatever else you have lost, you still recognise shifting emotions no matter how hard I try to hide. I used to love the way you could see right through me but I could do without your perception these days. With neither truth nor memory to make sense of what you feel it has become the most volatile part of you. You tightened your grip on my arms and I could see your trust in me wavering.

Baptiste, I'm sorry. I used to say lies were for cowards but this has made liars of us all and I am the worst. If you can't rely on those you love to be truthful, then who can you trust? With no words to make it better, I tilted my face for a kiss and thank goodness you responded. The roughness of your skin against mine pulled the blood to the surface, away from the hard knots tightening under my heart.

After I became Chouette you didn't touch me for days. We had been one of those couples that held hands, that always kissed goodnight and good morning, and even years into our relationship, the bedroom was as much for sex as it was for sleeping. But that person was gone, and not only in name. There I was, your little Chouette, in your bed, and you weren't sure what to do with me. You became shy and uncertain while I ached for your kiss, longed to feel the weight of you upon me, felt hollow without your constant desire.

When, finally, you took me in your arms again, you made love to me as though it were the first time. You gasped at my body as though you had never seen it before, traced it with your fingers as though mapping me out. 'Is this OK?' you asked me. 'Do you like it when I touch you there? Tell me what you want.' And I became nervous again, unsure if I should do the things I knew you craved in case it seemed odd that a new lover could predict you that way. I resisted the temptation, falling instead, into my new role, and getting to know you all over again.

In a way, all of that was novel to us both. The first time around we had never had those delicate, trepidatious moments. The first time we lay together you were so certain of me, as though it were the most natural thing in the world. You had known me already for so long, seemed to have memorised the length and curve of me. You anticipated what I would like, how I wanted to be touched. You took my breath away. When I look back on those times it feels like another world, another me, another you. I ache for who we were, before I became unknown to you, and you to me. Now you keep your eyes closed when we make love and I know why that is. You can't look at me because you are thinking about her.

Your eyes were closed then as we kissed. 'I'm not jealous, Baptiste,' I whispered into the crook of your neck. 'I know there's no need.'

Your hands slipped to my shoulders as you stepped back, holding me at arm's length. I stood my ground, looking back into the plunging darkness of your eyes. You are still so handsome.

'I should have married you,' you said at last. Your chest rose and fell heavily, your eyes looked as tired as mine felt.

'Baptiste …'

But you had already moved on, distracted. Your voice became bright again. 'Chouette, do you know who you look like?'

My heart jumped. I cursed the needling hope that refuses to die. 'No, who?' I said.

I had to drop my eyes from yours as you slid your hand behind my neck, your thumb soft against my cheek, and said, 'Sophie. You look just like her.'

My father is deep in the sunflowers. I am still at a distance, watching his short figure rise and stoop. Even when he is fully upright I can still barely see him, just a flash of his grey cap above the bowed and desiccated flower heads. I am standing at the edge of the field, leaning on the warm skin of his rusting, duck-egg blue Citroën truck beside a large pile of stones, pink-grey against the clear skies. It could be any Sunday of my life from an age where I wasn't even tall enough to see over the sunflowers, sent running over from the cottage by my mother to bring him back for lunch. But in my mind this scene is from that Indian summer, the warm September with the wind still in waiting.

'Papa!' I called. A hand rose up from the flowers.

'Good morning, son,' he called back, and then he was gone again.

People we love have patterns and habits that give our lives their unique form. It is what breaks us most when someone dies, the way they will never finish another sentence we start, never sharpen the blade of a knife before carving the meat, never again sit in their favourite chair and sigh just with the simple pleasure of a good day ended. The routine is over and we are reminded that ultimately we are all just the same, all trying to find meaning where there is none. My father looked for his in that field of sunflowers and had for as long as I can remember. It shaped me. I grew up thinking that was what made him happy. Only when I understood more about his past did I realise I was wrong.

My mother retired back in the eighties, the same year I left home for university. That summer my father's absences became more noticeable than ever and my mother leaned on me for company. Leaving aside the fact that a teenage boy is no company for his retired mother, I worried what would happen in the autumn when I was no longer around. How lonely she would be.

'Do you think we could persuade him to spend less time out there now you're at home more?' I asked, leaning across the kitchen table to where she was kneading dough.

She looked up. 'No. And we shouldn't try.'

'Won't you be lonely at home?'

'I will find ways to live with it.'

'I'm sure if you asked, he would understand,' I said.

My mother had smiled at me. 'It's because I understand that I won't ask,' she said.

I was frustrated. What was it she understood about my father that I didn't? This was a part of his character that evaded me.

'How can he just abandon you like this?' I said.

'No.' My mother put her small, strong hand over mine. 'It's just the opposite.'

'Then what?'

'I told you when your father came back he was a changed man. Everybody could see it. Everybody knew something happened while he was gone. But he wouldn't talk about it, and whatever it was he seemed to have dealt with it in his own way.' Her hand trembled, specks of flour dusting off on to my skin. 'But once, just once, I glimpsed his demons, and after that I knew the best I could do was help him keep them locked away.'

Throughout the long years my parents tried to conceive, every time the blood came and my mother suffered the hopelessness of another barren month, my father supported her. He was like a star, she said, calm, unshakeable in his optimism and she in orbit around him. But then one night their suffering collided. They had been skiing at the small resort in the Pyrenees where they went every year. It had been a particularly glorious trip, perfect sunshine all week in deep winter-blue skies and full, thick snow on near-empty slopes. 'We were like two birds,' she said, 'skimming over the mountains.' But on the last evening of the holiday my mother came out of the restaurant bathroom with red eyes. Nothing was said, but although they had been ravenous neither of them could finish their meal. That night as soon as they closed themselves into the room of their chalet, locking the world away, he took hold of her. But this time he had no solace to offer, only regret. 'None of this is your fault,' he told her, 'it's mine. I can try and justify the things I have done, I can try and redeem myself, but I should have known there would be consequences. I accept them for myself, but I am so, so sorry that you are being punished too,' and when he wept into her shoulder the pain was more terrible than any my mother had known. That was the night she decided to stop trying. She had always known the chances were slim, she was already in her forties and all her persistence was doing was destroying the man she loved. That was the end of the matter.

When I was born just a few months later, an orphan boy falling right into the arms of his wife, my father, until then a cheerful agnostic, was convinced that God himself had sent me. It was a message. A second chance. And he set about repaying his lost years, showing his gratitude and devotion in the best way he knew how. He didn't start attending the village church, not beyond Christmas and Easter, because he didn't want to have to explain his change of heart to people, so instead, on the foundations of a ruined barn in the middle of a field of sunflowers on the outskirts of the village, he began to build his own.

I looked out over the field towards my father and thought about what Amandine had said, how so many parents want their children to be happy, and yet fail to be happy themselves.

I felt the breath knocked out of me at the thought of her and the rising anticipation of seeing her again the following day.

I bent to lift a rock and felt the pull of its weight in my lower back, a strain even for someone half my father's age. Picking my way through the broad stems to the clearing, the scent of oil was thick in every breath. The seeds were ripe; it wouldn't be long until the harvest and then the cutting down and the ploughing before the first frosts that would harden the earth and cause my father to stumble and trip over the stony ridges as he made his way to the chapel.

I put the rock down by his feet. 'Good morning, Papa,' I said. 'These are heavy.' We embraced briefly, and he pulled back to look at me, turning me through ninety degrees first so he didn't have to squint up into the sun.

'You look well,' he said, then bent with a straight back, lifting the rock I had brought and bracing it against his chest. His sleeves were long and rolled up to the elbow, the skin of his forearms slack and liver-spotted although the tendons were taut. He set his legs further apart, rotating the rock through degrees and scowling at it. I winced at the sight, half expecting to hear his vertebrae crack under the weight. My father pushed the rock towards my chest. 'I appreciate the offer,' he said. 'But humour me, please. Take it back.'

'Really?'

'Really. Sometimes there are things you just have to do yourself.'

I took it from him and laid it back on the ground at my own feet. Behind my father, the unfinished chapel stood in the clearing, open to the sky, with no roof or rafters although its walls had at last reached a height taller than a man all around. Taller than most men. The rocks tessellated beautifully, layers of large pearly pink stones interspersed with layers of smaller white oval pebbles. The white pebbles also bordered the tall thin windows on each side. Every one had been chosen carefully and every one placed just so. It was impossible to look at them directly. The reflected light from them was blinding.

'You look like you could use a break,' I said.

'No thanks, Baptiste, I don't have the time to rest. It's not going to build itself, you know.'

'How long do you need, I—'

'How long do I need? A year, maybe two.' He winked at me.

'Perhaps just take a moment for a drink, Papa. Some sausage.' I slipped my bag off my shoulder, but he waved me off.

'Sausage! I bet it's your mother that's sent you with sausage. I can't eat her sausage. It will spoil my lunch. What's she cooking? Is it beef?'

I smiled. 'She's roasting a duck.'

His face creased with delight. 'Wonderful! How long have I got?'

'Maman says it'll be ready in an hour,' I said. 'Let me help, Papa.' I turned back for the road. 'I'll bring over more rocks for you.'

He put his hand on my arm. It was rough as sandpaper. I took hold of it in my own hand and turned it over. 'Papa, you can't continue like this. Look at you.' Where the skin was not thickly calloused and yellow it was cracked and infected in places. He shrugged. 'I'd love some gloves for Christmas.'

I sighed. 'You know, Papa, you're too old for this now. I know you're still strong but you're eighty-four. Maman says some days you can hardly walk for an hour after you get up in the morning. That your back aches but you refuse to see the doctor because you know exactly what he'll say.' A gust of wind blew across the field, stirring the heads of the flowers, blowing my hair into my eyes.

'Your hair's getting too long,' my father said.

'Papa,' I said, 'we really need to talk about this.' I heard my voice pitch higher in exasperation. I sounded like a child, and indeed when he looked up at me what I saw in his eyes was the patience of a father. I slouched under his gaze.

'We don't give God our second best,' he said quietly.

'I can understand that,' I said. 'But what about Maman? She needs you. You've already given up half of your life for this. You were so busy being thankful for me when I was growing up that we hardly got to know each other. I missed you. And Maman must miss you too no matter how much of a brave face she puts on. She deserves more of your time.'

His face coloured. 'Baptiste,' he said in a low, calm voice, 'I love your mother more than anything in this world. It's not as simple as you think. If you have no faith that's your concern, but don't ever question the faith of another man if it causes no harm. Your mother understands.'

'Papa …'

'No more now. I'm still your father.'

I straightened back up. 'And I'm your son, I should be able to tell you when you're being stubborn.' My father braced his hands into the small of his back and exhaled. 'Papa, I'm worried about you, that's all. We are all worried about you.'

He looked up at the sun, high in the sky, and wiped his brow. 'Well, it is getting a little hot. Shall we go over to the house?' he said. I smiled.

My father set about carefully arranging his tools for his return. 'Could you bring that rock?' he said. I picked it up and the two of us walked slowly over the soft furrows, through the bent heads of sunflowers and back to the Citroën at the roadside. As I buckled myself in, I caught a glimpse of an old man worrying over his son's face. 'There's something on your mind,' he said. 'What is it?'

I shrugged.

'I see. Never mind. Your mother will get it out of you.'

My parents' cottage stood by the sizeable pond at the edge of their village. I never went near it. Melancholy willows leaned into the soupy water, trailing their sodden fingers along its surface, where indignant ducks turned sad circles. When I was a boy all the other children used to love going down there, tossing in small stones to scatter the fish, scooping up tadpoles and letting them slither about in soft pink palms before slopping them back into the pond weed. But everything about that place made my muscles tense as though to flee. My parents had thought I was afraid of water for years but it wasn't the water itself so much as its still, lifeless depths.

Nothing changes from one generation to the next, and that day too there was a brother and sister at the water's edge, throwing breadcrumbs on to the motionless surface. My father stuck an arm out of the window to wave at the children as he pulled the car up in front of the cottage, and they waved back, shouting, '*Bon appétit*, Monsieur Molino!'

The kitchen was roasting but my mother was in her usual place, sitting in her tapestry armchair by the stove under the benevolent watch of a fading Virgin Mary. Her face creased into a bright warm smile as we walked in. She clicked her tongue against her teeth, shaking her head. 'You two are as skinny as each other. Good job I've made plenty of potatoes, roasted nice and crispy in the duck grease.'

'My favourite,' said my father, moving over to embrace her.

'That sounds delicious, Maman, and very fattening,' I said.

'It's almost ready,' she said, 'and afterwards, Baptiste, you must come and see how the garden is getting on.'

For twenty years we had toured her garden after lunch, but every week she still raised the idea as though it were a novelty, as though there were great excitements she simply had to show me. It was true that every week her garden was a little different. New jobs, small successes, tiny tragedies and the treachery of various unwelcome wildlife. My mother's life revolved between the garden and the kitchen, and her good humour relied on her steady progress in each. The predictable seasons and the unpredictable gluts and blights were her weathervane.

'I'd love to, Maman,' I said. 'How are the apples doing?'

'Still coming out of my ears,' she said, beaming, 'and so sweet this year. You can take some home with you. I should have made you a tart, I didn't think.'

Over lunch, as my mother spooned out extra helpings, my father rapped a yellowing fingernail on the table. 'Bernadette, have you noticed something different about Baptiste today?'

Without looking up from tumbling golden potatoes on to my plate, my mother replied, 'Oh yes, he's got feelings for somebody.'

I laughed. 'I do?'

'The problem with Baptiste,' she continued, adding an extra slice of duck, 'is that he spends so much time listening to other people that he no longer listens to himself.'

'That's because other people are far more interesting,' I said.

'Physician, heal thyself,' mumbled my father through a mouthful of green beans.

'What's that?'

'Nothing. I made the mistake earlier of asking Papa about his health.'

'I'm sitting right here,' my father said, and placed his knife and fork on his plate by way of punctuation.

My mother sat back in her chair. 'Well, do bring her over for lunch, Baptiste,' she said, 'when you've worked out who it is.'

Later, kneeling in the garden, my mother put her secateurs down on the grass and removed her gardening gloves.

'Do you want to tell me about her?' She smiled.

'There's nothing to tell, Maman. The only new people I ever meet are clients, I'm afraid.'

'So it's a client? Or is something developing between you and someone you already know?' I shook my head. 'Well, unless I'm badly mistaken you definitely have that look about you.' She reached out a finger to touch a lock of hair that fell across my forehead. 'It's a pleasure to see,' she said, 'and not before time. I'm surprised I've lived to see you going grey.'

There was an undercurrent of longing in her words. We never discussed it, she wasn't one to pressure others to fulfil her desires, but I know she was disappointed that there had been no grandchildren. All I had given her was another twenty years of fruitless hope. 'Perhaps love doesn't come to everyone,' I said.

My mother gave a little huff and shook her head. 'Baptiste, love doesn't come to anyone.'

'What do you mean?'

'Do you think love is like a butterfly that you have to catch, or wait for the chance to settle it on your hand? No. Love is a garden, you have to put your mind to it and you have to grow it.'

Her metaphor made me smile. 'Not everyone's a natural gardener,' I said. 'I've killed enough pot plants in my time to know that.'

'And now? Your plants are doing well, aren't they?'

'Because I stick to the ones that survive despite me.'

'We all have to learn. If you keep at it you'll get there. It might not be the garden you imagined, but eventually everything will work out for the best.'

'Has your life worked out for the best?' I reached for a handful of earth, crumbling it through my fingers. 'Ever since I was born Papa has been building the chapel. You hardly see him. Don't you ever regret—'

She put her small, strong hand over mine. 'I don't regret a single moment,' she said. 'Every day I wake up with your father beside me I am thankful for that. The first thing I see is his face, the face that means I'm home.' She studied my expression. 'And I wish the same for you. You seem lonely. Don't you want someone?'

'I don't know,' I said. 'The whole thing makes so many people miserable. Is it worth risking a perfectly happy life at my age?'

I've seen what it does to people, this inability to be satisfied. People are always chasing something more: a better job, a bigger house, a fatter pay rise, a more exciting lover, the things they crave quickly becoming things they think they need, holding power over them until the minute they hold them in their hands. Then the magic evaporates and it's on to the next thing.

'Better to appreciate what you have,' I said, 'than strive for more, until what used to make you happy is no longer enough. Of all people I thought you would know that.'

Kneeling there by the flower beds my mother looked at me as though she were seeing me for the first time. She waggled a knuckly finger. 'Don't you start your happiness nonsense with me,' she said. 'It's not about if you strive or not. None of us has any choice but to strive. It's about knowing what you're striving for and why.'

I felt suddenly precarious in my mother's garden, my certainty ebbing away. I wanted to be back in the yellow light of Candice, the piano keys under my fingers and the canal on my doorstep, to be reassured that my life was enough, despite what my mother said and despite what Sophie said. I looked back at my mother. 'I already have a lot to be grateful for.'

'Yes, yes, I know,' she said, 'and people can live blithely in a valley their whole lives. Whereas those that climb the mountain for a wider view, they're the ones who take a risk, but they're the ones most likely to see something spectacular. You were always so curious, I never thought you'd settle for the valley.'

I was taken aback. 'But if there's one thing I learned from you and Papa it's to find a way to be content with what life gives you. You two have stayed in the valley and you said yourself that it's enough for you.'

The soft furrows in her brow deepened. 'No, Baptiste, we are on the mountain. You just don't see that yet, and that's what worries me.'

At breakfast today you were agitated, pulling small pieces off
your croissant and heaping spoonfuls of jam on to each one.
You never used to like jam, now we get through pots of the
stuff. You used to dip your croissant into your coffee in the
morning but you've lost your taste for coffee too unless I add
an unreasonable amount of sugar to it. With each small bite
you cast your eyes around the wheelhouse as though searching for a point of reference. The wheelhouse is crowded with
plants sheltering from the cold and your eyes continually
flicked back to them. 'Something about the plants,' you said
under your breath, 'something about the plants.' Then you put
down your croissant and lay your hands flat on the table, your
fingers still sticky with jam.

'When was the last time we saw my parents?' you said.

In the seconds that followed I asked myself if I had the courage to be honest or the courage to lie. Then I smiled at you

and took the prudent path. 'We saw them at the cottage,' I said. 'It was a lovely day. Your mother made quail, and your father drove out to the library.'

Your eyes flashed, and your face soured. I put down my own croissant too, suddenly sick with nerves. These half-truths walk dangerous ground, the pretence at an answer that does nothing but buy me time until you have forgotten the question. But what better way is there? You see straight through lies and the truth only hurts you again. Then later, when only the spectre of your pain remains, you are angry at me, knowing that I have hurt you even if you don't remember how.

'My father never goes to the library,' you said, your jaw tensing.

Why had I said the library? 'Did I say the library?' I said. 'No, I meant the—'

'The chapel I suppose.' You regarded me over the top of your glasses. 'You mean the chapel.' I dropped my shoulders, took a breath and watched as your eyes fell on something behind me. 'What's that?' you said.

I turned to look. It was the notebook. I'd left it at the side of the wheel, the pencil tucked into the last page I wrote. 'Oh, it's that memoir I've been writing for you,' I said. 'The stories you told me.' Frowning, you rose to your feet, your breakfast forgotten. I joined you by the wheel, looking out over the mooring, where a thin grey mist shrouded the banks and hovered over the green water. I could hear the rasping call of a crow.

'Stories,' you said. You flicked through pages and pages of my handwriting, looking but not really reading, pausing only on the double pages where small sketches sat alongside the blocks of words until you came to a page where the ink is blotted and blurred (I had thought a fountain pen would be elegant but experience teaches us to be practical). When you came to that page you ran the tip of your finger over the gap where the words should be. The question of what was once there held your attention for a moment, but without it you couldn't make sense of the surrounding words and you turned the page in frustration. You stopped, finally, at the sketch of a kingfisher. 'Sophie,' you said emphatically. 'Sophie drew that.'

The way you say it. Sophie. The end of the name soft on your tongue like a whisper. I bit my lip. I thought about the sea, how it pulls all the water on Earth towards it, and how the fresh and salt water meet and mingle in the estuaries. 'Yes,' I said, 'she did.'

'It's me.'

'Yes.'

'I like it.'

You handed me the notebook back.

'I'll just go and wipe it,' I said.

You followed me down to the galley, licking your fingers, still on edge. Rather than sit you skirted around the room peering out of the windows over the misty canal. 'Boat,' I heard you say under your breath. 'Candice,' and all the while you kept your back to the piano as though it were a tiger crouched in the corner. You used to play most mornings after breakfast, it used to be the one thing sure to save you. Your hands could guide you to places where your conscious mind can no longer take you. But now more often than not you are afraid to approach it. As though it may not recognise you. As though it might bite. It is suffering the same fate as us all, but that piano is part of who you are and I'm not giving it up without a fight.

'Why don't you play for a while, Baptiste?'

'I don't know. I think I should call my parents. I can't remember the last time we spoke.'

'There was a problem with their phone,' I said. 'Something wrong with the line.' We had had to change the number at the cottage months ago after the time you called and Lucas answered. You had both upset each other. Neither of you understood.

'Oh, yes.' You frowned, your eyes moving but unfocused as though sifting through memories for confirmation that that had happened. Then your face lit up. 'I'll call my father's mobile. Why didn't I think of that before?'

I dried my hands, came out to stand by the piano and picked out one of your favourite scores. 'I love it when you play this one,' I said.

You took it from me, your index finger tracing along the first stave, tempted. 'I'm not sure.'

'Please,' I insisted, 'for me. Once you start, everything will fall into place.' I say these things because it seems right to be encouraging even if I don't really believe them. Everything is losing its place and neither of us know what will be next. But today at my request you sat at the piano and began to play.

You used to talk about muscle memory, and perhaps it's true. Perhaps a body shaped by repetition can hold a memory longer than a mind alone. There's so much about this that none of us understands. Then again I have seen the exasperated way you look at your door key sometimes when all you need to do is turn it in the lock. No matter how often our hand has described the same movement, touched the familiar curves and edges, in the end we can still forget.

Your head dropped and your eyes closed as you fell deeper into the music, letting your body judge the distances, trusting your fingers to know precisely where to rest. Waves broke in my chest as I stood mesmerised at your side. I could watch you like that for hours.

The day I first saw you play was the day I knew I wanted you. When you first sat at the piano you looked as awkward as Alice after biting the 'Eat Me' cake, the size of you making the piano seem miniature, almost absurd. Then you set your hands upon it and I saw how they fit perfectly, the effortless span of your fingers across the keys. The music was not a love song, but it may as well have been. You caressed every single note from the piano, whether discordant or harmonious, as though it were the only thing that mattered in that instant, and that was what made the whole so breathtaking.

When you reached the end of the piece you kept your eyes closed, letting your arms drop by your sides. You were calm again. The crow had fallen silent, and the only noise was the lapping of water upon the boat and the sound of our breath.

I saw Amandine on Mondays, when she took appointments only rather than a general surgery. Sometimes she could stay for a full hour, sometimes less. 'I'd get into all sorts of trouble if they knew I was sneaking out of work for a clandestine rendez-vous in the middle of the day,' she had said once, as though coming to see me were an act of mischief.

'I know many people like to keep these things private,' I told her, 'but there's no need to feel guilty.'

She laughed at me then. 'I'm too old to feel guilty about taking something for myself. If I don't put myself first some-times, who else is going to do it?'

'While you are here,' I said, 'I will.'

Amandine would inevitably arrive earlier than agreed, while I was still on the piano finding my focus. 'Don't let me stop you,' she'd say, 'do finish.' But I couldn't play in her presence, I couldn't shut her out. Even if she were out of sight I could sense the shape of her in the room, the way she changed the light. Even if I closed my eyes I could smell her perfume. Even now the thought of her makes me feel agitated.

It had been weeks, and I still hadn't got the measure of Amandine Rousseau. Something was fundamentally awry. My failure to figure it out had got under my skin so much it was distracting me from my other work. I still remember entire conversations with her, what she wore, how she sat, and yet I couldn't tell you anything now about a single other client from that time. She was all I thought about. I had started to ask myself if I was being affected by the particular empathy I felt towards her, a feeling that was becoming hard to deny. I would never have committed the professional transgression of striking up a personal relationship, but nevertheless it is possible my judgement was becoming clouded. It was on a wet Monday in the autumn proper that something finally shifted.

The sound a raindrop makes depends upon where it falls. On Candice a rainstorm was a three-part harmony. Raindrops rapped on her roof, pattered on to the towpath and plopped into the water. In the minutes before Amandine's arrival I was diverting myself by inventing a melody on the piano to accompany their percussion. The first I heard of her arrival was the clang of the bell. My heart leaped and as I stood to answer the door the bitter taste of nerves was already spreading from my stomach into the muscles of my legs and the back of my throat. I paused for a moment at the bottom of the stairs, willing myself to breathe normally. It's important to appear calm. But as hard as I tried I was still unsettled when I opened the door.

Amandine, sheltering under a dove-grey umbrella, smiled like an old friend. She shook off her umbrella and stepped in. I held out my hand to her, but she was already inside, leaning forwards as though to kiss my cheek. She wasn't keen on formalities. As she leant towards me my hand brushed against her waist and I stepped back quickly. 'Sorry,' I said, flustered.

Amandine regarded me coolly, then straightened up and offered her own hand. When I took it she held my eye, tightening her fingers around my own then retracting her hand, the brief pressure leaving an evaporating warmth. 'You'd think by now we'd at least have that sorted,' she said with a wry smile.

Deepening my breaths in an attempt to slow my speeding heart, I stepped aside to let her pass. 'Come through,' I said. 'I was about to make peppermint tea if you'd like some? It's fresh cut.' The rain had set my mint growing so enthusiastically that I couldn't use it fast enough.

Amandine slipped off her wet coat and hung it up, making herself at home. Underneath her raincoat she wore a dress the colour of a moth in a soft fabric that moved around her like a breeze. I watched her as she backed carefully down the four wooden steps into the cabin.

'Peppermint tea,' she said. 'Hmm.'

'What is it?'

'Nothing, it's just been years since I drank mint tea. It reminds me of someone.'

While I boiled the water she stood at the breakfast bar that divided the galley from the sitting room. She held the mint, still wet with rain, up to her face and breathed in its scent. 'You grow your own herbs?' she said, looking around the small sparse galley. 'Do you cook?'

'I don't cook, but my mother insists everyone should know how to garden,' I said. I took the mint from her fingers and tore the leaves into our cups. 'I'm quite good with herbs.'

'I can't keep houseplants alive longer than a few weeks,' Amandine said. 'I'd be terrible let loose on a garden.'

'I've killed off lots of plants in my time too. But it was my own fault. Every spring I would buy the ones I liked the look of most and put them out on deck any old how, wherever I thought they looked good. I watered them if and when I remembered and still managed to be surprised when I had to buy new ones every year. Eventually my mother took me in hand.'

'What's her secret?'

'She says it starts with choosing the right plants for the garden you have. No matter how much you like the look or the scent of something, if your garden is too exposed or doesn't catch enough light then no matter how carefully you look after them, they'll soon perish. The other thing is intimacy. She spends a little time every day just seeing how they are doing. She treats every plant differently. A little effort every day and knowing what your plants need to flourish, she says, is paid back many times over.' I carried our tea through

83

and placed the two cups on the chest. Amandine took the Louis XV as usual.

'She sounds wise,' Amandine said. 'Does she live nearby?'

I checked myself. The opening pleasantries of Amandine's visits could go too far if I let them run too long. It was easy to be seduced by the amiable conversation but too many times already she had managed to turn the discussion around to me. She did it so naturally I almost admired her ruse, but it wasn't helping me to help her. 'Just a few stops on the train. I visit them on Sundays,' I said. 'How about you, where do your parents live?'

'Oh, they live in Paris,' she said. 'I rarely see them. My mother isn't a gardener though. They've lived in a city apartment their entire lives.' She gave a slight shrug and crossed her legs. 'Like me, I suppose.'

I looked at her carefully. There was something pointed in her voice, a thread to pull. I waited to see if she would continue. When she didn't go on I shifted slightly on the couch and reached for my drink. Outside the rain fell and fell. Leaning back against the chair, Amandine now looked as relaxed as if she had simply popped in for tea. I watched as she lifted the cup towards her face, staring into its steaming surface, black and glossy with the oil from the mint. Again conflict flashed in her eyes.

'What is it the tea reminds you of?' I said. 'Tell me.'

'It reminds me of how I used to be,' she said. 'Of a younger version of myself. It's strange how just the smell of it now can make me feel so much. Nostalgia, but more than that.'

Finally, something. I put my own tea back down. It was still too hot to drink. 'Go on,' I said. 'Describe it to me.'

'It was a long time ago. In Morocco.' She looked over at me, as though appraising my interest. 'I had just left home, taken myself to Africa to find myself.' She laughed. 'I drank mint tea every day there, but much sweeter than this. They served it in scratched glass beakers on low tables. I would sit on the edge of the square watching life happen around me, the sun already hot and the whole day stretching ahead like an adventure. The colours were so much more vibrant there, scarlets and golds everywhere, not to mention all the colours of the stories woven into the carpets in the souks. And along with the smell of mint would be scents of leather and cooking spices. I walked endlessly around those winding streets. I felt intensely alive, alert to everything. Even the dust on my feet felt good, and washing it away at night in cold water felt even better.'

She looked down at her shoes and then used her toes to push them off, heels first. They were not green that day, but the same dusky colour as her dress. She slipped one shoe off and rubbed the bridge of her foot against the calf of the other leg, pressed her toes to the floor and arched her foot upwards, her dress slipping off her knee slightly as it rose. A long scar, pink and white, ran across the surface of her foot, and her toenails were tiny oyster shells visible through pale, sheer fabric. I caught myself and looked back to her face, to find her regarding me with amusement.

'Well,' she said, 'one night an old man stopped me in the souk and asked if he could put kohl on my eyes. When I asked him why, he said, "Because it would suit you." I let him do it. If that were me now I'd …' She made a brushing away movement with her hand. 'I wouldn't want to be touched by a stranger. I wouldn't want to be bothered when I was alone. But back then I felt like someone else. Or perhaps I felt like myself after a long time trying to be someone else. And then –' her gaze drifted out past me towards the drenched towpath – 'then I met someone who changed my life.'

I held still, afraid to move, as though a wild creature were tentatively approaching me.

'I can see myself as though I'm an observer,' Amandine said, 'as though it were a dream. I am riding a grey horse along a beach, the wind on my shoulders and the pink sky turning to dusk. His horse is darker, he is keeping it perfectly alongside my own even though the horses are starting to race each other along the shoreline.' Then something snapped in her. She looked at me directly and just for an instant her mouth hardened into a tight line. 'I thought I was in love then,' she said. 'I was naïve, of course. Happy because I didn't know any better.'

The rain drummed its long fingers. Amandine's eyes left mine. I watched as she looked around the room once more, her gaze settling on the piano and at the score covered in my corrections in pencil. 'What were you playing as I arrived?' she asked. 'I didn't recognise it.'

'Just something new I'm trying,' I said.

'You write music?'

'Sometimes.' She was changing the subject. It was fine. We could come back to this.

'I was wondering the other day,' she said, 'how you got your piano on board? The windows are tiny and there's no way it could have come down those steps.'

'I had Candice cut open,' I said.

She raised her chin. 'You're joking.'

'I'm not.'

She wasn't sure. 'Like a caesarean in reverse?' she asked.

'With Oscar as the midwife,' I said, although the image disturbed me.

'Oscar?'

'It's a long story. He had Candice before me.'

'That piano must be really important to you.'

'Yes,' I said. 'So, Amandine …'

'Would you play for me now?'

'If you want a piano recital I suggest a concert ticket would be better value.'

Amandine met my eye, looking amused. 'I'm serious,' she said. 'I'd love to hear you play.' She motioned to the violin case in the corner. 'Do you play that too?'

'No.'

'Is it broken?'

'No.'

A shadow of uncertainty clouded her face. 'So who does play it?'

I felt the hairs rise on the back of my neck. 'No one,' I said. 'Do you play an instrument, Amandine?'

'You know, it's sometimes impossible to get a straight answer out of you, Baptiste.'

'Because I want to talk about you.'

'And I like that,' Amandine said, 'don't get me wrong. But it can feel a bit much sometimes.' Alarm bells rang. In my experience, when people stopped wanting to talk about themselves it was because I had put my finger on the one thing they needed to talk about. 'And you have to admit it's curious to own a violin which you do not play. Which no one plays,' she said.

Torn between pressing her to pick up the thread of her young love with the risk of pushing her too hard too soon, I decided to let her run with her interest in my violin. We all make mistakes. 'Why?'

Amandine thought for a moment and straightened her shoulders. 'It's a question of possession. You don't strike me as a man who is interested in possessions. So why would you, as a musician, possess something as beautiful as a violin, only to keep it in a corner like an ornament?' She threw the question down like a gauntlet. 'What does that say about you?'

It had become darker in the room, the entire sky thickening with cloud. I reached for the switch on the standard lamp, which cast us both in a pool of amber light while the violin crouched in the shadow of the piano. I felt its presence more keenly than usual, as though it too were waiting for my response. It's about Amandine, I reminded myself. Keep it about her. 'Is that a metaphor?' I said.

She raised her eyebrows in amusement. 'Or a cliché?' she said. 'No, Baptiste, it's just a question.'

The rain on the roof was starting to get on my nerves, making it hard to concentrate. I couldn't shake off the sense that I was missing something hidden in plain sight. People pay me to listen. They want to be understood. But Amandine was making a game out of it. She constantly deflected that kind of intimacy and yet physically she was completely at ease. I looked over at the two instruments, side by side, chalk and cheese. What did I have to lose? I rose from the sofa and crossed to the piano. 'Come here,' I said.

Without hesitation, Amandine did as I asked, moving to my side in front of the piano, reaching out a delicate finger to stroke one of the deep scratches in its side. 'What's this?' As she breathed her chest rose and fell lightly, her dress shifting and sighing.

Beyond the window the raindrops spun ripples on the water, the canal stretching away like a thread. 'War wound,' I said. 'Take the stool.' I pulled it out for her and she sat askew, her body turned towards me, her legs crossed at the ankles. I unfolded the desk chair and sat down beside her. 'You're right, this piano is important to me. I spend a lot of time talking, but words can make it hard to think. They get in the way. On the piano I can express powerful, subtle, complex emotions without saying a word.' I leaned across her, running my fingers from the low, dark notes to those so high they barely resonated. Chords and arpeggios, majors and minors, muted and sustained. 'Down here you have anger, sadness, grief and power,' I told her. 'And up here's where I find happiness, joy and delight.'

Amandine was still as my fingers moved across the keys. Watching my hands. Sizing me up. When I stepped back, putting space between us again, there was a glint in her eye. 'Are your parents tall?' she said.

'I want you to try it,' I said. 'Express yourself.'

Amandine reached tentatively towards the keys. 'I don't play,' she said.

'It doesn't matter at all. Go ahead. Shut your eyes if it helps.'

Her fingers explored the keys, testing out scales, finding discordant groups of notes, reaching for the lower octaves and then up again to high bright notes. Eventually she settled on middle C, and played a scale. *Do, Ré, Mi, Fa, Sol, La, Si.* I waited. 'That's it,' she said. 'That's how I feel.' She played it again: *Do, Ré, Mi, Fa, Sol, La, Si.* Seven notes, one of each, an unfinished octave. I fought an extraordinary desire to press down on the final key.

Amandine laid her hands in her lap, a challenge in her eyes. 'Did I express myself well enough?'

'You feel unfinished?'

She shrugged, but her cheeks were slightly flushed. 'Not unfinished,' she said. 'Unresolved.' She looked down at the violin. 'And you still haven't answered my question.'

I sighed. 'It's a long story.'

'I like stories.'

There was so little between us at that moment, the smallest of spaces and the thinnest of fabrics, the spark of a shared awareness. I suddenly had an overwhelming desire to take her face in my hands and kiss her. The only way I can explain what happened next is that I was so thrown by that unexpected desire that I would have accepted the first available distraction.

'I inherited it,' I said.

'But never learned to play it?' Her voice was almost a whisper. She was leaning towards me slightly. She had sensed my discomfort.

'I never wanted to. I like to understand how things work and I'll never understand the violin.'

'Why?' she said. 'What's the difference between that and the piano? Surely music is music?'

'How many notes on a piano?' I said.

Amandine scanned the keyboard, counted the keys. 'Eighty-eight.'

'And on a violin?'

She thought for a moment and frowned. 'I don't know.'

'Well, in theory there are infinite notes on a violin,' I said. 'That's my problem.'

'That doesn't make sense,' she said. 'Show me.'

I lifted the piano lid. I was trapping myself. Why was I doing this? Amandine rose on to her toes to look down inside the box and I felt a pang of déjà vu. 'Eighty-eight notes, eighty-eight strings,' I said. 'A piano is tuned so that each key has its own note. You press the key and inside the box the hammer hits the string, the vibration makes the note. Nothing ambiguous about it at all.'

'And a violin has only four strings,' Amandine said. 'And they're all there on the outside. Even simpler, surely?'

'Just because you can see it doesn't mean you can understand it,' I said.

Amandine frowned. 'Show me,' she said again. A surge of panic rose within me. That violin had not been played for forty years or more. I could feel the woman on the train, my other mother, right there in the room with us, holding her breath, waiting for something. Amandine regarded me carefully. She too seemed suddenly, uncharacteristically, on edge.

'What is it?'

'Nothing.'

The fasteners on the case were tight and stiff. When they gave with a snap I opened the case and breathed in the musty odour as I reached for the violin. On the periphery of my vision the rain traced glittering paths down the windowpane. 'Here,' I told her, 'take it.' I felt as though I were handing her a vital organ of mine that had somehow been extracted and kept aside. Amandine's fingers closed around its neck and her face stilled.

'It's light,' she said. She was holding it like a newborn. A knot lodged in my throat, but I had no one to blame but myself.

I reached for the piano and played a middle C. 'So here is where you started, at C,' I said, as the piano gave up the note. 'We can go up the white keys as you did, or we can include the black semi-tones too, taking us all the way to B, where we have to stop, leaving you unresolved.' I left my little finger hovering over the last note of the octave, the final C. 'But on the violin, between that last B and the C that you need, there are other notes, other tones, each taking you a fraction closer towards resolution but never quite getting you there.'

'How can there be other notes?'

'How can there not be? As you slide your fingers down the strings, theoretically you can change the tone in infinite fractions as you go.'

'How can there be infinite possibilities on a finite length of string?' Amandine said. 'It doesn't make sense.'

'Try it and see,' I said. Try it and see. And of course she did. Taking one last look at me, Amandine pressed the instrument under her chin and brought up the bow. I could barely breathe. Then she slid the bow over the string in one smooth, unhesitating stroke. The instrument let out an ugly wail and I closed my eyes against the miserable sound. When I opened them again I found Amandine looking back up at me, crestfallen. She shook her head and held the violin back out to me. 'I'm sorry,' she said. 'There's a reason you don't play this violin and it's got nothing to do with music, has it?'

I sighed. I may as well have been standing naked in front of her.

'It's OK, you don't have to tell me,' she said, patting my knee. 'Game over. I'm sorry.'

I was coming undone. 'If I hadn't wanted you to play it I wouldn't have offered,' I said.

'You didn't offer, I pushed you,' she said. Her voice had changed, softened. 'You don't want to go on, do you?'

I was falling back into an old daydream. In my heart the notes were soaring, a crescendo of strings. My violin safely cupped under the chin of a woman I had imagined into life. The woman on the train. My mother. Her arm guiding the bow, her dark hair framing her face, her feet bare on the floorboards. Not a wail from its strings in my dream, but an ecstasy. And Amandine couldn't hear it. 'No,' I said at last.

'Put this away, then,' she said.

I took the violin gently, and returned it to its case. When I had put it back down on the floor I let all my fingers rest back on the piano keyboard. The tension drained from me. It felt like coming in from a storm. I played her seven notes one last time. 'You know, Amandine,' I said, 'I am going to find out what makes you happy. We're going to find your resolution.'

Amandine tilted her head slightly and tucked a loose strand of hair behind her ear. She was about to say something, then the clock chimed and we both looked up, startled. 'Sorry,' I said. 'I have a client coming in fifteen minutes.' It was a lie.

Amandine nodded, picking up her shoes and carrying them up into the wheelhouse. 'You know, if I didn't know you were a therapist I would never have guessed. You just don't seem …'

'Don't seem what?'

'Never mind,' she said, pulling on her coat. 'But let's do something different next week. What about lunch?'

It wasn't a bad idea. A change of scene might help us both. 'Why not,' I said. 'I know a nice quiet place in Toulouse. Can you make it to the city centre for midday?'

Amandine looked pleased. 'Yes,' she said. 'It's a date.'

I came around the corner of the towpath and stopped dead. You were standing naked on the deck, silhouetted against an evening sky fading to violet and pink. You appeared perfectly yourself, tall and relaxed with your back to the towpath and your face turned downstream to where martins swooped over the water picking off insects that hovered above the surface, the fresh evening air blowing your hair around your neck. Yet I knew that you could not be yourself at that moment. Perhaps you were unsure who you were, or where, or why. A crack of conflict split my heart. When I moved forwards again you turned. 'Chouette!' you said, throwing your arms open in delight. I smiled and relaxed. You didn't look like a man who had forgotten who he was, you looked like a boy who had remembered.

'Aren't you cold?' I asked.

'Cold?' The question perplexed you, and you laughed. 'It's not cold. Come on up.'

I joined you on the deck, barefoot but pulling my coat tight around me. 'Yes,' you nodded, 'the wind is coming. Don't worry, it'll blow straight through us, but you have to take your leaves off.' You pushed the jacket off my shoulders and lay it over a chair, then teased my blouse from my waistband, your fingers gently twisting the buttons. I raised my arms above my head.

Soon I was trembling with cold. 'Come here,' you said, folding me into an embrace. You were surprisingly warm. I wrapped my arms around your back and lay my cheek against your chest, looking out over the fields and feeling the beat of life flowing through you. I ached to treasure that moment, tried to let go and inhabit it with all my heart, but I couldn't. There was still daylight and we were standing naked on the deck of a houseboat. Even if your neighbours had already made it home we could expect the usual flurry of evening joggers on the towpath, and any minute now the pleasure barges would appear along the canal.

Almost every evening from spring to autumn they cruised past Candice, venturing just a little further downstream and then turning full circle before the lock and heading back up to Toulouse. I thought of them as safari boats, the tourists on board peering curiously into our windows, thirsty for a glimpse of our homes and our lives. You used to like it when they caught your eye and waved, but more and more often these days, they looked at us through the lenses of their cameras and their phones. When they did you laughed and called them the paparazzi, but I could see how it set you on edge.

I had always wondered what they did with all those photos, photos that must have looked so beautiful but told such thin stories. If we didn't go inside soon though, the photographs they took tonight would have some real flavour. The noise of a motor droned into earshot followed by a wash of panic over my skin.

As a girl, so I've been told, I would shed my clothes at every opportunity. There are no photographs of this phenomenon as my mother was somewhat prudish, but she insists it was so. Apparently our disagreement on this matter incited most of my tantrums as a toddler, not just at home but also in parks, at school and at other people's houses, and the arguments continued far beyond that age. She said it took puberty for me to find the appropriate level of decorum. Only then did I learn to dress myself up with all the things that pleased her, and which came eventually to seem not just important but necessary. It started with clothes and haircuts, then diplomas and jobs, the right friends, the right boyfriends, the appropriate points of view. I could only go so far and I never got it quite right for either of us. What would my mother say if she were to see me like this now, a grown woman naked in public, embracing a naked man?

I cast my eyes to the only way down to the inside of the boat: the ladder on the canal side leading to the narrow foot-way around Candice's edge. Perhaps there was just enough time to retain my dignity. Then I looked back up at your face. Calm. Happy. And I remembered for the first time in years how little any of it matters. How little any of it says about who we are. How little it takes to strip us back to nothing.

I turned my body towards the water, your hand cradling my hip, my arm around your waist. I felt the cool air skim across my skin and I waited for them to come.

The fire blazed in the bar, the fresh, damp logs crackling like autumn leaves. As I squeezed through the crush of people a couple bristled past me, arguing. Since the counter was already more crowded than I had seen it in weeks I slipped quickly into the table by the hearth where they had left their drinks unfinished. When Sophie appeared at my side she leaned down to give me a quick peck on the cheek, sloshed some red wine into a clean glass and took my order quickly. 'Better make yourself comfortable,' she said, whisking up what the arguing couple had left behind. 'Jordi's swamped.'

'Right.' Usually I was more than happy with time to stew in my own thoughts but recently they'd been so tangled that the more I tried and failed to unravel them, the more irritated I became. I needed a break from myself. I'd been hoping for company. Without Sophie to distract me I turned instead to observing the crowd of faces in the bar. Some looked familiar, others I was sure I had never seen before. Jordi's was one of two bars that served the apartment blocks nearby and came to life in the summer months when he spread tables out on the pavement for those wanting to pause and enjoy the warm evenings on their way home. Since the nights had drawn in we had been back to just the regulars, but that night the weather had washed people in from their walk back from the metro, for fireside drinks that might well turn into dinner if they were tempted by the meaty smells coming from the kitchen. A weary-looking man wearing a felt hat wet with rain stood alone by the door, holding a pastis and staring up at the television. Two older men played dice at the table beyond the fire. A young couple on bar stools, their knees turned towards each other and interlocked, bent over their clasped hands, their drinks almost untouched on the bar beside them. One small room, full of other worlds.

Sophie returned eventually with a round tray weighed down by an array of dishes and began pushing aside the cruet and the bread basket to make room on the table. She swiped my fingers away as I tried to help. 'Leave it to me,' she said, deftly tessellating the seasonings for my steak tartare. The colours and scents were acid bright: the sour green and white of finely chopped cornichons and white onion, an egg yolk cracked into a shot glass, a small heap of vermillion spices, hot sauces, a steaming bowl of fine-cut *frites*. 'There's your man-food,' she said. 'Enjoy.'

I gave her leg a gentle poke with my elbow. 'So sexist. I'd have expected better of you.'

Sophie rolled her eyes and shoved my shoulder. 'Knock it off. Anyone would think you were my father.'

'Oh, and ageist too. Is this how Jordi teaches you to treat his customers?' I smiled up at her. 'Or is it your idea of flirting?'

'Baptiste, pack it in, I'm busy.' She refilled my glass and scribbled on my tab. When she lifted her hand my kingfisher was there, cocking his head and looking at me askance.

As she turned away the fire billowed abruptly. I looked to the door to see a group of young men hustle in on a rush of chill air, broad rugby-playing types jostling and joking. Before they had even closed the door behind them their eyes had scanned the room and settled on Sophie. One of them raised a hand. An urge to reach an arm around Sophie's waist and pull her closer rushed through me. What had got into me lately? Sophie had seen them too. 'Later,' she sang, and sidled over to greet them with kisses and smiles. I watched as she joined their huddle, slipping between them as they bent to kiss her cheeks. One of the men, not the tallest but the heaviest, was leaning too close and when she returned behind the bar to serve them drinks I saw her draw something on his place mat. I turned back to my dinner with an inexplicable pang of annoyance and devoted myself to the ceremony of mixing the steak tartare: seasoning the meat, folding in the pickles and spice, making the perfect mix of meat and vinegar, balancing the richness of the yolk with the heat of Tabasco. When it was perfect, I looked back up into the room. Sophie was busy, the men at the bar laughing amongst themselves. I began to eat slowly, letting my mind drift to other things.

'You're picking at your food.' The whispered words were right by my ear. I snapped out of my reverie to find Sophie leaning over my shoulder. I had almost finished and the bar had emptied out. 'Which means there's something – or someone – on your mind,' she said. 'So who is it?'

I always kept client business strictly confidential and Sophie knew that. Occasionally I would tell her anonymous stories of clients long past, but I was careful with details and I didn't make a habit of it. 'I was just taking the time to enjoy my dinner, that's all.' I glanced off into the fire, but she stepped around the table, peering into my face and gave a triumphant smile.

'You're lying.' Sophie slid into the chair opposite me. Her legs stretched out under the table, pushing against my own as she searched for free space. She let them rest there, and gave a sly smile. From the corner of my eye I could see one of the rugby-men watching her, the one who had been leaning over the bar. She followed my eye over to where he was standing, helped herself to one of my chips and made a show of eating it with great relish. When she turned her face back to mine it lit up in delight. 'And you're blushing, Baptiste.'

'It's the fire.'

'Come on. Why does nobody tell me anything? What's the word from your floating temple of happiness? Who's been lying on your couch?'

I thought of Amandine, and felt the floor sway slightly beneath my feet. I laid down my fork. 'I can't say, sorry.'

'I've never seen you like this.' She rested a small hand delicately on my knee under the table and scrutinised my face. 'Baptiste, are you in love with somebody?' Her voice softened to a whisper. 'Anyone I know?'

I looked at her bright teasing eyes and felt suddenly confused and defensive. 'Absolutely not. What kind of question is that?'

She leaned across the table conspiratorially. I kept my eyes on hers and away from the low scoop of her neckline. 'Perhaps you can't spot an opportunity when it's right in front of your eyes.'

'You're probably right,' I said, 'although not all opportunities should be taken.'

'Love isn't going to come and bite you in the arse, you know.'

'I could say the same to you. Although I suspect you'd find a willing volunteer amongst that nice group of boys,' I said.

'Probably.' She shrugged. 'Look, all I'm saying is maybe you spend too much time intellectualising about making others happy and never thinking about yourself.'

'I love my job,' I said emphatically. 'That's who I am, Sophie.'

She could see she'd gone too far. 'You're right,' she said, 'I'm sorry. And I think it's great that you spend your life trying to make people happier, it's one of the things that makes you so different. But there's more to you than what you do. There's more to life than work. Aside from your job, who are you?'

I pointed to the kingfisher. 'You know who I am,' I said, 'and I count myself lucky that I do too. Many people never find out who they are, and it wasn't always the case for me either.'

Sophie straightened up, pushing a dark strand of hair back off her face. 'Oh? So who were you before?'

I was born on a train. That's another story, but it might explain why I never learned to drive a car. Which in turn means I regularly travel by rail, and one thing I've learned about trains is that no matter how set you are on your destination, it only takes one set of points to switch and you are veering off in an entirely new direction.

I was going to be an engineer. It was what my father had always told me I would be. It had seemed so obvious to him that I took it as a given. I asked myself a lot of questions about where I came from, but never thought to question where I was going. I would become the man my father had imagined I would be, I would have a good career and make my parents proud. I studied hard, won a place to study engineering in Toulouse, and my life would surely have continued on that track had I not dared to challenge Professor Arrouet.

The professor was notorious amongst my peers. They said he had been brilliant in his day, but now he was known only as a rite of passage for second-year students. He was easy to spot. He was the one for whom crowds of students would part as he strode through the corridors and campus grounds, lost in his own thoughts, muttering to himself. His lectures were dense and delivered at breakneck speed. He refused to repeat himself, his patience was brittle and beware the student who dared to ask a question, it could mark you out for the rest of the year. Students quickly learned to enter his tutorials with a thoroughly researched essay and all the facts at their fingertips. I had been warned. But I still hadn't been prepared for that first one-to-one meeting with him, sitting in his dusty chamber, face to face across a scuffed wooden desk piled at either side with papers and books.

Although I was reading from my essay, my eyes were fixed on his pencil as he waved it round in tight circles as I spoke, urging me to move on, to speak faster and get it over with, my words accompanied by the perpetual tap of his foot. If that wasn't enough, my concentration was also tested by the way he constantly looked from his notebook to his watch and back again. Never at me. I had never been treated in such a way, and found it incomprehensible. Finally I couldn't help myself any longer. 'Professor,' I said, 'is what I'm saying wrong, or am I just speaking too slowly for you?'

The professor stopped what he was doing and regarded me darkly. 'If you are going to be insolent, Molino, you can leave.'

'I don't mean to be disrespectful,' I said, 'but I am here to learn.'

The professor jabbed his pencil at my essay, snapping the sharp point off and splintering the wood. He glared at me from beneath dark, profuse brows. 'Molino, what you have written will probably get you through your exams, but there is nothing to mark it out from every other student I see these days. You have summarised other people's thinking in a satisfactory manner and nothing more. Nothing in this tells me you can think critically. There is, as usual, nothing extraordinary about this work. Just because I am obliged to listen to every one of you tell me the same thing, year in, year out, does not mean I'm obliged to pretend it is anything but dull.' He leaned across his desk. 'One day you will graduate, get on with your life and forget all this completely. I, on the other hand, am condemned to repeat the damn thing eternally. Time is frittered away as I live the same moment over and over with only the face changed. Molino, Badot, Thibaudeau ... for twenty-five years the same thing over and over.'

I looked back at the professor. 'Then why do it?' I said.

The tapping foot stopped. For a moment there was a chill silence between us. 'Because,' he growled, 'that's my job.'

I wasn't even twenty years old then. When you're that young you're certain that your own life is yours to direct. The idea of doing a job you hate for a quarter of a century seems ridiculous. Yet he was a fiercely intelligent man. I was bursting with questions. Why would he accept that situation? What would he rather be doing? What was stopping him? We said no more for seconds, minutes perhaps, as I stared at the professor and the professor scowled out of the window as though he had seen armies coming across the campus.

'Twenty-five years,' he said again, turning to face me. I felt myself somewhere between a child and an adult, intimidated by his status and yet firm in my own convictions.

'What would you rather be doing instead?'

The professor laid his hands flat on the bare expanse of his desk and stared me hard in the eye.

'Impertinent boy. What interest is that to you?'

I had to ask myself the same question. 'I don't really know why I'm here either,' I said. 'I never wanted to be an engineer. I'm more interested in people than things.' The points had switched. My life was about to take a new direction and there was no going back. My father would be so disappointed.

But the professor had softened. 'Too much to tell and no time to list it all,' he said. 'So much to learn, so much to see. What I don't want to do is to give this tutorial one more time. I don't want to go home one more evening to spend a thin hour watching my children bicker with each other followed by an evening trying to read while my wife watches television. As if we had time for television. As if we had half the time we need to live before we die.'

He took a pencil sharpener from his drawer and began twisting his pencil around in it in sharp, staccato movements, the curls of shavings spiralling into the wastepaper basket. A bead of sweat rolled over one eyebrow and down into his lashes. The professor wiped his eyes and checked his watch once more, saw our half-hour tutorial was done and sprang to his feet. Wrapping a scarf around his neck in an unwieldy tangle he threw open the door. On the chair in the hall sat round-faced Bertrand Pigal, who began to rise, but the professor rushed past him. Almost as an afterthought he shouted back, 'Pigal! Go away and have a unique thought for once.'

Then there was just the clatter of his footsteps hurtling along the corridor and down the stairs, and the bewildered huff of Pigal's indignation.

The professor continued his lectures that next week, but rumours about this new turn of events spread fast and eyes accustomed to his peculiar comportment now followed him with renewed interest, as though he were a bomb about to explode. The next week I returned to his office, taking nothing with me but an empty notebook. He was there, waiting.

'Molino, good.'

'Sir.'

'Well,' he said, 'go on then. Let's see what you've got.'

'Sir?'

'Impertinent questions. Ask them. Get on with it.'

So I did. You can't even begin to imagine the chronic state of that man's mind. It was driving him and his family mad. He probably had half a lifetime ahead of him, yet all he could see was time closing in. He slept two hours a night at best and most of his meals were eaten on the move. Even when he did sit at the table with his family he was distracted, making notes and lists and sketches of his ideas and his things to do. His wife was exhausted by his behaviour. His children found his intensity frightening. They were all withdrawing from him and he knew it.

'You,' he said after twenty exhausting minutes, 'are going to tell no one about this. And you are going to keep coming here asking your questions until we work out how I get as much out of my life as possible without destroying everyone I love in the process.'

I had no idea what I was doing, my only qualification was a burning desire to figure him out, but logical questions seemed to evoke surprising answers, and somehow it worked. The next weeks and months changed his life. It changed both our lives. We both realised who we were supposed to be, and when you know that there's not much can stop you.

Sophie leaned forward. 'Where's that passion now?' she said. 'When did you become so afraid of life?'

'I'm not afraid, Sophie.'

'I think you are.' She took a deep breath. 'But I don't think it's too late.'

She picked a stray hair off my shoulder, brushing it from her fingers on to the floor and glanced back over at the men at the bar. 'What plans do you have for next weekend?'

'The usual. Reading, music, see some friends, take a walk, visit my parents.'

'You are too young to be so set in your ways. That was a good story, but it's what, twenty years old? Are you still going to be telling it in twenty years' time or are you going to make some new ones?' One of the rugby players was calling her over. She lifted a finger in acknowledgement. 'We'll start this Saturday.'

'Sophie, you're young …' I stared down into my empty glass.

She stood, straightening her skirt ostentatiously. 'More wine?'

I shook my head. 'I'm done.'

'Look at it coming down outside. Wait for a break in the rain or you'll get soaked.' She pushed her sleeves up to her elbows and put her hands on her hips. A tattoo of a vine trailed over the fine skin on her inner arm. 'I mean it,' she said. 'You have no opinion about the news because you never watch it and you can't talk about your work because it's confidential. But women like it if you have a passion in life, something to talk about. We can't live on philosophy alone.'

Drowsy with red wine and the heat from the fire I shrugged hopelessly. 'Since when have you been interested in how interesting I am to women?'

'It's a recent development,' she said. 'But I'm serious. Keep this Saturday free. Meet us in town. Big things are going to happen in the next few months. Be a part of it, not just an onlooker.'

'Us?'

'Me, a couple of my friends … and that lot.'

I looked over at the group of men by the bar. One of them caught my eye, and waved his fingers with a wry smile. Again, the knot was there in my stomach. I rose to my feet, making myself as tall as possible. 'What did you draw for him?' I asked casually.

Sophie raised an eyebrow. 'Jealous?'

'Hardly.'

On my paper square, as far from the kingfisher as she could get, she drew a tiny, angry dragon. 'So, will you come?' she said.

'I might.'

'You will,' she said, the flames' reflection burning gold and copper in her eyes.

The song of Spanish guitars rising into the evening air announced the first arrivals to the Last Sun party, a tradition I'd known as long as I'd lived on Candice and that some of my neighbours had known their entire lives. It was a farewell of sorts, the last towpath party of the year, held just before the long season where the sun stayed so low in the sky that we wouldn't see it rise above the trees for months. The music was the sign for the rest of us to join them.

Sabine from the *Yvonnick* was firing up a barbecue on the broad, cluttered deck of her barge. Plastic chairs and tables had been set on the path, but her two teenage children and a handful of their friends were sitting cross-legged on the ground with their guitars. No one told them to get up; after the next rains, unless we had a very dry winter, the towpath would be humid until spring. Seated at the table, Marcel and Yvette from the *Rouge-Gorge* just upstream were wrapped up warm in coats and scarves, sharing a rolled-up cigarette. I walked over, my arms full of my contributions to the meal: a huge loaf of bread, cheese and some wild mushrooms I had found earlier in the week. 'Good evening, Sabine, Marcel, Yvette.' I waved over at the teenagers. 'Hi, Manon, Gaëlle, everybody.' Having no children of my own it was such a pleasure to spend time with Sabine's kids. They were lively and bright, and their friends seemed to gravitate towards the canal too, so there were often several of them hanging about the towpath. There was a little one that tagged along too, too young for the other kids I suppose, but happy to call in and see me if I was around. He took a shine to Candice and her little garden. Always asking for a go on the piano, or planting olive stones and cherry pips in yoghurt pots up on deck. I was always pleased to see him. Having kids around makes us all feel younger.

'*Voilà*, Baptiste!' The music paused to allow a small chorus of greetings.

'Ooh, are those ceps? Hand them over.'

I passed Sabine the bag of mushrooms and pulled up a chair with Marcel and his wife. 'I'm not the last?'

'No, we're still waiting for Etienne and René.'

'It's been a while, Yvette. Where've you been hiding?'

'Busy times at the hospital.'

'More than usual?'

'For my ward at least. A lot of breaks being brought in from the protests.'

'Really? People are getting hurt?'

She looked over my shoulder in the direction of the city. 'Nothing too serious at the moment, mostly crowd-related injuries: ankles, noses, dislocations. But it's getting rough on the streets. I don't like the way it's heading.'

'Some people are spoiling for a fight,' muttered Marcel.

'That's what they always say before sending the police in heavy-handed,' Manon said, getting to her feet. When had she grown so tall? She was becoming a woman. And the spit of her mother, apart from their hair. Manon was blonde and cropped short whereas Sabine had long carmine hair, but it was clear the red was dyed in. They even shared the same expressions, like the impatient one Manon shot at Marcel. 'To silence any voice that is inconvenient to the establishment.'

'Ha!' Marcel looked up at Manon. 'You remind me of myself in sixty-eight.'

'Then you know why it's important.'

'I think it was different back then,' said Yvette. 'What we wanted in those days seemed more fundamental. Or is it just that I've got older?'

'No. We were fighting a corrupt state.' Marcel blew a thin line of smoke out towards the water.

Gaëlle put down her guitar. 'And so are we,' she said. 'I don't mean to be rude, but you've had work, you have your pensions when you decide to take them. But our whole generation is looking at a system that's broken. We'll soon become a lost generation, going straight from college to unemployment to being unemployable. Which will mean when we're your age we'll have no pension to speak of. We can't just sit back and accept that. What happened to *Égalité?*'

Marcel offered me the cigarette. The smoke was sweet and heady, but I passed it on. 'And if you ruled the country?'

'We need to get the old into retirement and free up some jobs for the young. That would be a good start.'

'People like me for example?' said Yvette. 'Does it make sense for a perfectly healthy surgeon to spend the next thirty or forty years doing crosswords? Can your generation afford to pay me to put my feet up, because I've no plans on dying soon?'

Marcel grinned and gave his wife's leg a squeeze. Gaëlle scowled. 'It's not funny,' she said. 'There's nothing out there for us. No work, no money, and as for the environment ...'

'Exactly,' said Manon. 'The world has been left in a mess for the young and now we're expected to pick up the pieces.'

Marcel waved a single index finger. 'Manon, if you're going to discuss the economy then try not to make yourself look ignorant by speaking before you think. We were born after the war. We had plenty of pieces to pick up ourselves.'

Manon shrugged. 'Maybe if the government made better use of our taxes and spent less on wars we'd have some hope for the future.'

'Since when do you pay taxes?' called Sabine from the deck of the *Yvonnick.*

'That's not the point! I want to one day.'

'And you will. And oh boy, then will we hear you complain.' Sabine punctuated her phrase with a wave of her tongs. 'Now, can you two lay the table please? These sausages are nearly ready.'

Etienne and René arrived at last, walking briskly up the towpath, their feet in perfectly synchronised pace. Etienne carried a plastic bag whose clinking grew louder as he approached, René a salad bowl covered with a cloth. He peeled off in Sabine's direction and soon the two of them were bent over salads and bread boards, conspiring in whispers and back-ward glances.

'What excellent timing,' said Etienne, pulling up a chair. 'A cold beer with friends is just what I need tonight.'

'I thought that too,' I told him, 'but the conversation isn't all that relaxing. We've gone straight on to politics I'm afraid.'

'We're going in to the protests on Saturday,' said Manon, setting out plates and cutlery.

'No you're not,' called Sabine, now cooking the ceps on a griddle over the flames. Their woody scent blew over to where we were sitting and my stomach rumbled. How did she make food so delicious in no time at all? It seemed there was no end to her extraordinary talents. Sabine had arrived after a messy divorce five years earlier, and renovated the *Yvonnick* from scratch herself. It was a big boat, almost twice the length of Candice, but with two teenagers she needed it. Even to this day she was constantly out fixing things. I'm not sure I'd ever seen her sit and simply relax. There was a time when Etienne and René were convinced we were perfect for each other. Sabine had found this hilarious.

'We have to go, Mum,' said Gaëlle. 'It's fine in the city centre. You know all the trouble is out in the suburbs.'

I put two and two together. I was meeting Sophie and her friends in Toulouse at the weekend. Now it made perfect sense. 'Actually, it seems I'll be going too,' I said.

Etienne laughed. 'Really? I never took you for a politico, Baptiste.'

'It appears I promised a friend before I really knew what I was getting into.'

Ears pricked up. 'A friend? Is she pretty?'

Sabine came over with the meat. 'Men will do any old foolish thing for a pretty girl,' she grumbled. 'Did you not hear Yvette saying people are getting injured?' A chill wave of foreboding coursed through me. I suddenly had my own doubts about going into Toulouse. I didn't enjoy the city at the best of times and the thought of crowds made me shudder.

'Baptiste can look after us!' grinned Manon.

'I've told you, you're not going.' Sabine looked over at me. 'It's no place for children.'

'We're not children,' protested Gaëlle.

'Well, yes, in this case you are.'

Etienne flipped the cap on a bottle and poured the beer slowly into a glass. 'Your mum's right,' he said. 'It might have been fine in the centre so far, but they're expecting real trouble. Everyone's on edge at the bank. You should stay out of it.'

'What kind of trouble?'

'We've been making a riot plan.'

'You're kidding.'

'Nope.' Etienne shook his head. 'I think all the banks are. There's plenty of precedent already in Europe and we could be next. Better to be prepared for the worst.'

I thought back to the newspaper article, what had they called it? Boiling point? 'So you really think there could be riots?' I said.

Etienne took a long drink of his beer. 'All I know is it's a powder keg out there. It would only take one spark to set the whole thing ablaze. Maybe it will happen this year, maybe not for ten years, who knows?' He unfurled on his chair, stretching his legs out and his arms up to the sky, taking a deep breath. 'Anyway, I'm not here to talk about work, so back to pretty friends,' he said. 'I happened to notice *the* most beautiful woman visiting you earlier this week. Is that who I think it is?'

'That beautiful woman is expecting me to make her happy, not miserable,' I told him.

'My darling stupid friend. Why would you think you would make her miserable?'

'Even if she weren't a client – which she is, making her strictly off-limits – what would a woman like that want with a middle-aged bachelor who lives on a boat? It would all be very romantic to start with, but when the novelty wore off she'd only want to change me, move me on to dry land and cut my hair. I'd be nothing but a disappointment.'

'Ah, just a client. But I see you've put some thought into it anyway,' said Etienne with a grin.

I shrugged. 'Well, as you say, she is beautiful. But she's my client so that's that.'

'Surely there could be an exception to the rule if …'

'No, there can't. And no, before you ask, the friend I'm meeting on Saturday isn't going to get you an excuse for buying a new hat either.'

Marcel laughed. 'There are plenty of smart, beautiful women who are happy to live out here,' he said, winking at Yvette. 'Some of them insist on it.'

'It's such a pity about you and Sabine,' said René, finally taking his seat.

'OK, enough of that,' Sabine said, raising her glass to the rosy skies beyond the plane trees. 'We're all here. Here's to the Last Sun, and our good health until we see him above the trees again.'

'Good health!'

'And Baptiste,' she said, 'If you can't stay away from town at the weekend, at least don't go starting any riots.'

'Are we on holiday, Chouette?' you asked, gazing out of the
window at dragonflies skirring across the water.

'We're on a canal boat,' I said gently.

'I can see that.'

'Candice.'

I waited. You frowned at the brown water slipping silently
past. Please, not this, I thought. If you lose Candice you'll
have lost yourself. You reached for the piano, softly pressing
down a single chord and letting it fade into silence. 'But this
is not the sea. I thought ... I had this dream once where I was
on a canal boat on the sea,' you said. 'It's been so long since I
saw the sea.'

I put my hand on your shoulder. 'Come upstairs,' I said.

It was warm in the wheelhouse, the sun pushing through
a haze of stratus clouds. I opened the canal-side door and
joined you by the wheel. 'Look at the wheel,' I said. 'See

where the varnish has worn? This boat has seen some adventures.'

You looked uncertain, but you laid your hands on the wheel as though there might be magic in it.

'You've told me a lot of stories, standing right here,' I said. 'I think it's my favourite place on Candice.'

Your chest rose and fell, rose and fell. I stood at your side and told myself I must remember the good in this. Not why we are here, but that we are here, together. The way your hands look at home on the wheel, and the length of your eyelashes, which I only noticed recently because I didn't dare look right into your eyes. The smell of you, like fresh air and tree bark. Make this what I remember later, I prayed. But of course neither of us gets to choose.

More and more your mind lets precious moments perish as though they mean nothing, creating blind spots that you fill in with fear and fantasy. There's a cruelty in that, as there is in my mind, which discards nothing. The shape of the place in my life that was empty before I met you. A kiss. A cool breeze that came like a caress across my skin as I lay on my back on your bed in the sweltering heat of an early summer, the burn of your toes touching mine and the zither of cicadas in the night. It was your bed then, not ours, a strange and exciting place to be naked. You had won me, or I had won you.

Then there is the time I found the violin case open and the instrument missing, the hurt in your eyes as you accused me of stealing it. The time you were panicked and furious with me for suggesting you put on your glasses, convinced you had never worn glasses despite being unable to read your own handwriting. I couldn't calm you that night and had to walk the freezing towpath in my nightdress to rouse Marcel from his sleep. Then there is the woman from St Sernin calling to tell me you were there at her door yet again.

With every one of these moments I feel myself change a little, the firing of neurons, the chemical pathways, the memory-makers making me someone different. The shifting DNA of our life together. You shared it with me for a while, but your memories were never identical to mine even at their birth and they've been diverging ever since.

Your brow was furrowed. 'What were we talking about?' you said.

'Candice, the sea, your stories ...'

'Oh,' you said. 'The water is so vague about these things.' You looked out over the decks to the canal curving away, to the towpath, the tall trees and the high wall that hides the world beyond, screwing up your eyes as if searching your mind for something you're sure used to be there, like a mis-shelved book. 'So are we on holiday?'

'We're on Candice,' I said again. I knew I didn't have much time to help you find yourself again before you became frightened. I had to find a hook. 'I'll never forget that story you told me about how you came to be here,' I said, 'after that day in September, when you lived in the Mirail.'

You looked at me anxiously. I flicked through the notebook, it was in there somewhere. 'Your windows were broken,' I said, rifling through the pages. 'Yes. Here it is.' There is the sketch, an old man in a park, holding a dog and staring into the sky.

'Oh, yes,' you said, reaching a finger out to touch the drawing. 'They flew planes into buildings. My apartment exploded. I never went back.'

I always sat by the windows in that place, craving the light and the open space beyond the apartment. It was stuffy by the smeared glass of the east window where I bent over the table studying my notes, but it was too early to open the windows yet. The south-side balcony would have been cooler, but it looked out over the ring road, shuddering with traffic and giving me vertigo. On days when I had no clients I kept the windows thrown open whatever the weather. I would rather wear my coat indoors than breathe the stench of disinfectant from the stairwell. It got everywhere, seeping under the closed door and giving me headaches. But that day the chill autumn mornings had already set in and I needed the place warm enough for my client's session. I would open the window just as he arrived, a balancing act of comfort and fresh air.

In the end that's not what happened. When the shrilling telephone disturbed my thoughts I considered not answering it, but capitulated after a few rings. When my client told me he wanted to cancel his appointment I tried to change his mind, but failed. When I felt the throbbing in my temples from the combination of heat, bleach and disappointment, I thought of opening the windows wide and sitting there until I felt well enough to play the piano, but decided instead to take a walk. When, later, I returned to the flat and found the shards of shattered glass flung across the room so hard that two fragments had embedded themselves in the side of the piano, I could see the ghost of myself still sitting by the gaping window where I had been sitting all morning, where I would still have been sitting, had I not …

The shards of glass looked surreal, piercing the wood of the old upright, the one from my parents' cottage that had belonged originally to my grandmother and which my parents had passed on to me ten years before as a housewarming present when I was finally earning enough to move out and pay a meagre rent of my own. It was impossible not to imagine the trajectory of that glass as it sliced across the small room from one side to the other. Impossible not to picture the alternative, myself thrown back in the blast, the shards that had lodged in the piano lodging instead in my flesh, my blood on the parquet, a young man gasping for his last breath. The more I thought about it the stronger the images became until they seemed more like a dream, an old film or a hazy memory. I am not normally that macabre, but a brush with mortality can bring it out in us all. I still half remember that death that never happened.

The east window looked out over the small scrap of park seven floors below, just a playground and a few shrubs, and beyond to a cluster of shops, a bakery and a tobacconist. A woman was pushing a baby in a pram round the gravel path that circled the park fence and an old man was walking a small dog, which was squatting right by the swings. I stared out at them, hoping the man would pick up his dog's mess and considering what to do with my morning, now an empty page. Any thrill of liberation was tempered by the setback. The inertia of a missed appointment often turned into a lost client, which closed the door on the chance of a referral. I was just setting out. I needed every client and every appointment I could get if I was to pay the rent and make this work.

I took my time setting things straight. I dried the plate and bowl that had been sitting on the draining board. I paid a bill. Before leaving the apartment I took a breath deep enough to get me most of the way down the seven foul-smelling flights of stairs at a jog. It would be the last time I had to do that.

As I skirted the park around to the pharmacy there was a roar overhead, the kind that vibrates you in your skin. A chill rush of adrenaline drenched me, my body snapping into a half crouch as my eyes shot to the sky. We were all jumpy that week. It was only a few days after the planes in New York, the burning city, and there were plenty of reasons to attack Toulouse. The airport, the satellite industries; what made us proud also made us vulnerable and we all had our eyes up every time a plane came over.

The rumble grew louder as I scanned the sky for a clue. North, east, south, and there it was. A plane rising into clear blue skies, twin trails of condensation blossoming in its wake. Just another plane taking off from Blagnac. I allowed myself a small, relieved laugh and wondered when this fearfulness would retreat. The young woman with the pram looked over at me and smiled weakly, a shared acknowledgement that we were wearing our humanity close to the surface. For an instant before the adrenaline subsided I felt the urge to embrace her, to offer something beyond an awkward smile, but I knew she would take it the wrong way. She looked away from me to another child, a boy scrambling up the ladder on to the paint-peeling slide. He was young, distracted, unconcerned by the noise of planes overhead. The image freezes there.

Everything goes white and the air is sucked away. As I fight to fill my lungs there are explosions. Three, maybe five. It is all so fast, so surprising.

The green neon cross of the pharmacy comes back into focus first. Then the park. The boy is at the bottom of the slide screaming. The old man is lying on the floor. His dog has fled under a hedge and the long lead is a jagged scar on the playground floor.

For a moment we were held together by our incomprehension. Then the woman pulled her baby out of the pram, clutching it tight against her chest, her hand covering its tiny head. She was looking up and spinning, trying to figure out where the danger was so she could put her body between that and her baby. Behind her a mushroom cloud bloomed and billowed and then it began to rain glass.

I put an arm up to cover my head and the other over my mouth. The air filled with something noxious and hot – sulphur, ammonia, chlorine, maybe, burning my eyes and throat. I ran to the old man first. He was trembling, terrified. I thought his heart might go. 'My dog! Peanut!' Peanut. What kind of name is that for a dog? It still sticks in my mind. The woman had gathered her children, the pram abandoned, scouring the surroundings for safety. I wanted to help her, but I had no idea where safety was. Sirens begin to wail in the distance. Were the buildings around us going to crumble and fall like those on television? We had to move.

The five of us lurched out of the shadow of the apartment blocks towards the shelter of the parade of shops, keeping our backs to the cloud. The baby was screaming, her brother was weeping, and the old man clutched the wriggling dog to his chest. 'It's going to be all right,' he said to anyone who would listen. 'Everything will be all right.' But for many people everything was not all right. The explosion had been catastrophic. In the blink of an eye, thousands became homeless.

On the long train journey out of the city we stood crammed into the stifling carriages like refugees, rebreathing our exhalations, all the windows closed against the toxic air. By that time you could no longer smoke on the trains, but the shabby velour upholstery still leeched a nauseating odour of stale tobacco. I thought at least a glimpse of the fields would settle my stomach, but the view out was blocked with bodies. Instead I looked down the carriage over the mumble of shocked men and women, reliving the explosion and its aftermath, caught up in the "what ifs" and the "whys".

The Christmas tree was already up when I arrived at the cottage, the lights twinkling in the window as my mother rushed out to greet me at the front gate as though I had risen from the dead. I hadn't been able to call to let them know I was coming. My father stayed back, framed in the doorway and scratching his head as he wondered out loud who the tallest person in the village might be. He was right, I would need to borrow some clothes; no one on the TV had any idea when it would be safe to go back. I ended up sitting around the house in overalls from the local mechanic until we were given the all clear to go home a few days later.

I say home. That apartment had never really felt like home, and after this, how could it ever? The landlord had already warned me that there wasn't a window left in the block and although people had started patching them up with plastic or wood, making sure that the elderly and those with children took priority, supplies were almost exhausted. Until the glass could be replaced even those with a temporary fix were unsure how they could make it through the winter. If it had just been our blocks, which were closest to the fertiliser factory where the explosion happened, it might have been all right, but the blast radius had been kilometres wide. Most of the city's windows were shattered. The waiting list for a glazier already stretched into months.

On that train journey back into Toulouse, still feeling philosophical and raw, I settled myself into the idea of a cold winter and, at least for the foreseeable future, a regular job. Thankfully people were returning in a trickle and I was able to stare out of the scratched window and retreat into the depths of my spirits. Pulling out of the small station of my parents' village we cut immediately through acres of ripe sunflowers, their heads withered towards the earth as though they had forgotten where the light comes from or were too tired to remember. No matter how glorious and invincible those fields of flowers look in summer, by autumn it's always a battlefield. I was glad when we emerged from the sunflowers and the land opened out into gentle swells of ploughed fields, the sparrow-brown earth peppered with short golden straws, and wood smoke blowing across the horizon as though a steam train had recently passed. The vines, too, were already harvested, the grapes gone and their blood-stained leaves settling in drifts against the gnarled stems, waiting for the October winds to invite them to dance. Beyond the fields the blue-grey shadows of the mountains rose slowly from the dark of the land, becoming a faint haze where the sky met them in rosy-white, before falling away into itself, vivid blue above.

The emptiness was hypnotic and calming. There were few signs of human life, all the villages and towns along the route set well back from the tracks. There were occasional little stone barns standing in the middle of the fields, each orange roof peppered with holes to a greater or lesser extent, sometimes with entire walls collapsing through their own windows.

Every now and then the odd field of scrub was occupied by a lone house, a couple of grazing horses and a handful of ravens. As we passed by I could see that most of the shutters were closed, keeping the houses dark and airless. I imagined tiled floors inside, dark wooden tables, dressers and wardrobes, all crouched in the shadows like a mausoleum. I felt suffocated just looking. It made me want to fling open the shutters and let the people breathe.

Somewhere along the line we stopped at a station which looked all but deserted. The platform was crumbling and a forest of weeds pushed through the rocks of the track ballast. I knew that place well. Every time I passed through it I would feel a surge of sentimentality. Somewhere along the next stretch of track, I knew, was the place where I was born. Where my mother died. That day as we set off again, the rattle and sway of the carriages provoking the familiar lurch in my belly, it was accompanied by a deep irrational panic. I pressed my forehead against the cooling glass, believing that if I could ride that train through those fields for ever I would.

The residents met in the town hall to fix what could be fixed. We organised ourselves into a kind of cooperative, some of us cleaning up, some making repairs, some running a soup kitchen and still others watching those children who were too young for school. The women complained that it was too crowded in the town hall, but there was nowhere else safe to let the children play. I would have given anything right then to stay out of those apartments so I volunteered to start by cleaning up the playground, but by the time I had crossed to the park the trembling had set in. I steadied myself on the fence as I closed my eyes and took a moment to breathe and to calm myself.

I felt a hand on my arm. 'Are you OK, son?' I found myself looking into the soft brown eyes of a man almost as tall as me. He was standing on the other side of the fence, his grey hair sticking up at all angles, his mouth hidden below his riotous moustache.

I nodded. 'I'm fine, thanks. Just a flashback I suppose. I was out here when the explosion happened.'

'Thank goodness you weren't hurt' – his eyes scanned me quickly just to check that was the case – 'but it must have been traumatic for you.'

'Lucky escape,' I said.

He looked at me appraisingly. 'Oscar,' he said, removing his hand and holding it out.

'Baptiste.' I took his hand and instantly felt better for his company. 'I came down to get this place cleaned up, the kids are driving the parents mad cooped up in there, but it looks like you've already made a start.'

'Great minds think alike. I got sick of watching the news and feeling bad for you all so I decided to come and be of practical use. I hope you don't mind?'

So that was why I didn't recognise him, although in that place you could pass your neighbour on the street and never realise. 'No, on the contrary. Thank you.'

We worked together in companionable silence, sweeping shards and splinters from the slide, raking them from the surrounding soil, pulling out the poisoned shrubs. 'You know,' Oscar said to me after a while, 'it's years since I've been in a playground. The one where I grew up used to be my absolute favourite place to spend time. It can't have been much, a lot like this one I suppose, but to me then it seemed vast and extraordinary. So many other worlds there to explore.' He had one of those smiles on his face, the kind when you are recalling a memory so perfect you feel its pleasure all over again. I thought of my childhood in the village. There had been no playground there, except the swings by the hateful duck pond which I avoided at all costs.

'What kind of worlds?' I asked.

'Oh, a climbing frame like this could be a rocket, a pirate ship, a fortress or a submarine, or each one in turn. And a boy could time travel on these swings.'

It was true, I could see it. 'Yes,' I said, 'that slide could take you to the centre of the earth.'

'Or the bottom of the sea.' He smiled at me, a rueful smile. 'It's such a pity, the way we lose it,' he said.

'Lose what?'

'Our imagination.' He was brushing the rope climber with a toothbrush, painstakingly examining each strand, working from top to bottom and running his own thick-skinned fingers around the strands he had covered to ensure not even the tiniest chip of glass remained. He paused to examine his fingertips. 'Terrible business, this. They're still saying it was an accident, but what with the timing and all … well, what do you think?'

'Hang on,' I said, 'we don't really lose our imaginations, do we? As we get older we might not imagine our bicycles flying any longer, or dragons guarding the bathroom door, but we can still lose ourselves in stories and we can still imagine the future.'

He shrugged. 'You're still young,' he said. 'Maybe you can. But not me. Not any more.'

The familiar thrill of excitement raced through me. Here was a puzzle to be solved. I looked at him harder. He wasn't that old, fifty at a stretch. He had an air of resignation about him, but beyond that he seemed uncomplicated, clear as water. 'What do you do for a living?'

'I'm a lawyer,' he said, avoiding my eye and running his hand through his crazy hair. 'And no, it's not what you're thinking. I'm really just here to help, so do me a favour and don't tell anyone.'

'I wasn't thinking anything.'

'Really? Most people do make certain judgements, I'm afraid.'

'That can't be easy.'

'Oh well,' he said, 'it was a terrible career choice, but that's what comes of choosing a career when we're so young. I was an argumentative child and everyone told me I'd make a brilliant lawyer. It seemed like an exciting, well-paid profession and I do have a certain aptitude for it. But law school trained facts and logic in and my creativity out. Can you imagine never enjoying a novel or a film properly again because you can't suspend your disbelief long enough to enjoy the story? Can you imagine every case you work on resulting in at least one unhappy person?'

'Getting what you think you want doesn't always make you happy.'

'No, son,' he said. 'That's true.'

'Perhaps it's time for a change?'

'Well, I'm trying not to grow old and cynical, no one likes a grumpy old man, but no matter what I do, I don't think I'll ever be happy again like I was when I was a boy.' He put his hand on my shoulder. 'Don't be a lawyer. You're not, are you?'

'No,' I said. 'In fact …' After what he had said it seemed opportunistic to suggest he made an appointment, but I still had the rent to pay after all and I really thought I could get somewhere with him. I explained what I did, and told him that despite a minor issue with my office, I'd love him to come and see me. Payment only on satisfaction.

'Where's your office?' he asked.

'Seventh floor,' I said, pointing up at the ravaged apartments.

'Ah,' he said. 'Yes, I can see the problem. How is it up there?'

'It's a wreck. No windows and no likelihood of getting any until spring,' I told him. 'Not that I ever shut them anyway, but it's no place to invite my clients. I can figure something out, though. I'm going to have to, or my business will be done for.'

'I take it that's your home too?'

I thought of the train ride back, the sense of displacement that had nothing to do with the physical damage to the building. 'Well, it's where I live. I'm not sure I've really found my home yet, if you know what I mean.'

He smiled. 'I do,' he said. He looked me over and then looked back up at the rows of dark cavities where windows had been, all the while nodding to himself. Something was shifting inside him. 'Have you ever bumped into someone by chance,' he said, 'and suddenly everything becomes clear. When you've been avoiding something, and now you know what you need to do?'

I thought of the professor. 'Yes, I have.'

'Well, now I have too. Who'd have thought it? I'm so pleased to have met you.'

A new client, I thought, a silver lining to a dark cloud. No need to go looking for jobs after all. 'If you don't mind the unorthodox environment we could start this week,' I suggested. 'My diary is pretty clear.'

He shook his head. 'Thank you, but you've already helped me enough. I know exactly what I need to do.' My spirits fell. 'But on the other hand,' he said, 'maybe I can help you. It transpires I shall soon be going away for a long time, who knows how long. I don't really want to rent my place out, but I could do with someone to stay there and keep an eye on things.' He smiled at me. 'It would be a bit of a change from this place, but I have the feeling you wouldn't mind that too much. What would you say to house-sitting a boat?'

Oscar went to Scotland, only returning for his first visit last year. Yvette told me later that he had always preferred the coast, often taking long trips on Candice, and it didn't surprise them when he finally moved to live by the sea. It did surprise them that he chose Scotland, or rather, Scotland chose him. He had intended to travel for a while apparently and took very little with him, but quickly fell in love with one of the Scottish islands, set up a pottery and married a wood-turner.

Yvette says he was a lot like you, and for a while she called you Oscar by mistake, even though you were twenty years younger than him. When she talks about him there is something more to her words than the words themselves, and I sometimes wonder if she wasn't a little bit in love with him herself, if it wasn't just his job as a lawyer he had to leave in the past.

Whatever my speculations, Oscar stayed in touch with Yvette and Marcel and they still plan to visit him one day, although no matter how much Oscar and Miriam tried to persuade him that they enjoy plenty of sunny days, Marcel is still worried about travelling all that way to be rained on.

When Oscar and Miriam did visit, apparently a spur-of-the-moment decision, they arrived by taxi and had to walk past Candice to get down to the *Rouge-Gorge*. Oscar couldn't resist dropping by to surprise you.

The first I knew of it was the clang of the cowbell, and the wavering note in your voice as you called down to me from the wheelhouse. 'Chouette?' When I came upstairs you were standing just the other side of the glass door, looking through at the two strangers standing there with their suitcases, smiling. I was as surprised as you, and assumed they were lost. It was possible they were looking for one of the other boats downstream that sometimes took paying passengers on weekend cruises.

When I opened the door, Oscar stepped towards you, effusive. 'It's me, Oscar. I suppose you don't recognise me after all these years.' Once he said his name I realised it would have been impossible not to recognise him; he was the most striking-looking man I think I've ever seen. He had the air of a benevolent wizard, tall and graceful, with long grey hair and chocolate-coloured eyes set deep in lines like starbursts. He reached both hands up to place them on your cheeks, like a father would a long-lost son. You flinched, and Oscar pulled away in surprise. No one had thought to warn him.

'Not his face,' I told him. 'He's sensitive since ... well, it's a long story. You'd better come in and sit down.'

A white mist skimmed the surface of the canal. Ducks swam in and out of it like ghostly flotillas. I made my way upstream under fallen clouds, tramping through leaves and the damp gravel on the towpath, north and west up into Toulouse. Most boats already had smoking chimneys, the salt-oak smell pitted against the sweetness of the hedgerows, redolent of the time of year. After over fifteen years by its side, I knew the scents of that path intimately. Each season has its own flavour. Winter is the sharp smell of snow, bright as glass, and soups that simmer so long that everything around takes on their warmth. Summer is the smoke-tang of charring meat. Spring smells yellow-green, a fresh salad of scents that rise and fall like a wind-blown veil. My favourite, autumn, smells of wet earth, red wine and burning wood.

I knew the sights just as well: the pattern of the boats I would pass, strung together like beads, red, green and blue. The lines of every curve of grass, every swell of hedgerow. I knew where I should place my feet carefully because the path was old and had crumbled away, and where I could lengthen my pace and raise my eyes to the scenery. I knew where the water in the canal picked up speed and where it slowed, the parts of the banks where branches leaning into the water caused eddies and where the light fell in such a way that on a damp morning you might see rainbows just above the water. I knew how a full moon looked on the water in both winter and in summer. I knew where the smells of the wild garlic would accost me as I rounded a corner, and how the acacia blossom would feel, falling on my skin in May round by the lock; the places where you could take shelter from the weather and where you would take its full force. I could tell you the words on every milestone and canal marker, and often where filaments of spider silk would be stretched across the path, catching your face. I was connected to that small corner of the planet like no other. As I walked I let daydreams flicker in and out of life, and reflected again on the discussion I'd had with Etienne and Marcel. I began to wonder, if circumstance ever forced me to move, could I come to love another place the same way? It would be like asking a man who has been in love with his wife for years if he could love another. How can you imagine any alternative when you are saturated with the way her body fits into yours, the smell of her neck, the way she always sits in the same chair?

As I approached Toulouse the wind picked up, spreading the clouds like butter and allowing hesitant sunbeams to push through. Buildings rose on either side of me to meet the dappling skies. By the time I reached Riquet's statue at the top of the broad avenue that led down into the city centre there was a spreading patch of blue above his head. As I turned, leaving his canal behind I found myself in a rising tide of people flowing down the wide pavements. By the time I'd passed the entrance to the metro I was submerged in the weight of bodies and their low-level clamour. I unwound the scarf that earlier had felt snug but now felt suffocating. Not far to go, I told myself, nearly there.

Sophie had asked me to meet her by the carousel in the Place St Georges. I began to wonder if I would ever find her in the crowd, but most people seemed to be heading further into the city centre and once I arrived in the square itself there were only a few bored-looking students with placards and a handful of police keeping them off the grassed areas and away from the carousel where parents looked on, edgy and ambivalent as their children turned circles under the golden canopy. I remembered what Sabine had said. 'It's no place for children.' Cool hands closed over my eyes.

'Sophie!'

'How did you guess?' She removed her fingers and I turned and looked down into her face, wind-blown and bright. Away from the bar she was transformed. It wasn't in her clothes or her hair, but in the way she held herself. She took up more space, like a carousel horse come to life. She embraced me on tiptoes, planting a kiss on each cheek, then stepped back a pace, holding me at arm's length.

'It's good to see you. You look different outside of the bar.'

'I was just thinking the same thing.'

Sophie looked pleased. 'Right, come on then, everyone else is over near the Capitole.'

'Some kind of a date this is.'

'Knock it off, or I'll tell my mother.'

'I'm sure she'd tell you the same thing.'

'OK, whatever.' She took my hand and began to lead me along, winding through people and down side streets. 'Hurry up. There's such a great turnout, if we're not quick we'll never find them.'

I took one pace for every two of hers. 'So you've brought me here to persuade me that we need to do more to get young people into work, and get old people to retire as soon as possible, is that right?'

Sophie had to raise her voice to be heard, shouting up at me as she walked. 'You know what, I don't really care if you think we're right or wrong. I just want you to have an opinion. I want you to realise that this matters. We have to burst that bubble you've made for yourself so you remember what passion feels like.' We broke through into the vast Place du Capitole. 'It matters to me,' she shouted breathlessly, 'and it matters to all these people. Look at them all.' Hundreds, maybe thousands of people were filling the square, now so closely packed that they no longer looked like individuals but a single mass. There was a fluidity to their movement as they shifted slowly in and out of any available space.

I saw a flock of migrating starlings late one autumn down near the Spanish border, in a city where the rise and fall of mountains abruptly turns to waves. Every year in November all the starlings in France gather there. They blacken the skies and defecate on the streets, on the parked cars and on the people of the city. Every wire strung across the sky is covered with them like iron filings. Red rooftops blacken. Not a flock but a swarm. City officials shoot at them, but they won't disperse. They stick together, rising up in a clattering wave, up into the clouds, turning and swelling, billowing out and then settling down again, half a kilometre further along. They leave only when they're ready, when something finally tells them it's time to take flight. I watched those starlings for hours, mesmerised, trying to work out what made them lift, what made them turn, what made them settle, what made it all work.

'These people care about their future,' Sophie said, tugging me into their midst. 'They care enough to do something about it.'

I held back. 'Is protesting really doing something about it?'

'When people come to you because they are unhappy, is that doing something about it?'

I smiled. She was sharp. 'They don't know what the answer is yet.'

'Maybe we don't either, exactly. But we know it's time for change.' Sophie pulled me again, down into the crowd. 'And maybe you could help?'

'Me?'

'If unhappiness bothers you in one person, how can you not feel moved by so much discontent all in one place?'

I looked at the buzzing, jostling men and women around us. Now I was in amongst them they looked like individuals again. Mostly young, laughing and joking on the surface but with a hard energy rising up somewhere in their midst. I thought again of the starlings. Every bird an individual until it joins the flock. 'Do these people even know why they are here, Sophie? In my experience most people haven't a clue why they're unhappy. We latch on to the first explanation someone offers.'

'Baptiste, some of these people are struggling to eat.'

'And some of them clearly are not.' I pointed out a group of students all talking or texting or taking selfies on their phones. 'Why are they here?'

'Solidarity? Because they know that they could be next. Baptiste,' she urged, tightening her grip on my hand and looking up at me, 'you're the kingfisher, remember? Do your thing. This is the society you live in, these people are the future. You can't just ignore it.'

'There's a reason the kingfisher fishes in a quiet corner of the canal, Sophie,' I said, 'and not in the ocean.'

Eyes flickered over us and then away again as we inched through the throng until Sophie finally caught sight of her friends by a dais in the centre of the square. I didn't recognise either of the girls, but I knew two of the men from the bar, the dragon and one of his friends. The dragon turned to watch as we got closer, keeping his eyes fixed on our approach, flickering between Sophie and me. I saw him say something that made the others turn too, and as I fell under their regard

I immediately felt old and out of place. I let Sophie's hand drop, but she slipped her arm through mine and pulled in close enough that I could feel the heat of her against me as we drew into their small circle.

'This is Baptiste,' she said with a smile, 'from the bar.'

'We've heard so much about you,' said the dragon. Was I being sensitive, or was there scorn in his voice? I held out a hand. He considered it with a scowl. Anger came off him like lightning looking for a place to earth. So Etienne was right, a storm was brewing. 'You know, if you're here to complain about your pension,' he said, 'you'll not find a lot of sympathy. Sophie's brought you to the wrong demo.'

The others sniggered. Sophie clicked her tongue against her teeth and rolled her eyes at him. 'Didier,' she warned.

'I'm just kidding,' he said, taking my hand and shaking it hard, 'but my point remains. Sophie will be the first to admit that she didn't go to university to end up serving you drinks every night in a crappy bar in the suburbs.'

'At least I have a job.'

'That pays pin money, Sophie. That you're forced to do because our degrees mean nothing. That you'll probably have to do until you're eighty if you want a decent pension. There's not enough work for all of us. Something has to give, and it's either our generation or' – he looked at me pointedly – 'yours.'

My generation? Just how old did they think I was? Sophie stepped in, trying to broker peace. 'He's just generalising. He doesn't mean you specifically.'

'I mean the establishment,' Didier said, 'the people who make these policies that only help themselves. And who run a government that claims they have no money to help us yet still welcomes in people like you.'

We were being jostled closer together. 'People like me?'

'Immigrants. It might be hard for you to swallow but the French people have to help themselves before we can help everyone else who wants to live here.' He folded his arms. 'No offence.'

For a moment I was taken aback. What had Sophie shared with him about me, about my mother? Then I realised it was more likely he was just making his own assumptions based on my appearance. 'No offence to you either,' I said, 'but if life's not giving you what you think you deserve, do you plan to actually do anything about it or just spend your time blaming other people?' It was snappy, but Didier had started off aggressive and the weight of people around me was making me agitated.

Didier bristled. I could see now why Sophie had drawn him as a dragon. 'Oh, that's right, make it my problem. You have a job, so you're just fine. No need to worry about anyone else.' He squared up to me. He was well built but still shorter than me by a good few inches. I squared back, the air between us crackling.

'With all due respect, Didier, you know nothing about me, you know nothing about my life.'

'And you know nothing about ours.'

I saw Didier look over at Sophie then, rolling his eyes, but she refused to take his side. 'Pack it in, the pair of you,' she said. 'Put your dicks away. How can we achieve anything if we're fighting amongst ourselves?'

'I don't know what you were thinking of, bringing him here,' Didier said. 'He's got no intention of listening to any of us.' It wasn't true though. Sophie's instinct had been right. There was something exciting, if a little overwhelming, about being there in that moment. I wanted to talk to every one of those students, to ask them what they were really doing there, what they were looking for and where they were going. Were they going along with things, as I had once, heading down a track they hadn't really thought through, waiting for the points to switch?

'It's not that I'm not interested,' I said.

'Good. Here we go then.' Didier pushed a loudhailer against my chest and propelled me backwards, up the steps of the dais.

'Didier, that's enough.' Sophie tightened her fingers around my arm, but Didier had put his body between us and she was forced to release me, pulling an apologetic face as she did. I looked at her in confusion. Faces had turned to stare, the loud conversations around me fading to an expectant rumble. The timber was hard and unforgiving under my feet.

A young woman met my eye. 'Hi,' I said.

'Hi.' She continued to stare. 'Are you going to say something or are you just going to stand there?'

'What? No, I—'

Didier stepped in. 'He's here to tell us to stop complaining,' he shouted. Heads lifted like a dog's hackles, all eyes suddenly on me. I looked out at them. So many young faces, already dissatisfied, already disenchanted, already fuelled by a sense of entitlement.

'Who are you?' someone called.

'What do you study?' shouted another, to a ripple of nervous laughter.

'I'm just here to listen,' I said quietly, putting down the loudhailer at my feet. 'Apparently my generation don't listen. So I'm here, I'm listening now. That's all.'

'Hey, listen, give me a job!' someone called out behind me, accompanied by more mirth from those nearby.

I turned to look at him, a short, slightly built young man with the kind of haircut your mother takes you for. 'What kind of a job do you want?' I asked.

'We can't hear you!'

Didier's friend moved forward then, climbing the steps until he was standing next to me, looking out at the wind blowing through the crowd. I felt another lurch in my stomach. Why didn't I just get down off the dais? Why was I letting myself be intimidated? Sophie was nowhere in sight, swallowed up in the sea of faces. The dragon's apprentice grabbed my hand and spoke into the megaphone. 'What would make me happy would be a job when I leave college next year, decent pay when I work, and a pension when I'm sixty. Anyone else feel the same?' There was a flutter of applause.

I tried to focus on him. To drown out the others. To see just that one person. 'It's what you're concerned about right now,' I said, 'but will those things really satisfy you?'

'Those are my basic rights. Once I have those I can take care of the rest myself.'

I tried to think back to myself at his age. Had I felt that way too? No, I had learned better from my parents than to expect providence, divine or otherwise. I rubbed my eyes. 'I don't like being the one to break it to you,' I said, 'but who told you you have the right to anything?' This brought a tumult of howls from the students within earshot, causing still more to turn and close in, a thunderhead gathering.

Sophie's friend stepped closer, tightening a hand on my shoulder. 'Wait, give our friend here a chance to change our minds. Maybe he's right. Maybe we don't deserve the respect! The support! The commitment of this government we didn't even vote for! Maybe our generation doesn't deserve the rights that he has enjoyed! I want to hear what he has to say!' The crowd jeered.

'Look,' I said. 'This is a mistake. I'm sorry.' I moved towards the steps.

But the young man held up his hands. 'Not yet,' he said, blocking my exit. A hungry silence fell over the crowd. They were waiting for me to make a fool of myself. I could have got past him if I'd tried, but still I stood there. Why? I thought of my mother, of her valleys and mountains. Never mind what the students were doing there, what was I doing there?

I turned to face the sun, letting it hit my face so I could see nothing in front of me but shadows against the white light. That was better. Beyond the crowd and the city, beyond the river and the canal, somewhere to the south, the mountains rose up to the sky. I could almost see them. They were calling to me. 'I've never complained about a thing in my life. Funny, I hadn't really thought about that until now. Maybe I'm too easily satisfied. Maybe I should have looked for more than I had. My mother certainly thinks so.' The mountains, I had seen them from the train, so many shades of violet, rising up, rising away. 'But to do that you not only have to be clear about what's important to you and be ready to fight for it, you have to be willing to give other things up to have it. You can't have everything, even if it's right there in front of you, no matter how unfair that seems.

'There is no easy answer, and there's no one and nothing to hold accountable for what we have or don't have but ourselves. None of us are children any more.'

I suddenly became aware of myself again then, realising that I was speaking out loud, and turned to see the crowd's reaction, but my voice must have been almost inaudible and the spark of energy in the crowd had dissipated. A few at the front were shaking their heads, some had lifted their phones and were taking my photo, sniggering with their friends, others had already turned their backs. Then Sophie scrambled up the steps to my side. 'I'm so sorry,' she said, waving her hands at the front row of students, shooing them back. 'Do NOT take my photo.' No one paid much notice to her. Some kind of disruption had broken out on the far edge of the square, and the crowd was already turning away of their own accord, the flock shifting under its own weight. I sat down on the edge of the steps, feeling my heart pounding in my chest, and Sophie sat beside me, putting a hand on my knee. 'Where did that come from?' she said.

Before I could answer, Didier stepped up. 'I thought you knew how to make people happy, Baptiste,' he said, sinking his teeth into my name.

I looked up at him. 'We all have to learn the difference between wanting happiness and wanting life to be fair.'

If only we had known what that first time would lead to. It was just a whim to take you there. We laughed when we planned it. We thought it might light a fire under you, shake you out of your inertia. It was such a mistake, but how could we have known?

That day changed you. You felt for those students. You could see yourself in them I suppose, how you might have been if fate had not nudged you towards your perfect job, your perfect home. You did want to help them, not as a crowd but one by one, and how could you ever do that? It has troubled you ever since.

Not so long ago I had to collect you from the police station. They had arrested you in the Place du Capitole, where you had been preaching or trying to tell a story, they said. That hadn't been a problem as such, but when a crowd had gathered around you one of the pavement cafés on the square had called the police to complain about the disturbance. By the time they got there you were curled on the ground asking to be taken home. There was a woman sitting beside you with a badly cut arm from where she had fallen, or (witnesses said) been pushed. No, it had been an accident, she insisted. She didn't press charges, and left her number with the police for whoever came for you, 'in case they want to talk.' As if she didn't have enough problems of her own. Sometimes the kindness of others overwhelms me.

At first the police just wanted to help you get home, but the problem was you wouldn't give them an address, just kept repeating, quite calmly, that you were Baptiste de la Candice. There was no one of that name in Toulouse, or anywhere, as far as they could work out. Eventually you had begun to panic and struggle. It took three officers to overpower you, they said. I saw the bruises. I doubt you will ever trust anyone in uniform again.

By the time they got you down to the station you were in tears. Thank goodness someone there had been compassionate enough to fetch you a drink and just sit and listen to you until eventually you were calm enough to explain that Baptiste was your name and that the Candice was where you lived.

'It must be difficult for you,' the sergeant said as I signed for you. 'But you really ought to think about getting him into care.'

'Of course I've thought about it,' I said. 'But most of the time he's fine. You just have to know how to—' I stopped myself. What was the point? The sergeant was right.

You had never wandered off alone before, it was unusual for you to be awake in the daytime anyway, but now you had. Things would have to change. I could no longer leave you alone, but how could I be with you all the time? I'm not strong enough for that. It was time to admit I needed help.

Heart-breaking as these practicalities are, I had been expecting them. What I hadn't expected was people's cruelty.

I had a call from Sabine later that week. Gaëlle had recognised you in a video that was being shared around her friends: 'Jesus in Toulouse'. It's a shaky recording, taken over someone's head with a mobile phone, but there you are. Your arms are up, your palms out, the sun on your face and your eyes half closed against it. Your feet are bare, your face half hidden by your unkempt hair and the unruly beard that you won't let me trim. You are calling out, 'There is another way. Don't compare yourselves to others. You have to listen to your heart.'

Most people are just walking by, embarrassed or disinterested or simply getting on with their lives, but others, like whoever shot the film, have stopped and are standing at a distance, pointing and giggling. As you continue your homily more and more people join them, wide-eyed, their arms stretched up, snapping photos on their phones. Then, just before the clip ends, there is a woman pushing her way through, trying to get to you, clearing some space. 'Leave him alone,' she is shouting. 'You should be ashamed of yourselves.'

I had the same nightmare every time I slept for weeks afterwards. In the dream it is me who is trying to get to you, but the more I push my way through the crowd the more it swells and swells. I lose sight of you, and even as I am shouting your name, futile over the roar of the crowd, I am telling myself I should just turn away. Just go home before it gets worse. But I can't. Something draws me on. I keep going, insisting that I have to help you, and why is no one else helping? When finally I reach the place you had been standing you are gone and there is blood smeared across the paving stones.

When I arrived at the bar that evening the place was empty and the television blaring. Sophie huddled on a low chair behind the bar, her head down, concentrating on something. I leaned over the bar to catch a glimpse. Her shoes were off, her feet resting on the crossbar of the chair with the toes curled under like a bird on a perch. She was bent over a pad of thick creamy paper that rested on her knees, sketching something in soft, dark pencil. She caught sight of me and looked up with a start.

'Baptiste! Don't sneak up on me like that!'

'Sorry,' I said, 'I can't hear you over the television.'

She handed me the remote. 'Here. Turn it down if Rémy doesn't mind.'

'Rémy who?'

Sophie stood up in surprise, and took note of the coins on the table in the corner. 'Oh, right.' She lifted her chin, her eyes drawn towards the TV. Even on mute it was intrusive, the electronic ticker tape scrolling along the bottom of the screen. Violence on the streets of Paris, more rallies planned, more strikes, more political rhetoric, Europe looking on with morbid interest. I clicked it off. 'I think I've had enough demonstrations for one day.'

Sophie watched wordlessly as I pulled up a stool, resting my elbows on one of the brass bars that ran the perimeter of the bar itself, and my feet on the other. 'I'm not disturbing you, I hope?'

She shook her head. 'I'm glad you're here. I didn't think you'd come tonight. Have you forgiven me?' She looked up at me, her eyes almost yellow in the shadow of the dark twists of hair piled around her face.

'Don't do it again,' I said. Sophie pushed the pencil in her hand behind her ear and closed the sketchpad. 'Wait, what were you drawing?'

She gave me a pre-emptive scowl. 'The *primeur*,' she said. 'It's just in.'

The first red wine from the year's harvest, generally unremarkable, certainly not something I could imagine would inspire anyone to art. 'Can I see?'

Sophie's colour rose, her tawny skin deepening in tone, but she retrieved the book and showed me her sketch. 'Don't you dare laugh.'

Her drawing was beautiful. Grape vines poured out from a tilted bottle, curling out and around the page, filling it with bunches heavy with grapes. Surrounding them were the wisps and curls of smoke rising from a fire at the bottom of the page, its flames licking up over the bottle. Beside the fire was a small congregation of tiny stick-people, some bent over walking sticks, some holding infants, others holding banners. At the centre of the fire, piles of money were set ablaze.

'You got all this from the *primeur*?' I said.

She filled a glass and pushed it towards me. 'Try it.' I took a sip, feeling the alcohol descend swiftly to my knees, making them buzz. When was the last time I had eaten? I would order a steak. 'What does it taste of to you?' she said.

I certainly couldn't taste burning money. The wine was thin and sharp. 'It tastes young, raw, a little bitter.'

'I think it tastes of change.'

'If you can taste revolution in this wine you really are wasted as a waitress.'

'I know,' she said. She closed her sketchpad again and slid it under the cash register. 'Taste it again. Even when a wine is young you can taste the past year in it. Every year the wine from the same vines is different because every year is different, the essence of the earth they grow in, the air around them. This hasn't been a peaceful year. This isn't a peaceful wine.'

'Next year's isn't looking too cheerful either then,' I said.

Sophie rolled her eyes. 'I was thinking about what you said earlier, at the demo. You were right.'

'Right about what?' I could barely remember what I had said. At the time it had seemed amorphous, more like a thought than words.

'That rallying on the streets is as useless as complaining to our parents. The young have no money, no power and no influence, why would anyone listen to us there? No, you're right. To make any difference at all I need a plan. I've been thinking about it all afternoon and I know what I'm going to do.'

'You're going into politics?'

'No. I'm going to get a job on the trains.' I stared at her, dumbfounded. 'What?' she said. 'If I can tend a bar here I can just as easily be a barista on a train.'

'And how would that be different? How would it make better use of your talents?'

'Oh, it's nothing to do with what Didier said. I like working here, don't get me wrong. The hours suit me and the customers aren't too annoying.' She tilted her head and smiled in a way that I supposed was meant to be charming, but which didn't suit her at all. 'But what effect can I have on anything here? It's as though I don't matter.'

I felt a stone swell in my stomach. I had never expected Sophie's company to be any more than friendship but I had come to count on it. I had thought there was something special between us. Could she really leave just to prove a point? Without thinking I put my hand over hers on the bar, as though to hold her there. 'You matter to me.'

Sophie dragged her hand from under mine with an exasperated sigh and turned to mix herself a drink. Grey storm clouds of liquorice syrup bloomed up into the water as she stirred. 'But not to those who make the decisions that affect me,' she said. 'Not the government, not the establishment. I need a job where I can join a union and go on strike.' I opened my mouth to speak but she continued. 'Don't,' she said. 'You can't tell me to make my own choices then criticise the choices I make. You can't have it both ways.'

I fixed on the small bowl of olives she had placed on the counter between us, uncertain if at that moment I could look at her and remain composed. Despite my distress my stomach growled and Sophie responded by shoving a menu into my hand. 'Cheer up,' she said. I feigned interest in the menu and Sophie left me to it for a minute, although we were both aware I knew it by heart.

Eventually she poked my arm. 'You're still mad at me,' she said. 'You're sulking. Look, I'm sorry about the thing with Didier, it was my fault, I should have known he'd do something like that. He gets very passionate, that's all. But he was a total arse to you and I gave him hell afterwards.'

I shrugged. 'Not my business.'

She grinned. 'I think he's jealous of you.'

'Is he your boyfriend?' I said. Sophie put her face in her hands and shook it in mock exasperation. 'Well,' I could hear the petulance in my own tone, 'he wants to be.'

'Yeah, I know.'

I felt a small thrill as she waved a dismissive hand and quickly checked myself. Why should I feel so absurdly pleased at that? What was happening to me lately? Whatever it was I needed to snap out of it. I leaned towards her. 'I'm sorry. It's been a strange day. But I am glad you took me. It did me some good. If nothing else it set me thinking about what I really want these days.'

She sipped at her drink thoughtfully. 'I got that impression. And what conclusions have you drawn?'

'Just how little consideration do you think these things deserve?' I said. All I knew was that I had surprised myself by even thinking about it.

'Well, don't take too long.' Sophie tugged the menu from me with one hand and refilled my glass with the other. 'Now, since you are clearly feeling indecisive, shall I just order you a steak and have done with it?'

'Thank you.'

She pulled the pencil from behind her ear and started to sketch on my place mat. A few swift, deft little strokes and there was my kingfisher again. I felt calmed, as though a connection between us had been restored, reinforced.

'Baptiste?' Sophie lay down the pencil on the counter.

'Yes?'

She pushed a wisp of hair back off her face and looked hard straight into my eyes. Her pupils were as black as the water in a new moon. 'When you said you can't have everything you want, what, or who, were you talking about?'

I looked back at her, trying to shake off the strange feeling of déjà vu it gave me. 'Is that what I said? I don't remember.'

She arched an eyebrow coolly and turned for the kitchen. 'Right. And Baptiste?'

'Yes?'

'I'm not kidding. I'm going for that job.'

I saw Amandine approaching from the far end of the street, where the low sun warmed the bricks of the library from ice pink to salmon. Even in the shade it was pleasant enough to eat outdoors and I had taken a table for two on the narrow pavement. There was a second restaurant on the other side of the street, so between us we caused eddies of pedestrians to converge on the cobbled road.

Amandine stepped out of the flow and I stood to greet her. Our cheeks brushed as I kissed the air beside her smile, dizzied by her proximity, the whisper of her perfume. As she turned to sit down I saw her fingertips move briefly over the curve of her chin. Instinctively I raised my hand, touching my own face and finding it rough with stubble. I thought back hastily to that morning: what could have distracted me from my usual routine? I had, despite myself, paid particular attention to my appearance, or so I thought.

I would have said something, but my apology tied knots in my throat so instead I sat down again as though nothing were wrong.

'How are you?' she said.

'That's supposed to be my line.'

Amandine ran her finger along the mosaic around the table's edge. 'Sometimes, Baptiste, you have an amazing ability to complicate the simplest things.'

For a moment I was doubtful; was I being complicated? No one else had ever challenged the way I did things. I ask how the client is, they talk, I listen. Why did everything with Amandine have to be so different, so unsettling? 'I'm sorry,' I said. 'I'm fine, thanks. How are you?'

'The stubble suits you.' No. It certainly wasn't me that was complicating things.

The menu was written on a small chalkboard between us. I turned it to face Amandine, but she didn't even look at it, flipping it around again. 'You choose.'

'Is there anything you don't eat?'

Softly, 'I eat everything.'

And everything looked appetising. I wanted her to taste it all. Even with my best efforts at restraint the waiter raised an eyebrow as I ordered far more tapas than we could reasonably manage between us: the patatas bravas, the chorizo, grilled aubergines, manchego, king prawns with aïoli, razor clams with parsley, anchovies, bruschetta, grilled mussels. Amandine said nothing, leaning back in her chair and taking in the surroundings. Above us a jumble of ironwork curls and bright blue shutters angled across the sky. Yellow paint peeled like lemon rind off the walls.

I was glad when the wine arrived. 'It makes a nice change to meet you off Candice,' Amandine raised her glass. 'I hope this doesn't sound strange, but I think because it's your office as well as your home, sometimes meeting there can feel neither one thing or the other.' What did she mean by that? Was I being too informal? 'And it's lovely to discover somewhere new so close to where I live. It's a romantic little spot.'

'Do you think so?' I looked around. It was true that most of the diners did seem to be in couples. 'I picked it because it's secluded.'

Amandine laughed. 'I'm sure most people do. If I bumped into anyone from work I'd have a lot of explaining to do.'

One of the advantages of Candice for my clients was the discreet location, but then this lunch had been Amandine's idea. I realised I should have put more consideration into the venue. 'People come to all kinds of conclusions without thinking, or even looking properly,' I said. 'If you're worried, feel free to tell them I'm an old friend.'

Amandine put her elbow on the table and rested her face in a cupped hand. 'If you're to be an old friend then I need to know more about you.'

I was drawn in by her smile. 'OK, go on then, quick, ask me something.'

Amandine didn't hesitate. 'Where did you grow up?'

'In a village not far from Toulouse.'

'How many times have you been in love?'

'I said one question,' I sighed.

'No you didn't. How many times, old friend?'

'Never,' I said.

Amandine looked at me appraisingly. 'Never? Are you sure?'

'You'd think I would remember something like that.'

She shrugged. 'Sometimes we just don't see love for what it is,' she tucked her hair back behind her ears. Tiny diamonds glittered in her earlobes, 'even when it's right in front of us.'

The sun pricked my eyes. I thought of the call of the mountains and of Sophie's question in the bar. Sometimes life doesn't let up until you hear what it's trying to tell you. 'Just because I've never been in love doesn't mean I can't recognise it,' I said.

'OK, what about that couple there?' In the restaurant across the street, a man and a woman in their twenties, both wearing sunglasses, sat at an angle to each other sharing a heaped platter of seafood – all fleshy pinks and rocky greys, oysters, mussels, cockles, clams – and a large basket of fresh bread. The woman had slipped off her shoes (Spanish espadrilles, cobalt and green) and the soles of her feet were bare against the pavement. The two were not touching, no hands held across the table, nor feet touching underneath. 'Are they in love, do you think, or are they just "old friends"?'

Before I could reply, a second man arrived, greeted them both with warm embraces and animated exclamations. He asked the hurrying waiter for a glass but remained standing, leaning against the brick wall as he helped himself to wine from their carafe. The three fell easily into enthusiastic conversation, the couple smiling up at their friend and he making expansive gestures with ape-like arms.

'Maybe they're brother and sister.'

Amandine sat back. 'Nonsense. It's clear they're in love, regardless of if they are old friends or not.' She ran a fingertip around the rim of her wine glass. 'Why can't you admit it?'

A jolt. A chemical rush through my blood from head to toe. A quickening heart. A longing for the familiar security of Candice. 'Maybe they are,' I said, 'or maybe it's a professional relationship.' I put my wine glass down for fear of dropping it. Or maybe it's both, I thought.

'Excuse me.' The waiter began to rearrange our table, moving the salt cellar to the periphery, tightening the liaison between wine glasses and cutlery, making room for plates. Then the dishes were spread before us, filling the air with the rising scents of garlic, sulphur, lemon and grilled meat.

'Mmm, it all looks delicious,' Amandine said, the momentary tension falling from her shoulders as easily as if she had shrugged off a coat. 'It's hard to know where to start.' Her hand hesitated over the plates of food, then she pierced an anchovy with her fork. Olive oil, red with chilli, glistened on its skin and she leaned in to catch the drips in her mouth. I watched as she sat back and chewed slowly, pleasure settling on her face. She replaced her fork on the table, took a sip of wine and smiled. 'Well? Don't be shy.'

We ate slowly and in silence for a while, allowing me to put my personal feelings aside, gather my thoughts, think analytically and plan my approach. Right from the start, Amandine had told me she was looking for love. Knowing from experience that that wouldn't address something deeper, I had tried my best to steer her in another direction. But I'd failed, and now it was obvious that she was projecting her desire on to me. I'd be lying if I said I wasn't flattered, but I had a job to do and I knew her feelings had no substance; they were symptomatic of something deeper. I couldn't allow either of us to be distracted by such a trick of nature. There was the option to skirt around the issue, especially tempting since I was part of it, but sometimes we have to face these things head on.

'So,' I said eventually, wiping my fingers, 'let's talk about sex.'

Amandine clasped her hands above the table. 'Is that the end of foreplay then?'

'You tell me. We can't play games for ever. I'd like you to feel you can be open with me, but you're holding something back.'

Amandine affected incredulity. 'You think it's me that's holding back?'

'I do,' I said firmly, 'yes. So just be honest. What exactly is it you're looking for, Amandine. If not happiness, then what do you expect from love? What is this mysterious quality that you need to take your breath away?'

'You think when I said I want my breath taken away I meant sex?'

'I don't know what you meant,' I said. I genuinely didn't.

'You're unbelievable.' Amandine's fingers closed over the tiny silver ladybird hanging from her necklace and she closed her eyes. When she opened them again she was looking straight at me, her turquoise eyes brighter than ever. 'It's not sex,' she said. She bit her lip. 'Well, not just sex. I think there can be an intimacy so profound between lovers that they become empaths, one for the other. Can you imagine how exhilarating it must be to step out of ourselves and truly feel for another person?'

'You crave intimacy?'

'I crave connection.'

'You'd let your happiness depend on someone else's?'

'You wouldn't?' Amandine shook her head. 'Look, you're the expert,' she said, 'but I think you're looking at it the wrong way. You're so concerned with finding the happiness inside ourselves that you refuse to believe we can also find it outside ourselves. Why can't there be both?'

'How many kinds of happiness do you think there are?'

'More than we have words for.'

'But true happiness—'

'Is an idea that only serves to make us feel unhappy.'

'So then why are you …'

She held up a finger. 'Listen. I agree there's a kind of contentment inside ourselves that only we can find. And I agree that without that everything else can only brush the surface. But if you have that already it should liberate you, it should make you bolder, not more afraid.'

Perhaps Amandine should be doing my job. 'And you feel you have that already?'

She glanced down at her plate and then back up at me. 'I think I must, yes. Do you?'

The waiter was at our side again. 'How is everything?'

Not good, I wanted to tell him. I'm drowning. But instead we both nodded politely and praised the food.

'Baptiste,' Amandine said quietly as he left, 'for weeks now you've tried not to encourage me. You've done everything in your power to persuade me that falling in love is a bad idea. You've challenged me, you've offered me alternatives. Someone less confident might think there was something wrong with them. But you're never going to convince me. Maybe it's because you don't know what falling in love means. Maybe it's because you are scared of love. But I'm not. So give it up and let's move on.'

'I've seen a lot of people made miserable by love.'

'So what?' She squeezed lemon over a razor clam, teasing it from its shell and eating it whole. 'A lot of people don't like shellfish,' she said. 'But does that mean you shouldn't try it? If you've never tasted it for yourself, how would you know? It would be a pity not to taste what life has to offer.' She waved her hand at the half-eaten meal before us. 'It's obvious you have the appetite.'

'I couldn't help myself,' I said. 'There were so many good things on the menu. But it wasn't for me. I wanted you to enjoy it all.'

Amandine reflected briefly. 'Yes,' she said. 'I can believe that. You find your satisfaction in others' pleasure.'

'You say that as though it's a bad thing.'

'Passion runs both ways.' I thought of Sophie and smiled. 'What?' she said.

'Nothing. You remind me of someone I know.'

Amandine scrutinised my expression for a moment, then looked down at her hands. 'Well,' she said, 'you asked what the mysterious thing is that I'm looking for. This is it. I think when two people genuinely pool their lives, something stronger is forged, something fundamental that can ride out both waves of happiness and tides of sorrow. How could that not take anyone's breath away?'

I was out of my depth. The table felt unsteady under my hands and the ground seemed to tremble underfoot. 'Amandine, I want you to be happy. Truly. But if that's what you believe it takes, I wouldn't know where to start. I'm not sure I can be of much help.'

Amandine looked exasperated. 'Let's not do this again,' she said. I couldn't let it go, though. Where had she got this idea? Had she imagined it? Experienced it for herself? Had she already tasted this connection she craved? When I asked her, she folded her arms. 'With a man, no, not even close. But ...' her defensiveness turned to uncertainty. 'I don't suppose you ride horses?' I shook my head. 'Pity. It's not a bad comparison.'

'Tell me.'

'There's more goes on between a horse and rider than meets the eye. With a good horse it takes just the slightest shift in your weight, the slightest pressure on its mouth or its flank, and the horse understands. It responds. You move together, both bound and liberated. Neither of you is truly in control, neither of you passive. Complicit. That's how I imagine it should be. And then, when you see the field stretching ahead, the horse tenses beneath you and you feel its desire, asking if it's OK. You lean forward slightly and release, just barely, the reins. And together you can fly.'

Her face was radiant with pleasure. It was the first time I'd seen her look genuinely happy. I was finally glimpsing beyond the surface of Amandine Rousseau. I had never ridden a horse, but she just as easily could have been talking about me playing the piano. The way it responds under my hands, the way I can channel my emotions through it in such a way that someone else could understand them without me having to say a word. 'Riding is important to you,' I said.

Amandine dropped her shoulders, the light in her eyes fading. 'It was once. I rode all the time when I was younger.' She smiled wistfully. 'And even before that I was horse crazy. I had posters of ponies all over my room. Wild ones, mostly, in Iceland, Mongolia and of course the horses down in the Camargue. I fell in love with those animals just from the photos. I dreamed of travelling to see them one day. I still haven't got round to it.'

'Why not?'

'Life gets in the way of these kinds of fancies. I haven't really thought about it for years. Of course I could still go, at least to the Camargue, it's only a morning's drive away, there's no excuse really.'

'You still ride though?'

A sigh of resignation. 'Not for years. I can't afford broken bones these days.'

'After how you just described it?' I recalled the scar I had seen on her foot. 'Did you have an accident that put you off?'

'No.' She shook her head. 'I fell off plenty of times but never really hurt myself. But if I took a fall these days I'm sure I wouldn't bounce as easily as I did when I was a girl. It's called growing up.'

We give up these elements of ourselves so easily, I thought, and then spend our adult lives grieving for them. Something within me would die if I ever stopped playing the piano. 'Isn't growing up about learning what's important to us?' I said. 'What's really stopping you?'

For a fleeting instant, Amandine's composure failed her, and I saw a conflict in her eyes that I didn't understand. 'Nothing. Not really. You're right.' Her smile was an indication that the discussion was over, the closing chord of a melody. I thought of her melody on the piano, unfinished, unresolved.

'Go riding this week,' I said. 'Promise me.'

Amandine sat tall, her hand reaching to touch the exposed skin above her breasts where her blood had risen to the surface. 'I'll take a chance if you will,' she replied. Then something caught her eye, and without turning her body she shifted her gaze over to the couple across the street. 'They're watching us!' she whispered, as though they could hear. I glanced over at them. Their friend had left. They had finished their meal and were drinking coffee. The woman was angled forward, her bare feet now resting on his shoes, their hands clasped across the table in a shaft of light that slanted away across the cobbles. I had the uncanny sensation of looking in a mirror. They were looking at us.

What did they think of us? I wondered. What must we look like to them?

A cloud had settled over everything. My laundry flapped damply on the line I had stretched across the bow. Even on the brighter winter days it never dried properly and I would eventually have to bring it in by the wood stove. There were months of steamy windows ahead, until the crisp March mornings would open them again and bear in the deeply satisfying sound of shirts snapping in the fresh spring air.

Etienne and I sat in silence on the gloomy deck, listening to the lick of the water, watching the low clouds swimming in the soupy sky and the scraggy late ducklings scudding across the water in the wind. The deck was all shades of grey. Candice was as deciduous as her surroundings, life retreating into her core to overwinter. In winter I ate downstairs by the stove, allowing upstairs to become my conservatory. With the temperature falling fast, that morning I had brought my garden inside, picking off the last ripe fruit before covering the lemon tree against the cold and retiring the geraniums to the table inside the wheelhouse. This process always seemed to make the wildlife indignant, and sometimes in a certain light butterflies would fly up to the window of the wheelhouse and flutter against the pane of glass, unable to land.

It was on days like these when the joggers, walkers and cyclists would all hurry by Candice without a second glance. She was just another houseboat moored along a muddy towpath in a small damp corner of a suburb. The yearning would not return to their eyes until spring, when I took the plants back out on deck and their light would fall all around the boat, reds and violets and greens. In summer I was living the dream. In winter I became an eccentric. People see what they want to see.

'What is it?' Etienne asked. He lit the cigarette that he'd been rolling. I liked that his habit forced us outside, and although I'd never been a smoker and nor had my parents, I loved the smell of his tobacco on the cold air. Etienne didn't care for tea and had made us strong black coffee, short measures dressed in a thick caramel froth.

'It looks like rain today,' I said into the whispers of steam trapped and swirling in the high walls of the too-large cup. Etienne said nothing. With rare exceptions, weather was not a legitimate conversation between us. He waited. The coffee at the bottom of my cup was grainy. I swirled it around, inhaled the essence of the grounds.

'Baptiste?'

I unwrapped my scarf and wrapped it again, a little tighter this time. 'Someone told me,' I said finally, 'that when two people are in love, they can feel as much for each other as for themselves. That they sense each other. Do you feel like that with René?'

Etienne regarded me with dark eyes. He let smoke drift slowly from his lips, out across the water. 'Hmmm.' After a few moments, when he had put out his cigarette, he said, 'If you're asking me to explain how love feels, you'll be disappointed. Many smarter men than me have failed.'

'Just in your experience.'

Etienne inhaled. 'If you had asked me thirty years ago I would have told you one thing, twenty years ago something different, and today something else again. In my experience love doesn't only take one shape. It grows and adapts.' He paused. 'Or it doesn't.'

I looked down at the deck as he spoke, tracing the dark Rorschach patterns where the branches overhead kept it shaded and damp, trying to give shape in my mind to my own point of view. 'And in all that time have you felt that way?' I couldn't get the thought straight in my mind. I was failing to explain the idea that Amandine had described so clearly. How had she put it? I saw her on horseback, her fingers tangled in its mane, flying hooves along the sand. I saw myself at the piano, absorbed and transported out of myself. 'As though René were not separate from you but part of you, or that you were part of him?'

'Baptiste, I can't even begin to tell you about everything our love has been. My experience of love can't be the same as yours. It's not even the same as René's. You just have to let the bloody thing take its course and see for yourself.'

I looked over at him. 'But has it made you happy?'

His regard was wry and sympathetic. He shook his head. 'Of all the days to ask me this. Listen. Love has made me happier than anything else in my life, and it has made me the most miserable. It has changed me, sometimes for the better and sometimes for the worse. And it's not done with me yet.' He dropped his cigarette into the tin can that served as an ashtray. 'It's that woman of yours, isn't it?'

That woman of mine. I shrugged into my coat against the wind. I would ask Marcel and Yvette next time I saw them. 'Yes, it's her.'

Etienne leaned back. 'Tell me about her.'

It was hard to know where to start. I wanted to tell him about her green shoes, as if he would understand why that was important. Instead I told him that she was a doctor, that she was beautiful, that she was flirting with me without mercy. That there was something between us that shouldn't be there.

'And I'll ask you again: why not?'

'And I'll remind you again: she's a client. She doesn't really know what she wants yet. She just thinks she wants it. I'm supposed to be helping her, not taking advantage of her.'

'Give her some credit to know her own mind, Baptiste. Neither of you are kids. Why are you overthinking this so much?'

One of the dark patterns on the deck resembled a butterfly, its wings ragged and uneven. I felt a stirring of sadness. When I looked up Etienne was staring at me.

'Look,' he said, 'I'm not the psychology guy, all I know about is money and markets, but even I can see you're using that as an excuse. You have plenty of clients these days, you wouldn't miss one, right? Have you actually asked her outright which she'd rather be, your client or your lover?'

I thought back to the first time I met her. How there was something odd that I couldn't put my finger on, and at the same time there was something intoxicating about her. How that first night the only thing I had figured out was that things weren't what they seemed. How she had constantly evaded my questions by turning them back on me. 'No,' I said, 'but I'm not sure I'd get a straight answer. And even if I did, I'm not sure it would be the answer I want.'

'Exactly.' Etienne looked triumphant. 'There's your problem. Part of you wants it, but part of you is afraid.' I was sure my mother had said something similar, or was it Sophie, or Amandine herself? Everybody seemed to have an opinion about me these days. I shrugged. 'That's why none of these blind dates people try and set you up with ever work out. And now, even when the opportunity has fallen into your lap, you're still resisting it.'

'What blind dates?' I laughed. 'I've not been on a date in years.'

'People are always trying to set you up if you'd let them. That girl from the bar, for example, what's her name?'

'Sophie.'

'Sophie, right. Anyway, it's normal,' he said, 'none of us like to feel vulnerable. But you have to get past the fear. What's the worst that could happen? What have you got to lose?'

I waved my hand around the deck, the trees, the water. 'All of this. I'm happy here. I might never know where I come from, but I know where I belong. Here. This is where I've put down my roots.'

'Roots can tie you to one place and put the rest of the world out of reach.'

'Roots are what nourish you,' I said. 'I don't want to give up what makes me happy for something that might not last.'

'You're getting ahead of yourself.'

'Better to envisage that scenario now than to fall in love blind and have to face it later.'

'Too late for that, I'd say.' Etienne reached over and put his hand on my knee. 'Seriously,' he said, 'take my advice on this. Don't embark on love expecting it to last for ever. Don't embark on love worrying about if it will make you happy or unhappy. Just embark on love for the sake of it. If in the future you realise it's no longer what you want, you'll be sad but you'll get over it and you'll figure out what to do next.'

Etienne's smile was at once encouraging and melancholy. I took my friend in properly for the first time that day. He looked exhausted. I felt ashamed that I'd been too self-absorbed to notice before. 'Is something wrong?' I said. 'You look pretty terrible.'

'Oh, it's probably just the weather,' he said with a wink. 'Or too many late nights. We're trying to work out what to do about Christmas. The usual questions about where we will spend it. Every year it's the same thing. René wants a party, a big family get-together, but the boat's too small and our families live so far apart. We usually end up dashing about the country to make sure we see everybody. Just for once I'd love a quiet Christmas, with just the two of us, or even a holiday away somewhere, but René wants to be near children. He says what's Christmas without children? It's times like this I think it would be easier to be alone. One set of parents to please, a quiet home to come back to.'

'After all you just said.'

'Don't you dare use that as an excuse. We'll figure something out. We've managed it every other year. I never said it was easy.'

A wet gust of air blew through the plane trees, skimming my cheeks. I closed my eyes and let myself sense the wind. Broad, papery leaves were coming down in droves now, I could hear them landing on the deck and skittering off again into the water. It reminded me once more of the first day I met Amandine, when the first leaves had started to fall. Then a sharp clatter on the deck made me open my eyes with a start. At first I didn't realise what it was, then I saw that my cup had slipped from my fingers and broken in two at Etienne's feet, a tiny splash of coffee joining the pieces.

'Shit,' I said. 'Sorry.'

Etienne shook his head. 'You're in a bad way, Baptiste,' he said. 'There's only one way to fix it.' He picked up the pieces and stood to leave.

'Wait, you never answered my question,' I said.

'Which question?'

'If you can feel that way about someone you love. That connection between two people. Does that really happen?'

'Take my advice,' Etienne said. 'Go and discover that for yourself.'

It's all very well, this romantic idea of being in tune with someone you love, but sometimes it's just too hard.

I've done it. I've felt the profound pleasure of seeing you happy, been swept up in the waves of your desire. But I have also felt your fear and frustration as keenly as if it were my own. I've let your anger become my anger. I have become so engulfed in you that I almost lost myself.

You once described to me how you managed to stay detached from your clients' malaises. You were so logical about it, if I hadn't known you better I would have thought you cold-hearted. 'There's a reason we can't truly empathise with those who are suffering,' you said. 'If we did it would overwhelm us. Our impotence would paralyse us, and what use would that be? Empathy is useful in short bursts, but no one can keep it up over the long term, it doesn't help anyone.'

You were right. You didn't know it then, but you had given me the words I would fall back on later to change myself. To love you I had to learn to let things be as they would be. I had to learn to let go.

Before, when I was still affected by every setback, Lucas overheard a conversation we were having down in the garden. He must only have been three or four. I was upset. I had allowed your deterioration to come as a surprise. It wasn't that I didn't know what to expect, but for some reason I had still clung to the hope that somehow it would be different for us. It wasn't different for us.

'When life gets hard, most of us can at least console ourselves with memories of good times,' I was saying. 'But now Baptiste remembers so little that's real, never mind if he was happy or not. What comfort can I give him?'

Even at that age, Lucas was very pragmatic. 'I've got a good idea,' he said, when he came downstairs to join us. 'If he's lost all his memories we'll have to make him some new ones.' It was the best advice anyone could have offered. Every day since then we have made sure we do at least one thing that makes you happy or makes you laugh. We layer them up, tiny joy upon tiny joy. Every moment a pebble dropped in water, sinking fast and leaving only the disturbed surface to work out its passing until we can throw the next one in. We look at the stars, we cook, we walk along the towpath, we tear mint leaves into tea, we tend to your plants and try to get butterflies to sit on our fingers, we sit on the floor and read books together.

Lately even books are a minefield though, and I have had to become discriminating about what you read. Life and fiction blend together now in your mind. Just as you often don't recognise these stories as your own, so other stories that you have read become your truth.

You sleep mostly during the day now, like a cat. What at first was the occasional afternoon nap became a regular occurrence and you started slipping out of bed before dawn and pacing the boat, sometimes reading, sometimes playing the piano (but always softly, muting the sound with the pedal, trying not to wake me). I always pretended not to have been disturbed. Then you were tired in the mornings, and a morning nap took hold. Now you have given up on dozing in your chair, instead accepting your fatigue and retiring to bed whatever the hour. It was the last step in your transformation to a night owl. After dark you are generally at your most lucid and I stay awake with you as late as I can, but I still have to get up in the mornings. In the scant hours I sleep you are a voracious reader and I have often woken to find that you have temporarily become someone else entirely. You have insisted variously that you are a professor, a fisherman and a detective. All of this was manageable until the morning you became shifty and defensive because you had been reading a thriller and believed yourself to be a murderer.

I try to steer you towards benign characters now for the benefit of everybody concerned.

When Etienne left I put on my running shoes and took to the empty towpath, the autumn leaves thick along its sides. It was like running through a spice market, barrelling through piles of cinnamon, red chilli and cayenne, nutmeg oak and saffron acacia. Magpies scattered into the low skies and branches as I approached. But it was cold. Everything bled into grey and I soon turned for home. I had only just got back in and was stripping off to take a shower when the cowbell clanged. Etienne again I guessed, but the face at the door wasn't his. Still half way up the steps, I froze when I saw her.

When she caught sight of me, Amandine opened the door herself. At first I must have been partly obscured by the jungle of plants, but as she stepped inside she too stopped short. 'I'm so sorry,' she said, holding her hands up before her and backing off towards the door. 'You're busy.'

I was taken aback. What day was it? Did we have an appointment? 'No, I'm sorry,' I said, feeling suddenly exposed standing there without a T-shirt. 'I must have lost track of the time. Come in, sit down. I'll just go and make myself decent.'

When I returned five minutes later, clean and fully clothed, she was in her usual chair, but perched on the edge of it still wearing her coat. She looked misplaced, like a bird fallen from its nest. I felt such a strong impulse to approach her that I put aside my professional reservations and rather than accepting the awkwardness of the couch as usual I sat right by her, on the edge of the chest.

'I should have called,' she said. 'I was just passing ...'

Not the most believable of excuses. 'There's something on your mind,' I said quietly.

Amandine leaned forwards such that the silver ladybird became a tiny pendulum at her throat. 'I went riding,' she said, so softly it was almost a whisper.

'And?'

'It was like finding something precious that I thought I'd lost and would never see again. It made me extraordinarily sad, actually.'

'I'm sorry.'

'No, I wanted to thank you.' She put her hand on my knee and my breath caught in my throat. She would do these things as though they were entirely natural, as though she could see no limits between us. 'I needed it.'

'Tell me about it,' I asked her. 'Please.'

Amandine shifted in the chair, turning it to face me. As she did its deep violets reflected in the pearl of her hair in the low light. 'Do we all lose ourselves as we get older, do you think?' she said. 'Is that it?'

'You think who you are today is not really who you are?'

Amandine pursed her lips. 'Yes, because I've neglected those parts of my character that make me who I am. I've failed myself. I've become someone else.'

'Who have you become?'

As she paused I counted her breaths: one, two, three. Deep inhalations as though the air in the boat had thickened around us. My notebook was out of reach. I would just have to do without. 'I think like most people, I've become the person everybody else wanted me to be. It starts with our parents, doesn't it? Then our teachers, the media even, all the other influences on us. And then as we get older we have other responsibilities. Work. Family. Life gets to us.'

Goosebumps rose on my forearms, lifting the dark hairs. I was beginning to cool down after my run, my hair wet on the back of my neck, but I couldn't interrupt this now. I looked carefully at Amandine. Was she feeling the cold too? But no, she seemed fine, relaxed even. 'So who do you want to be?'

'I liked who I was before. I was less complicated then. It took the ride to remember that. But we can't go back, I know. We can't unremember things.'

When she saw that I was not going to break my expectant silence, Amandine gave a rueful smile. 'When I was a little girl,' she said, 'my father left my mother for a younger woman.'

She dropped her eyes to her hands. 'I missed him terribly. Of course I was angry with him. I couldn't understand why he had left us. My mother was the same person she always was. She hadn't become boring or unkind. She hadn't grown fat or old. Then I heard him one night, he must have come back for some things, his voice was agitated and loud, coming down the hall and through my thin bedroom walls. They must have heard in the apartment next door too. He just didn't love her any more, he said. I believed in happily ever after then, and I thought his idea of love was as stupid as you could get, as though you could just fall out of love like falling out of bed. And yet ... and here's the thing, once he left us, despite his betrayal, I loved him more, not less.'

After all this time. I could scarcely believe it. 'Go on.'

'When I was younger I thought it was because I felt sorry for him. He was making such a huge mistake and I thought eventually he would be lonely because of it. But as I got older and got to know myself better I realised it wasn't that at all. I loved him more simply because now I could see life without him. His presence had become more precious because it was transient. Do you see?'

'Yes.'

'I liked that feeling of teetering on the edge of loss. It made me feel so ... alive. I became almost addicted to it. Some people would say that's screwed up, I know, but I learned how to use it. When I was angry with my mother and I thought I hated her, I started to imagine losing her too, and it put everything back into perspective. When being with someone is painful or tedious, if you imagine the void they would leave in your life it clarifies how you really feel about them. You should try it.'

She lifted her eyes to mine. 'So in one way it has saved me when things got hard,' she said, 'but I'm aware it's not all positive. The cliché of a downside is that I've always found myself attracted to the wrong kind of man, the ones who are afraid of really committing to another person. The ones like my father, of course.' She laughed bitterly. 'I thought I'd got over that … but I haven't, have I?'

I felt the blood rise in my skin, an ache in my core. I looked out towards the canal to compose myself. Behind Amandine I could scarcely see a metre beyond the window, the brume closing around us like a cloak. Amandine crossed her legs, folding her arms across her chest. Perhaps she was getting chilly after all. 'Anyway, I know we can't stay children for ever, but it's a pity how such things can affect our entire lives.'

Sitting on the chest was starting to make my back ache. I stood and crossed to the galley to put some water on to boil. I hadn't even offered Amandine a drink.

'It depends on how you look at things,' I told her, leaning against the divide. 'If you believe that your experiences are the ingredients that make you who you are, then you can't rid yourself of past disappointments and pain any more than you can take a rotten egg out of a cake.'

'How else could you look at it? You think we can just forget what we've learned about life?'

'No, but I think we are constantly reinventing ourselves, keeping some elements, discarding others, and there's no need to hold on to the previous versions. We have to let them go.'

'So if you think that way then our childhood years, everything that came before, just doesn't matter?'

'Of course they matter. They're steps along the way, the ghosts you carry within you of who you once were. They have made you who you are. But they're not you, not any more.'

'It must be getting pretty crowded in there,' she said. I raised an eyebrow. 'OK, OK, I'll think about it.' Amandine sat back in the chair.

'I can't tell you how pleased I am that you felt you could tell me this,' I said.

We talked. I must have lit a fire at some point. Time condensed. I can see Amandine standing in stockinged feet at the window with her back to me. She has cleared a small gap in the misty pane and is looking out on to the canal. She is no longer wearing her coat. Her skirt is the colour of milky coffee, and just covers the crooks of her knees.

'So,' she is saying, 'what made you decide to close yourself off from the rest of the world?'

She meant the boat, of course. 'I don't, it's not ...'

'Yes you do. You keep yourself at a distance. You avoid intimacy.'

'You think because I live on the boat—'

She spun around angrily. 'Have you not been listening to me? It's not the boat. Although that's another thing. Candice is not really a boat to you, she's just a floating house.'

'What do you mean?'

'Have you ever gone anywhere on this boat?' I shook my head. 'Why not? Surely the idea of a boat is the possibility of adventure,' she said. 'You could go anywhere you want, Bordeaux, Carcassonne, down to the sea, and yet you never move.'

What is it about the times we live in, where we can at once condemn people for not seeing how privileged they are and yet still be suspicious of those who are happy with what they have? A contented child is praised but a contented adult lacks ambition. Why?

I switched on the lamps and began to draw the curtains. Amandine turned back to the window, making slight stretching movements with her neck as though there was tension in her shoulders. Her hair was not so long, and as she stretched the nape of her neck was briefly exposed, and then hidden, revealed, then hidden again. I was only two steps away from her. I could have easily kissed her then, standing behind her, my lips on her neck, then I remembered the roughness of my skin against hers at the café. I ran my knuckles along my bristled jaw. They say infatuation makes you absent-minded. Before I had made up my mind either way, Amandine stepped aside, reaching for her coat. 'I'd better go,' she said. All the energy with which she had arrived had evaporated, leaving only disappointment in her eyes. I knew it was me that had disappointed her.

The hands on my watch confirmed the lamentations of my stomach. What time had she arrived? We must have talked for hours. 'I'll walk with you over to your car,' I said. 'I'm going that way anyway.'

I followed Amandine as she crossed from the boat back to the towpath. The cloud had lifted and there was already a fat full moon, hanging low above Candice, champagne coloured and dappled against a dark green sky.

'This didn't go as I'd hoped,' she said with an arch look.

'I'm sorry,' I said. I was sorry. I knew I was messing this up even if I had no real idea what it was. 'I could buy you dinner?'

'Dinner?' she said, looking down at my feet. In my haste I had forgotten to put on shoes.

'They won't mind,' I said, pointing over towards the bar. 'I'm there so often it's effectively my second home. I'm best of friends with the waitress. If I missed two nights in a row she'd send out a search party.'

'The waitress.' Her tone was sarcastic, not unkind, but somehow implying that I shared the joke.

'Yes. The waitress. Sophie,' I said.

Perhaps there was something in the way I said her name, perhaps something in my expression, for a sudden tension came over Amandine. There was a strange look in her eyes, something territorial. Then as fast as it came it disappeared. My heart beat in the void. If I was ever going to take the leap, now was the time. Now was the time to tell her. Now was the time to kiss her. I put my hand on her shoulder but she shrugged it off, shaking her head with a half-smile, a wry exhalation. 'Of course, it all makes sense now. You're in love with her.'

What? For a confused moment her conjecture hung between us. Had I understood what she was implying? 'Sophie?' Amandine regarded me levelly. 'No. She must be half my age.'

'Aren't they always?' She rubbed her brow and looked over towards Jordi's. 'Maybe we're not so different. Maybe we have both fallen in love with the unattainable.'

From nowhere the image of my mother came back to me, the graceful, captivating woman I had imagined into being and had been infatuated with for years. Somewhere in the distance was the sound of a violin. I closed my eyes. When I opened them again Amandine had already taken several steps away from me. I was letting the moment slip from my grasp. She stood on the towpath with the moon caught in her hair, and looked back at me.

'You're wrong,' I said.

'Am I?' she said. 'I rode that horse, like I promised. And you said you would take a risk, yet here we still are. Nothing has changed. Nothing is ever going to change, is it? Goodnight, Baptiste.'

The glossy light reflected off the canal and on to Amandine, with her hair blowing around her face, her skirt blowing around her knees. She was quite the most beautiful woman I'd ever seen. I moved towards her, as though to kiss her cheek but as my lips drew alongside her face there was the slightest shift in the tilt of her head. I felt her breath on my cheek, looked at her mouth, and the energy rose within me like the wind.

As my lips met hers there was a heart-stopping moment when all I could do was wait, and then she was kissing me back, my fingers were in her hair, the other hand slipped around her back, drawing her in. She tasted like nothing I had ever tasted before. Fresh and wild and ripe.

There was an honesty in that moment that had been lacking between us for months. The relief sighed from us both and it became clear that we weren't going to stop at a kiss. I slid my hands under her blouse to touch her skin. The desire to bury my face in it was overwhelming. But instead I pulled her gently towards me, kept my mouth on hers. With my hands holding her at the waist and my fingers on the muscles of her lower back, the tips of my thumbs stroked the rise of her belly, where they slid over soft ridges, like tide marks on sand. And as though pulled by the tide, her flesh shrank away beneath my touch.

'Don't.' Amandine pulled back as though stung.

'Amandine.'

'I'm sorry. I really have to go.'

I stood barefoot on the moonlit towpath, my lips still wet with the taste of her, and watched her walk away. Whatever I had done, it was the wrong thing. But there was no taking the kiss back now. No unknowing her skin and the secret it had just revealed. I would be kept awake by it that night, lying there waiting for the sun to rise, listening to the groan of the ropes.

It tends to happen when you first wake up: they rise to the surface of you, haunting you, possessing you, insisting that they are you. You'll never know just how prescient your explanation was about our ghosts within.

I never know who will come next or for how long. Sometimes you are visited for an uncertain hour, sometimes a whole morning, sometimes longer than that. Sometimes they leave you alone for days, and at other times they are upon you one after the other: you're still living at home with your parents, or in your flat in the Mirail. You are still eating at Jordi's every night. You are still working. You are still young.

The first time it happened you were so convincing I was almost persuaded that it was true. You had become more animated than usual, fussing around Candice making everything tidy. Other than that you appeared perfectly rational. You were waiting for a very interesting client, you told me.

'He's the most positive man I've ever met. He's amazed by everything. He's drunk on life.' You checked yourself.

'I was thinking of going out to get something for dinner,' I said, uncertain what else to say.

'That's fine,' you said, distracted. 'Obviously you can't stay anyway.'

I hesitated, afraid now to leave you alone. 'Why is he seeing you if he's so happy?'

'He can't rein it in, so people can't abide being around him, they find him exhausting.'

'That's sad,' I said.

'You should hear him speak,' you said. 'He makes even the most insignificant things sound astonishing. The scent of an apple, the sensation of the sun, the colour of a shirt, the sounds of the city. It's as though he's reading from a wine menu.'

'Perhaps I will just stay until he arrives.'

'Fine, but I need to get ready now.'

I watched at a distance as you made extensive notes in long-hand, all of which seemed to make perfect sense, and then sat at the piano for hours waiting for him to arrive, playing from memory, music that I had never heard you play before.

When he didn't come, and it grew dark, you simply put the notebook away by the side of the bed, and said, 'I'm hungry, shall we eat?' By the time we sat down to dinner the ghost was gone.

I have never had the courage to try and convince you that things are anything other than how you perceive them. Your reality is what it is and I am a time traveller, privileged to meet these spectral versions of you that otherwise I would never have seen. Since I appear to be living with not only you, but all of your ghosts, I may as well fall in love with you all.

Not everyone agrees with this approach, and everybody has the right to an opinion. It is, as they rightly point out, living a lie. I'm not helping you by indulging your fantasies, and what will happen when you realise that there are inconsistencies in who and where you think you are? How will you ever trust me again? Fortunately for now your ghosts are untroubled by my presence. I am incorporated without question and without fuss, as is Candice and the canal, all seemingly just details without consequence. But it's true that everything is becoming more complicated.

I stood with you today at the wheel as you, or the ghost of you, told me about Sophie. How she was leaving for Paris. I listened with interest, asking questions in all the right places and you were satisfied with that. Maybe this will be a day like so many others that you will have no recollection of at all when you wake up in the morning. But maybe it will be one of those increasingly rare times that succeed in claiming a place in your memory. Then what? Will you remember it just as it was? Where will it sit in time? Will you remember the wind that blew clouds right over the top of us, causing sharp bursts of spring rain punctuated by floods of glorious sunlight? Will you remember the sweet smell of the mimosa blossom coming at us in waves from the table behind us and me close beside you, too close to only be a friend?

What does it matter now? Even if you were to remember these moments perfectly, the irony is that so much of it is already a lie.

The true heart of Christmas at home is the nativity scene that takes pride of place in the sitting room: the stable, as shabby as I imagined the original must have been, the crouching figures of awestruck shepherds, the mother beatific amongst the asses and the sheep. On Christmas Eve, almost every character was in place and only the manger remained empty. In the next room, the dinner table was already set with dried figs, nuts, dates and a plate of glacé fruit like a stained-glass window slick with sugar. First there would be church at midnight, thirty or forty of us villagers perishing inside its cold stone walls, and then back to eat in the warm cottage, fragrant with clementines and pine.

The small tree by the fireplace was hung, as every year, with the same ancient baubles and a scrap of red tinsel. My mother always put up the pagan decorations to make me feel festive; she knew my childhood Christmases were locked within them. That faded, threadbare length of tinsel held such power over us. On Christmas mornings when I was a boy, they would invariably find me up early, sitting by the embers in the half-light, gazing in awe at the gifts glittering below the tree. While we slept, magic had been visited upon us. I remember little about the presents themselves; the excitement was the thing. Somewhere inside me, when I see those faded silk baubles, that wonder still exists; a boy who believed, a ghost of Christmases past.

My mother was busy in the kitchen. When we got back in from church she would set out the rest of the food: the oysters and the foie gras, just a little, and the sweet wine, and we would give thanks as my father placed the Baby Jesus reverently into his manger. Apart from my mother's withdrawn mood – she didn't want any help with supper, thank you – this was the Christmas I had always known. It hadn't changed in almost forty years, except that these days I found it easier to sleep on Christmas Eve, and would no longer come downstairs at first light in my pyjamas.

After the roast goose on Christmas day my father excused himself to change; he was going out to the chapel. My mother and I sighed with relief. The fog that had smothered the cottage thickly since dawn had finally lifted. He had been fighting off a black mood all morning and we had prayed for the weather to brighten. On this of all days he was anxious to be out there in the field, and were it not for our beseeching he would be, heedless of snow, lightning or hail. Neither weather nor old age was going to stop him finishing his life's work, he said, but he was getting unsteady on his feet and we worried what he would do in case of a fall. That year I had given him a mobile phone to take with him, a gift that had not been well received.

'I've got by without carrying a phone around before,' he'd said. 'Phones are for in the house.'

'Well,' said my mother, 'even if you don't use it as a phone you can do crosswords on it while you're having a break. You can check the weather forecast. Marie-Thérèse has one, she says it's marvellous.'

'I can do crosswords in the newspaper,' my father said. 'I can look up and see the weather.'

'You're not too old to change.'

'You should talk,' he said. But he went over to where she was sitting and kissed her forehead. Her smile was sublime.

When he was gone my mother took to the sitting room with her sewing basket for an hour's quiet reflection, but she didn't lift the sampler, her attention drawn instead to the nativity. I followed her solemn regard, wondered what she was thinking. As a boy this would have been the time I'd have spent with a new toy, or gone out to play with friends while the adults rested. As a man I had taken to choosing one of the books my parents had given me and just sitting in peaceable silence with my mother. I always found it hard to relax though. I should have felt the warm, easy satisfaction that other people describe when they are back in their family home for the holidays, but instead I felt a kind of inverse seasickness. The room was too dark and too stuffy, the furniture too soft, but worst of all, the cottage felt lifeless – it never sighed and shifted like my Candice. I wished myself somewhere else and at the same time regretted that I was not enjoying these moments more while they lasted. I looked back at my mother, who was falling into a doze in her chair by the fire. Age had crept up and settled over her like a frost.

'Maman? Would you like to take a nap?'

She lifted her lolling head and looked at me through red eyes. 'I'm sorry, Baptiste, I didn't sleep too well.'

One of the things she prided herself on was that even at her age she still got a good full night's sleep. 'Are you OK?' I said. 'What is it?'

'It's that boy. I can't stop thinking about him and his poor mother.'

We had heard it on the radio on the morning of Christmas Eve, and after the mass last night a special prayer had been said. It had all started with a Roma boy from the camp up by the hospital in Toulouse. His name was Pesha. He had been sent out with his pregnant mother to beg, which was nothing new; a lot of those families were penniless and starving. But the bus driver had refused to pick them up to take them to the more affluent neighbourhood they usually worked. In desperation, because she knew she could not go back to her husband empty-handed, the mother said, they had gone into a shop in a poor immigrant quarter. The people there were disaffected French Algerians and Moroccans, who felt that a lot of local crime was blamed on their youths when in fact it was down to the nearby Roma. The mother had only wanted some staple foods – the box of lentils she had in her skirts was dropped in the doorway and spilled over the white shop tiles in the reports – but her hungry son had not been able to resist the displays of sweets by the tills and had pocketed some chocolate. The boy Pesha had been caught by the store owner and his brother and, the Roma claimed, beaten to death.

'It must have been an accident,' my father had said. 'No one would beat a child over a bar of chocolate. No one. How could anyone believe anything else?'

The boy's mother had tried to intervene but she too had been abused and pushed to the floor. It was unclear whether her baby had survived. When the incident hit the news later that day the Roma men had come out on the street seeking retribution. They had swarmed into the Arab quarter, and the Arabs had come out fighting too. Between them they had knives, planks of wood with nails in, metal bars, and they also had guns. Shops had been looted in the suburbs, cars were burning. Now the buses and trams were refusing to stop for Roma or Arabs, claiming their lives and those of other passengers were in danger, and there was a threat of a general strike in their support. The police were out in force.

'Think of the families,' my mother said. 'Whatever religion they follow, they must all have known what time of year it is. Is His message of peace forgotten?'

'Why don't you go for a nap?' I said again.

'No,' she said. 'I'll be fine.' She picked up her sampler and began to stitch, but after a few minutes it was abandoned on her lap and she was snoring sporadically into the empty hum of the air, her rasping breaths accompanied by the crackle of the fire and a wood pigeon calling out from beyond the window.

Thin white winter sunbeams washed through the nets and on to the nativity scene, on to Mary and the baby given to her, but not belonging to her. 'Hallelujah', sang the host of angels, as Mary gazed down on a son she was destined to lose. She already knew it, yet she was smiling. How could she still be smiling knowing what lay ahead? I thought of what Amandine had said, about how the foreshadowing of loss could make love stronger still. I thought about the soft furrows on her skin, where my thumb had traced over her belly. What had happened to that child? What pain had I inadvertently uncovered?

I rose silently, put the guard around the fire and picked up the tiny manger, where the pale face of the Christ-child now stared out from the custard-coloured hay. I turned it around in my fingers. An orphan boy, given into the keeping of strangers. Loved and loving, but nevertheless always something other. What a son to have, I thought.

When I was younger I was obsessed with finding my birth family. I tried to convince us all that it was because we owed it to them, but in truth deep down I believed it would help me find myself. Eventually, after years of uncomplaining support it was clear my parents wanted to put it behind them. It fatigued my mother especially, and one Sunday after I'd brought up the idea of searching again on the Internet, trying to get new leads that way, I found her crying silently into the dishwater and knew I couldn't raise it with her any more.

Later my father had taken me aside. 'Why are you still looking for answers outside yourself?' he said.

Perhaps, I thought, although I didn't say it, it was because my role model was a man who was too scared to look inside himself. 'Isn't that normal?' I said instead. 'Don't we all need to know where we come from, to make sense of who we are? If Jesus hadn't known he was the son of God, do you think he would have gone on to lead people as he did?'

My father had pressed his hands into the small of his back, stretching out his spine. 'That's not a comparison I want to hear again,' he said. 'And if you want to know what I think, it's that trying to understand who we are by understanding our parents is shirking responsibility. In the end you will be whatever you make yourself. You are who you are.' He lay his hand on my heart. 'The answers are all in there.'

I understood what he was trying to tell me. I agreed, mostly. But still I knew I carried a blind spot within me, a part of me that came straight from her, concealed by my ignorance.

'Christ is born.' My mother's voice startled me.

'You're awake,' I said.

'And there you are, a non-believer, staring at Jesus as though there was something he could teach you.'

I smiled. 'The light from the window was making the whole scene look divine. It made me think of the way you talk about my birth. You always make it sound miraculous. Was it like that for you every time, delivering a new life into the world?'

She laughed gently. 'Baptiste, maybe I do tell it like that, but in truth there's nothing religious about birthing a child. It's the most animal experience I know.' She pursed her lips and dropped her eyes. 'Death is a far more religious experience than birth.'

Her words hung in the air as I placed the model of Christ back into the stable beside Mary, who seemed to have become more radiant overnight. My mother stared down hard at her sampler. 'That was tactless of me,' she said. 'I'm sorry.'

'No, it's OK.'

'No, it came out wrong. I'm still upset about that poor boy. What I meant to say is that when a child is being born, there is such an immense effort from the mother, the midwife, even the child itself. In that moment they are just a few souls on a tiny corner of the earth, struggling to give life, to save life. It's a very human moment. Death is different. It always comes as a surprise. We find birth easy to accept. It's only in death that we seek answers from God.'

I moved Mary a little closer to the manger. 'It's sad,' I said, 'how she always knew she would lose him.'

'You can't lose something that was never yours to keep.'

I thought of Amandine again. It was rarer and rarer in those days to find a moment when I was not thinking about her. 'Do you think that made her love him more?'

My mother put down her sewing on the basket beside her and folded her arms. The soft skin below her elbows fell in folds against her chest. 'Who are we talking about now?'

I shrugged. I wasn't sure myself. 'I don't know. A friend.'

'A friend, yes, that's right.' She looked at me critically. 'When are you finally going to admit you've fallen in love,' she said, 'and do something about it?'

'I tried.' I shook my head.

My mother smiled. 'That's a good first step,' she said. 'Stick at it and you'll work it out. Now, I for one could use some air. Shall we go out into the garden for a while? I could use your help picking those last persimmons off the top branches, and you could tell me about her if you feel like it?' Yes, I thought, that was exactly what I wanted to do.

As I picked the soft fruits and handed them down to my mother, she told me how she was thinking of getting a gardener. She was still keeping up with raking the leaves, but the hardened soil needed turning and the apple tree pruning and she wasn't feeling up to it that year. 'You know I can always help you,' I said, 'you only have to ask.'

My mother tutted. 'I'd rather spend time with you than have you doing all my jobs when you're here.'

I turned to look again at the garden. From the top of the stepladder the perspective was different, and my eye was caught by the shutters outside my bedroom window, still thrown back against the wall, their vivid iris paint now faded to a pastel blue, peeling in splintered curls off the wood. I wondered if the bats were still behind there. The thought of it brought with it a sensation of falling and I felt a sudden wave of vertigo. I stepped down hurriedly from the ladder, resting a hand against the rough trunk of the tree. My mother eyed me with concern. 'Are you OK?'

'Remember the time I fell out of my bedroom window?' I said.

'What?' My mother's brow furrowed as though trying to remember. 'You never fell out of a window, Baptiste, what are you talking about?'

I couldn't believe she had forgotten. Despite her age she had always been very sharp. 'Because of the shutters, remember? That's why Papa put those bars up.'

She shook her head and lay a hand on my arm. 'You always did have some funny dreams.'

I was uncertain for a minute. 'No, Maman, I didn't dream it.' I pointed to the flowerbed below the window. 'I fell into the tulips.'

'Which tulips? That's lavender.'

'I know,' I said gently, 'but it was tulips back then.'

'That's been a lavender bed as long as we've lived here,' she said, but she looked doubtful.

'No, there were these beautiful, huge scarlet tulips. Almost too large for life, remember?'

My mother frowned, staring over at the pale slender-leaved lavender bushes. 'I must be going senile,' she said, 'you'd think a mother would remember something like that.'

It was the first time I'd seen any kind of decline in her mind. Of course you expect it to come to your parents eventually, but I had always relied on my mother as the keeper of my childhood stories. I faced the stark realisation that they were fading away.

The telephone was ringing. 'I'll get it,' I said, running back into the house. When I answered, there on the other end of the line was my father's grinning voice.

'Testing, testing,' he said. 'What took you so long?'

It was January, yellow-green catkins hanging like sherbet rainclouds over the towpath and the streets of Toulouse groaning with the weight of feet. The slate-grey skies matched my mood. There was no longer any need for me to imagine the void Amandine would leave in my life. She hadn't called since the kiss.

The rain came in sideways at Jordi's misted windows and despite the fire that roared up the chimney we all huddled in layers of clothes over our stews. There was fresh tarragon in the *daube de biche*, citrusy against the dark earthy game. I sat at the bar, drinking strong red wine to warm me from the inside and take the edge off the ache that wouldn't go away. I was hoping Sophie would provide some company but lately she had been giving me the cold shoulder too, always too busy to speak to me even when the place was empty. It was as though she were trying to spite me. If I sat at the counter she would always be around the other side of the bar.

This particular day she was leaning across the bar, talking to her dragon. She had a scarf the colour of figs knotted around her throat with ends that trailed down over her breasts. Didier's gaze flicked between her eyes and the place where the scarf ended, bringing knots to my own throat, but if Sophie had noticed that it didn't seem to bother her. They were deep in conversation and every now and then Sophie would point over to the TV, which had been permanently tuned to the news station since the new year, footage of the riots on perpetual loop. Riots was the only word for them now, spiralling out of control, going from bad to worse.

Down by the canal you would never have known anything was amiss, but the centre of Toulouse was starting to look like a war zone, slick with unleashed anger. Barricades had been set up across main roads. Shops and cafés remained shuttered during the day. One group had torn up the cobbles from Place Saint George and hurled them indiscriminately through any unprotected windows of shops, restaurants and apartments. Before they boarded them all up, a Molotov cocktail had smashed through a first-floor window at Galeries Lafayette. Students were blaming Arabs and Arabs blamed Roma. No one knew for sure who was who any more; the bare faces of autumn were long gone and in their place were hooded rioters with scarves or ripped cloth over their mouths. In the suburbs it was worse; shops had been looted in broad daylight and at night cars blazed in the streets. The union rallies still continued, now heavily policed and the various protesting factions moved together and apart like storms in separate weather systems. Toulouse needed reinforcements, but France's resources were disastrously stretched. Other cities were burning too.

In Paris the riots had spread fast into the heart of the unprepared city and there had been threats on the American embassy. The police were already using tear gas. In Marseille a gendarme had shot two immigrant brothers dead in the street and now there was hell to pay. There was a fresh clamour from fearful residents across the country to clear the Roma from their camps, resulting in an outcry from humanitarian organisations. It was winter, where could they go? An incendiary editorial in *Le Figaro* had called it France's Arab Spring, a headline catchy enough to be picked up on by the world media despite it being wildly inaccurate, and out of the shadow of this propaganda the far-right party rose. It was perfect fuel for their upcoming electoral campaign. Many of these rioters weren't even French, they said. This is not how we expect guests in this country to behave.

I can sense it all so vividly now. I can smell the cars burning, hear the smashing of glass, taste the sickly sensation of my own fear. The images I saw on TV have become indistinguishable from my own memories, as though it doesn't make any difference where the information came from. As though the television reports have become a part of me.

Sophie was refilling my glass. I reached over as she poured and put my hand on her wrist. She met my eye, defiantly.

'What?'

'I miss you.'

'You need to start hanging out with people your own age,' she said, pulling her hand away. But as I spun the stem of my glass in resignation, staring down into the vortex, she hovered there, and I wondered if she had decided to take pity on me.

'You do look miserable,' she said.

'I am.'

Her face was hard but her eyes were soft, and she leaned towards me a little over the bar. 'I think we should talk.'

Out of the corner of my eye I could see Didier watching us. We weren't going to get any privacy any time soon. Sophie followed my eyes and nodded. 'Perhaps later,' she whispered.

'I used to come here to relax,' I said. 'Do we have to have the news on permanently?'

'Most people want to know what's happening in the world, what's happening on our own doorstep right now. Most normal people.'

'OK, but the TV sensationalises everything. It doesn't tell us what's at the heart of all this. It doesn't separate the issues from the anger.' Didier was moving towards us. 'And then every fifteen minutes, with apparently no sense of irony, it gives us another lecture: want more. Expect more. Need more. Fast food and weight-loss miracles, a perfect family, an exotic holiday. When people realise they can't have it all, of course they get angry and frustrated.'

'You think we're all so easily persuaded?' Sophie pulled her wrist out from under my touch, put her hands on her hips.

'I think it's hard not to be.'

'I agree.' The dragon had stepped in by my shoulder, close enough for it to feel like a provocation. He winked at Sophie. 'The truth is not on the TV. The only way you can understand the truth is to be out there on the streets.'

'Good evening, Didier.'

'Baptiste.' He shook my hand firmly. 'I take it you'll not be joining us tomorrow?'

'You're not serious?' I looked at Sophie in despair, the wine souring in my mouth.

'Of course,' she said. 'You were right when you said the issues need to be more prominent. But no one is going to do that for us. We need to put ourselves out there. We need to be seen on TV too, a voice of reason in all this. Otherwise people will think all we are doing is fighting each other, which is exactly what the government wants.'

'Sophie, are you crazy? It's too dangerous for you out there now. Don't go.'

Didier rolled his eyes. 'Why, because she's a woman, or because you think she looks like an Arab?'

Sophie glared at him. 'It's no more dangerous going out to protest in the daylight than it is going home at night in the dark, and I'm not afraid to fight for what's important to me,' she said, 'unlike you.'

'And no one likes a coward.'

'Shut up, Didier,' Sophie snapped. 'You have no idea what we're talking about.'

'Sophie tells me that people assume she's your daughter,' he motioned around the bar with a vague hand. 'That must be embarrassing for both of you.'

Sophie glared at him as his greasy peal of laughter erupted. She grabbed me by the arm. 'Look, everyone needs to stop worrying,' she said. 'It's all organised. There's a police cordon. I'll be fine.' She was looking down at my forearm, writing something on the skin. 'I know you won't want to call me at home, so here's my mobile if you want to talk.' I kept my eyes on her face as she spoke, listening not to the words but the way she softened them by barely parting her lips, studying the curve of her nose, the dark eyebrows. She could have been my daughter, there was no doubt, although why Didier would think I'd be embarrassed by that I couldn't think. Yet as I looked at her I realised there was something uncanny in what I saw, like a faint note in a glass of wine that you know is familiar but impossible to place out of context. I strained to recall the grainy grey newspaper clipping of a dead-faced woman, but all I could bring to mind was the imprecise, dark-haired dancer of my own imagination.

We rarely go into Toulouse these days; there are too many places that make you edgy. I never know when turning a corner will trigger a flashback to a time when you were here before, so we tend to stay close to home. Sometimes there is no choice though. We were delayed this morning at an appointment in the city and you suggested eating lunch in a nearby restaurant, well known for its excellent meat. It seemed like a good idea at the time, but as we were shown to our table, a woman recognised me and stood to greet me.

You smiled as I made the briefest of introductions before leaving them to enjoy their meal, but once we were seated you turned to me accusingly. 'Who was that?' you demanded.

'Just someone from work,' I said. It was true in a sense, but I must have appeared guarded and your expression darkened. It wasn't the first time something like this had happened, and I thought I could brave it out, but I should have known better.

We ordered and began our meals with no more mention of it. It was only later when I returned from the bathroom that it became clear it was not forgotten. The contents of my bag were spilled across the table, in the food, on the floor. Fury came off you in waves. The other diners were self-consciously continuing to eat as though nothing was wrong and the waiter hovered nervously at a distance. I nodded to him apologetically. I've got this.

I forced myself to return to the table, sitting down calmly and looking you in the eye. There, small and insignificant-looking, in the palm of your hand you held the driftwood horse. 'Where did you get this?' you said. 'Where did you get this –' there was panic in your eyes, you were missing the word – 'this animal?'

I had kept that secret for so long, long after you thought you had lost it, long after I became Chouette, safe in my bag like a talisman. I had no choice now but to tell you the truth, and hope that even if you didn't understand it, you would see it for what it was. 'You gave it to me,' I said.

I woke in the dark. The cowbell was ringing a continuous, urgent alert. Something terrible must have happened, I thought, scrambling for clothes, for a hair comb, for the door. But no one was there, just millions of air particles crushing and blowing. The wind had come for me. The window frames rattled. Candice heaved. I unhooked the bell and brought it inside, standing it amongst the geraniums. Back in bed I tried to sleep but too many thoughts trespassed across my mind and eventually I capitulated and got up to make tea.

At first light the telephone rang, my Saturday client calling to cancel his appointment. I should have known then it was a portent of trouble. I offered to reschedule for later in the day. 'No chance,' he said. 'I'm looking out of my window right now and the traffic is already nose to tail all up the street. It's not moved now for half an hour. There's no way I can get to you.'

'Perhaps there's an accident?'

'An accident? It's *Operation Escargot*. The roads are blocked all around Toulouse,' he said. 'No one's going anywhere today.'

'Are there still no buses? The metro?'

'Don't you read the news? The metro has been out since Wednesday, the buses too. The trains are on strike and taxis are refusing commissions. It's chaos.' I suggested that I came in to him by foot. It would take me a while, but I always enjoyed a walk. 'Even without this foul weather I wouldn't take the risk,' he said. 'It was nasty last night in the centre, completely out of hand. Anyone with any sense is staying home today.'

Sophie, I thought. I had her number now. It was early but I could send her a message.

I remember standing for a while at the window after I had sent the text, looking out at the wind-lashed water and thinking what I would do with the day. And then a shortening of focus to the window itself. The glass was dirty. An irrational sense of panic rose within me. Something about the windows. I had to get away from the windows. I felt sure that something terrible was going to happen if I stayed there. I had to get out. I had a headache. I needed some air.

The wind howled around Candice. As I locked the door I was shoved hard back against the boat by a gust so strong I thought it might lift me off my feet and I could ride it like a carpet. Running was impossible, so I turned and set off along the towpath in the opposite direction to usual, walking against the wind, leaning against the weight of air, every hunched step an effort, my eyes stinging with dust whipped up by the blizzard of dead leaves. The wind scoured my cheeks and the cold scalded my throat. Yet high above, the ashen clouds hung motionless, draining away the light.

It was one of those winter days when the landscape appears pencil-drawn in sepia and grey. Even the catkins were a pallid green, all the life sucked out of them. Only the mimosa hinted at colour, already showing the first signs of yolky yellow on the early fronds of blossom that bowed and shook in the wind. Later, when everything froze, the laden boughs would bow low to the ground and snap under the weight of the snow. Not the other trees; the wind slipped and slid through their branches causing nothing but a shiver. They didn't resist it; they had known it was coming.

I passed under road bridges blocked by solid rows of cars, the drivers' frustration blaring. So much noise. I kept going. At some point it became apparent that I was on my way to the city centre and although nerves rose within me I didn't resist, just kept on apace, pushing against the wind so hard that by the time I arrived in Toulouse I was exhausted.

There was going to be no place to rest. The city streets were more crowded than I had ever seen them and yet the crowd seemed fluid, bursting open and contracting again. With each shift, an energy built. Just like the migrating starlings, new, smaller groups seemed to be joining the main buzz of the flock from all sides, sucked into the swell. I allowed myself to be engulfed in their dark, flapping coats and carried along on a wave of adrenaline, moving in on the centre, streaming effort-lessly around obstacles like liquid.

'Aren't you cold, brother?' A tall man patted me on the back. I turned, catching my distorted reflection in his sunglasses.

I shook my head. 'No, but thanks for asking.' It felt good to be welcomed, I thought.

As we approached the Place du Capitole you could feel the air thicken and rumble. Before we even turned into the square, past the television vans that crowded the entrance, I knew it wasn't like before. I was right. It was so solidly packed with bodies that the people already there, maybe ten thousand or more, could barely move. I looked over into the centre of the square where a thicket of placards, unmoving, pushed up from the sea of heads. That was the students. That would be where I would find Sophie, although the question remained what I was going to do when I reached her. Between me and the students was an unbroken row of police. Good, I thought, that's good, and I began to move forwards, inching into small gaps, excusing myself as I went.

As I reached the periphery of my group, I could see another crowd of people moving in from a side street. These were different again. They walked slowly, a dignified procession, with their heads held defiantly. The men were not wearing hoods, but what looked to be a form of Sunday dress: suits, but with ruffles and frills as colourful as the boats on the towpath. There were women too, the older ones wearing bright head-scarves, the younger ones in long colourful skirts, their bare arms glittering with bangles. Amongst the blacks and the blues their colours looked so out of place, like blossom fallen on the streets. I thought of the boy, Pesha, and shivered with grief.

A call went up around me like a ripple. I couldn't make out the words. Then one of the Roma shouted something back. The crowd thickened and boiled. And then the police were advancing in a hard line, yelling and pushing people out of the way, straight for us.

Where could I go? I would never get through the police to the students now, but the men behind me were becoming hostile. They were pushing forward and, unable to advance, those of us at the front began thinning out around the Roma like oil on water. Then, as though something had snapped, I found myself bustled out into their midst.

I immediately started to apologise, but the man I had stumbled into jostled me angrily, shoving my arm. 'Where do you think you're going?' His face was all shade and suspicion, but for a flash of gold tooth. By his side were two children, a boy and a girl. I was never great at telling ages. They were probably older than the friendly little boy from the towpath but I could see they were still younger than Manon and Gaëlle. What were they doing here?

'This is no place for your children,' I exclaimed, thinking of Sabine. 'You shouldn't bring your children here.'

A woman beside him, dark hair scraped back off her face, pulled the children into her side. 'Leave us alone,' she said. 'We have a right to be here as much as you.'

'No,' I said, 'I—'

'Having a problem here, brother?' It was him again, the man in the sunglasses, his voice now suffused with threat.

'No, no problem,' I said.

'Why don't you go home?' he said to the couple with the children, now flanked by others, tense.

'We've come here peacefully,' the man said, shifting in front of his wife. 'All we want to do is live peacefully. All we want is a chance at a good life. You treat us with contempt, you call our women whores, you call our children thieves—'

'What would you call someone who steals from us?'

'Wait, stop, both of you,' I said. I put out my hands, trying to separate the two men, and then someone cried out, 'Get your hands off me!'

A roar went up behind me, ahead of me people were turning and running, and then I was moving too. I was a leaf on the canal, swept along with the other flotsam, sometimes rushing forwards then all at once caught in an eddy, spinning back on myself, trying to stay on my feet, sinking and rising again until the screams retreated behind me and ahead of me the crowd began to thin out. I could see daylight through the mass of bodies. I gained impulsion, pushing through to the safety of the slim void ahead. Five deep, four deep, three ... and then my shins slammed sharply against the edge of something solid and painful.

I tumbled forwards on to the marble bench, disoriented for a moment, then got shakily to my knees, then to my feet. The bench wasn't high, but high enough that I could climb up out of the feverish smell of the crowd and raise my arms, untangling myself and stretching up to the magnificent desolation of the scowling sky. Sometimes the sky is all we've got.

When I had caught my breath and felt my heart beginning to calm, I took stock of what was happening around me. Behind me I was aware of a rhythmic banging, like drums, and in front of me something strange was happening. The crowd was moving away from me, opening up a space between us. Backing away, not turning away. In the distance, sirens wailed.

My telephone buzzed in my pocket. Without my glasses I had to hold it at arm's length. A text from Sophie, a beacon in the darkness. *Got your message. Where are you?* As I started to thumb out a reply, squinting at the screen, out of nowhere I saw the first stone arcing towards me. It had a perfect, slow trajectory, like the olive stones Etienne and I would throw into the water. I liked watching the way the small ripples would spread wide and then disappear as the stones sank to the bed of the canal.

The stone flew over my head, just missing me. I looked out at the crowd, still all facing me. Shouting insults, some waving their arms. What was it? The drumming sound grew louder. My mouth tasted of olives. Bitter black olives as though I had just eaten them. As though I could taste the memory. Marjoram and thyme.

After the first stone came a murmur, then a storm, flying out of the crowd in my direction. I suppose I overthink things, and while I was still trying to work out what was happening the first blow came across my left shoulder. Instinctively I put my hands out to shield my head and felt the crack of the bones in my fingers. Oh God, my piano. I crouched down, pushing my hands under my armpits and turning to jump off the bench.

Then I saw them, the wall of riot police advancing, their shields held up against the volley of stones. I ran towards them as the third stone cracked into my back, winding me.

There was a roaring in my skull, a pounding of blood. I reeled forwards, somehow remaining on my feet. Black boots marched across the broken cobbles towards me. I turned again, trying to suck in a breath, but there was nothing. I could feel myself getting light-headed. The next blow came across the backs of my knees, not a stone but a truncheon, and as I went down, something struck my forehead. Afterwards, I'm not sure. A kick in the kidneys. I curled tight, pulling my head underneath me as wild cries went up and the high black boots and blue trousers mingled with sneakers and legs, most passing thankfully around me but many stumbling over me as the dreams arrived.

When the storm had passed and the flock had dispersed, I felt myself pulled up by hands, lifted roughly into a sitting position. There was so much blood in my eyes I could barely see them, two young men, white-faced and shocked. They put me back down again quickly. 'Don't touch him! You could get done for that. What if he's got a broken neck?'

'Shit.'

The hot spread of blood. The hard pillow. The cool smell of city flagstones.

'Call an ambulance.'

The bed was narrow and too short. When my arms failed to find a place to tuck away under the small thin pillow and draped down the sides they brushed against cold tubular steel. People in green came in and raised the back, laid it flat again. I sat straight and reclined at their will, all the while covered in a thin bobbled blanket the colour of rust. Between me and the old man in the next bed with the bruised face and his leg in plaster was a night stand on which he or his family had already laid out his affairs. A puzzle book, a loupe, a tin of lozenges. There was a fox's face on the tin.

The chair in the corner was covered in padded plastic and smelled of disinfectant. The window wouldn't open, which filled me with alarm. Only by pretending it wasn't there at all could I ease the claustrophobia. It brought back my childhood, my room back home, the shutters I hated, leaning too far out of the window to pin them back. Bats in my room.

I tell you these superficial details because they are what my mind has deemed important about that place. Beyond that, beyond the smells and the fox and the useless window, nothing is clear in my mind. They gave me a lot of painkillers, allowing me to drift in and out of hazy consciousness, and in the weeks that followed I dreamed about that hospital so much that dreamscapes blurred into memories that found more purchase than reality. Walls moved. My roommate was sometimes there and sometimes not. Sometimes his face had changed entirely. Doors led into my parents' cottage or down to the sea and one night I dreamed that the door to the hospital opened out beside a glorious bottle-green canal as wide as a river. I followed it for kilometres, gliding above it as though swimming through air. Then, after what seemed like an endless stretch of long, straight water, the canal curved around a hillside and disappeared from sight. As I rounded the corner, the canal ended abruptly, petering out into a barren piece of land like the tail of a worm.

In another dream Amandine was there, sitting by my side. I was happy to see her, but embarrassed. She was looking me up and down. She seemed so concerned about me but all I could think of was how strange it was to see her in the hospital. 'How could I not come?' she said, although her face was pained and wary. She motioned to my chest. 'Show me.' I shook my head, but she reached forward anyway and untied the hospital gown, gently slipping it forwards off my arms to reveal the black plum and yellow stains on my skin. 'What were you doing?' she said.

'I don't understand.' I trembled under her touch, aching for her to take me in her arms, willing my subconscious to make it happen.

Doctors with clipboards came and went, trips to radiology with cheerful orderlies who wheeled me in and out of elevators, up and down endless corridors. Then there was a pinch-faced man who arrived wearing a suit and tie under his white coat, a small cluster of young doctors trailing in his wake like ducklings. He was less interested in my fractures than how I came to get them. He had an awful lot of questions. 'Tell me again why you went to the Capitole,' he said.

I thought about it, but the answer lurked behind whitewashed windows. They had told me the concussion should have cleared by now, but the memory wouldn't come back to me and my eyes ached with the effort of remembering.

'Still nothing?' he said. I told him about how the people looked like birds, migrating starlings that shifted and swooped. He took notes. 'And do you remember how you got into the city centre in the first place?'

'I walked,' I told him. At least I had remembered that. And I told him about the wind, and how the trees had known it was coming. How I had been so cold in its path because I had forgotten to wear a coat. At this the young ones with him shuffled and murmured excitedly.

'In January?' the pinch-faced man said, writing on his clipboard. 'Would you describe yourself as absent-minded?'

'No.'

'And what's this, then?' I followed his gaze down to my left forearm. 'Do you frequently write reminders to yourself like that?'

I put on my glasses with my least painful hand and read the faded characters inked on to my forearm: ten numbers finishing with a tiny but perfect little kingfisher. Numbers from every bar tab I'd had in the last five years, the six that looked more like a gamma, the one that looked like a mountain.

'A friend wrote that, not me,' I said. It was comforting to run my fingertip over the traces of Sophie's pen strokes. And then it hit me. Blue ink on skin. Just like the woman on the train. Not a phone number for her but a single word. Toulouse.

With sudden clarity, I knew what the doctor was going to say and why.

Etienne's voice stirred me. 'If you're not going to answer your phone maybe you should turn it off.'

I was slumped on the couch, winded by fatigue but flooded with the relief of being home, one bare foot on the cool leather, the other flat on the reassuring wooden floor. My eyes were heavy and my throat felt parched.

'I didn't hear you come in.'

'I've knocked a few times and I did try to call …'

'Sorry, I'm done in.'

He nodded, handing me a glass of water as though I had asked for it. I drank deeply, closing my eyes to enjoy the blissful feeling of hydration spreading under my skin. When I opened them again, Etienne had pulled the piano stool over and was sitting beside me. 'I expect it'll take you a while to recover. You took quite a battering. What on earth were you doing?'

I shrugged.

'Well I'd steer clear of Sabine for a while if I were you, you're in for a piece of her mind.' Etienne motioned towards the phone where it vibrated on the chest, the little red numbers of messages and missed calls now in double figures. 'Your parents, I suppose?'

'I shouldn't think so.'

'Your girlfriend?'

'No, it's Sophie, the girl from the bar.'

Etienne looked confused, then surprised, and finally as though he had had a revelation. 'The one who took you to the student demonstration?'

'That one, yes.'

'So she's behind all this. Is there something between you? She's not the client you were telling me about?'

'No, nothing to do with that. Sophie's just a friend,' I said with a sigh.

'Probably just as well since she's young enough to be your daughter,' he said. 'A man has to retain some dignity in middle age. But she is the reason you were in Toulouse?'

It would make perfect sense but I couldn't say for sure. Yet something about the flashing messages told me Etienne would be proved right. I thought back to the last time I saw her. We had talked for the first time in weeks. She had worn a scarf around her throat. Purple. She had said she was going to the protests and I had urged her not to. It had been cold and there had been tarragon in the stew. My stomach rumbled at the thought. I was famished.

Etienne smiled thinly. 'I'll make you supper. What have you got in?' But of course there was nothing. Perhaps some jam and butter in the fridge. 'Do you want to go over to Jordi's?' he suggested. 'I'm sure I could persuade René to come, it would do us good to get out.' But the idea overwhelmed me. I could barely sit without wincing. I shook my head dismally.

'Well, maybe they'll do a take-out. I'll call them.' He raised an eyebrow. 'Or I could just send a text?'

When Etienne returned from the bar he didn't ring the bell, just came in, and I woke groggily to find his hand on my shoulder. Beside him was a sheepish-looking Sophie holding a casserole dish. 'I'm sorry,' Etienne said, 'she insisted.'

Sophie put down the casserole on the galley counter and came over, squatting on the floor beside me. 'Oh my God, look at you.'

'I know. Who will love me now?'

A shadow crossed her face. 'Don't joke about it, you look terrible.'

'Thanks.'

'I'm sorry,' she said. 'I was spiteful to you. Neither of us expected you to come. Not after last time, not after what you said.'

'You weren't spiteful.'

'I was. I've been horrible to you. I should have minded my own business.'

I shrugged. 'Concussion,' I said.

Sophie allowed herself a grin. 'I can see how that could be rather convenient.'

'I'm going to leave you to it,' Etienne interrupted. He turned to Sophie. 'Now don't get him too excited, he needs to rest.'

As soon as he was out of the door, Sophie turned to me, her face serious. 'Look, I have to get back to work once I've seen you eat something, but I need to ask you a question first. Did this happen because you were jealous of Didier? Is that why you came? Your text that morning was so cryptic. Didier's convinced you've got a crush on me too, but I asked your friend just now' – she looked bashful – 'sorry about that, I couldn't help myself, and he said you told him you're in love with someone else. But to be honest he didn't look so sure himself.'

The evening was getting so surreal that I really couldn't be certain I wasn't dreaming it. 'What? No, Sophie, I'm not in love with you. Why do people keep asking me that?'

'That's what I told Didier. I think it's him that's jealous.' She stood to serve the casserole, opening and closing cupboards in the galley until she found a suitable bowl. 'Why then?'

'Goodness knows what possessed me, I don't really remember, but even if it was because of you it wouldn't have been to impress Didier, but because I thought you were in danger.'

'You were right,' she said. 'I was stupid to go. My mother went mad with me afterwards.' She glanced back at me over her shoulder, a look in her eyes that I couldn't put my finger on. 'So, then. Just how long is this concussion going to last?'

'Anyone's guess,' I said. I wasn't ready to tell people yet. I didn't want to watch their feelings towards me change until I'd worked out how I felt about myself.

Amandine arrived out of blue skies. I should have been pleased to see her at the door, perplexing as it was after not having spoken for so long, but the sight of her only gave a shape to the dismay that already lay heavy as rocks in my chest.

Her timing was abysmal. I was a mess, the boat was a mess, even the towpath was a mess. The wind had left signs hanging off hinges and litter strewn along the towpath and in the canal. But worse than any of that, this was the end. It was the end for all my clients. How could it be anything else? That was one discussion we needed to have. Then there was everything that happened the last time she turned up without an appointment. The kiss. The secret she had kept from me. I felt a welcome frisson of excitement at this unchartered territory. Five months of appointments and she had avoided telling me she had had a child. Why?

'You're letting all the cold air through. Aren't you going to invite me in?'

'I didn't think you'd be coming back.'

'Come on,' Amandine said briskly, stepping inside and closing the door behind her. 'Come and sit down. Even under all those bruises you look pale.'

She didn't seem at all fazed by the way I looked. I suppose as a doctor she would have seen much worse. I offered her a drink and she insisted on making it, bustling around the galley making small talk and tea.

She sat. We looked at each other. We looked at the tea. We looked out of the windows and back to each other. My heart swelled and ached. My eyes stung. I couldn't trust myself to speak.

'You were on the news,' she said eventually.

'Oh. That's embarrassing.'

She stirred her tea, the spoon chinking against the cup. 'Talk about being in the wrong place at the wrong time. How are you feeling now?'

Everything was amplified: a cyclist scraping past on the towpath, the ducks snacking their way around Candice's flanks like a troop of amateur tap dancers. Amandine stretched out her legs in front of her, crossing them at the ankles. In her hurry to get me sitting down she had kept her shoes on. Just like the first time. These shoes were the same colour as her skin, with straps that ran over the ankle bone. A tiny silver buckle on each. How was I feeling? Where to start?

'I can't see you any more,' I said.

Amandine shifted in the chair as though the swell of a wave had caught her briefly then set her down again. 'I'm sorry about last time. I shouldn't have just walked off, and I shouldn't have left things that way afterwards. I meant to call you to explain, but I was angry. Or confused maybe. Can't we talk about it?'

'It's not that.'

'Then what?'

'It's complicated.'

'I told you, you complicate things too much.' Her voice was soft, patient.

'I wish it were as simple as that.'

She smiled. 'You kissed me.'

'I know.'

'I'm glad you remember,' Amandine said. Behind her a butterfly tilted the light as it brushed through the dusty air by the window. 'I thought what with the concussion and so on ...'

'It's not concussion.'

I still don't know why I said that. But Amandine's eyes flashed, suddenly hard and alert. 'Baptiste?' I felt as though the weight of whatever I said next could capsize me.

'Did I ever tell you I was an orphan?' I said. Amandine shook her head warily. 'My mother died in childbirth and we still don't know who she was. It's a complete mystery and there are so few clues.' I pointed to the violin. 'Remember that?'

'Of course. Was it hers?'

'Yes. It's a funny thing, for years I wondered about those few possessions she had when she died. What did they mean? I tried to define her through them, as though that would help me understand myself.'

'Perhaps she was a musician?'

'Perhaps, although she could just as likely have not been.'

'What else do you have of hers?'

'Just the violin, a little money, her coat – a green coat – and a wooden toy.'

'A toy?'

'Well, an ornament maybe; a carved horse. But it doesn't really matter. The clues were never in her things. My mother has always been inside me, if only I had known where to look.'

'You're talking in riddles,' Amandine said. 'What is it you're trying to tell me?'

I spread my fingers wide, counted on my fingers. 'In a nutshell, what do we know about my mother? One: she was eight and a half months pregnant but travelling alone. Two: she carried almost nothing with her, not even a change of clothes. Three: she was travelling on a train from Barcelona to Toulouse, and four: she had *Toulouse* written on her arm.'

'So she had no passport or papers?' Amandine asked. 'How could she have come from Spain?'

'Something could have happened to them along the way if she wasn't thinking straight.' I looked down at my tea, going cold before me.

'Drink some,' Amandine said. 'It will do you good.'

I drank. 'Why would you write something on your own skin?' I said.

'Because it's a reminder you can't lose.'

'Exactly. It makes perfect sense now,' I said. 'I always imagined she'd had to escape something bad, that she was fleeing with whatever she could carry. But now I ask myself, what if she didn't really know what she was doing? What if she just left home one morning and never came back? What if back where she came from there was a family, if there were children who went to school one morning, a husband who went to work, and when they got home she had gone? Eight and a half months pregnant and she just disappeared like that?'

It had crept up on me so slowly that I hadn't noticed the way the edges had rubbed off my mind. But when the doctors had asked, when I thought about it, I had admitted that yes, I had been losing the names of things, losing the sense of things, and when I grasped for them they were not even just out of reach. Not on the tip of my tongue like before. Just absent, as though they were never there. Had it been the same for her, I wondered? Did she even know why she was on that train at all?

'Oh no.' Amandine covered her mouth, falling back against the Louis XV as though knocked. I have learned since that this is what happens around people like me. Grief follows us around like a thickening fog, suffocating those who get too close.

'Dementia.' I stepped over to the stove and pushed another log on to the waning embers, letting the wood smoke drift over my eyes. A jolt of pain shot through my ribs and I winced.

'Let me.' Amandine came to stand by my side, closing the glass door and looking up at me. Sunlight fell in layers over her face, cast through the windows dirty after the storms. 'I don't know what to say,' she said. 'I'm so sorry.' I shrugged awkwardly. I was sorry too. 'Your work?'

'A change of career I suppose.'

'Take some time to let it sink in before you start making any decisions, Baptiste. Speak to your doctor. If you need any advice, I'm here. I'm not a specialist, but ...' She put her hand on my arm.

'I'll be OK,' I said. Her eyebrows creased inwards. Of course I wouldn't be OK. The irony was that after all the searching and imagining, who I was didn't matter at all. What mattered was who I would become.

'Even if you don't want to talk about it,' Amandine said 'even if you just need some company, I'm here for you. I don't like to think of you having to deal with this alone. It must be a huge shock.'

'The last thing I want is for you to feel sorry for me.' The fire was blazing again now. I closed the vent.

Amandine stiffened. 'Don't insult me. You know me well enough by now. If you thought about it for even a minute you'd know that I'd never pity you. Don't let this define you, Baptiste. Don't shut yourself off.'

But I didn't know her, did I? I couldn't shake it from my mind, the way her skin had felt under my fingers, the fine soft scars on her belly. One discussion down, I thought, and two to go. 'Amandine, why in all this time did we never talk about you being a mother? What made you turn away from me that night?'

Amandine retreated to the safety of her chair and crossed her legs, her hand reaching up to the ladybird at her throat. 'Don't you have anything stronger than tea?'

'Maybe. I could look?'

She smiled wearily. 'I'm kidding, it's 11 a.m. No I'm not, what have you got?'

Amandine cradled the glass in her hand, looking down into the crimson pool of wine. 'I was an unmarried mother,' she said. 'It was shameful. Both my parents were angry and ashamed of me. They judged me. Other people judged me.'

'Did you think that I would judge you?'

'No. But even people who don't judge look at you differently. I never thought that keeping the baby would determine who I was, but it did. Even for people I thought loved me. Even to this day.'

'I'm sorry.'

She shrugged. 'I got over it. I never judged myself. But still it rankled. And then when I came here, when I met you, it was as though you didn't even consider it. There was something exclusive between us, as if when we were alone together we had shut everyone else out. I wasn't anyone's mother or daughter or doctor; all you could see was Amandine.'

She was right. There she was in the chair she had made her own, her pale hair cut the same as always, framing the same cool eyes, yet somehow in my mind she had changed. She was a mother now. She was different. It's impressive the way a single piece of information can transform how we see someone. I wondered how I had missed this. How long had I been failing at what I used to do best? I shook my head.

'No,' Amandine insisted, 'it was perfect. You had seen exactly what I needed. I was rediscovering myself. But it did feel like I was the one taking all the risks, revealing myself to you while you kept your distance. And then that evening on the towpath, after everything we had talked about ...' She extended a hand as though to touch me, but I was beyond her reach and she rested it instead on the curved arm of the chair. 'Baptiste, I'm sorry. I didn't mean what I said. About you being in love ...'

'With Sophie?'

'Yes.' Amandine sighed. 'It was an awful thing to say. It was an awful thing to think.'

'Was it something I did?' The wine was too sharp to be drunk on its own, but it took the edge off the seismic waves that rippled through me as though a fault line had opened in my heart. I wondered if she saw.

'Not really,' she said. 'It was a combination of things. Look, I know I'm not as young as I was. I'm already older than my mother was when my father left her. I know my body carries its age and I don't mind that at all. I'm not shy. But there was still a worry, a sliver of doubt in my mind.'

I thought again about the strong curve of her back, the softness of her skin. My hands ached with longing. If I could have had one wish at that moment it would have been either to make love to Amandine, or to play the piano. Both, given the state of my hands, were impossible.

She took another drink. 'This wine is rough.'

'Sentimental value. It's last year's *primeur*.'

'Ah.' She drank again.

'And now?' I said.

'Here I am. Back again.'

'Yes.' I smiled weakly. 'Thank you. And I'm sorry how this turned out.'

'No, wait –' she raised a hand to curtail my conclusion – 'I've thought about it a lot since then. The thing is, I saw the look in your eyes when you touched me and I knew after that there'd be no avoiding it: you would want to talk about that part of me, about motherhood, and I got cold feet.'

'I needed to know that part of you too. I needed to see all of you.'

Amandine shivered. 'I know. And we would have got round to it eventually of course, but I'd deliberately put it off. It was a side of me I wasn't ready to show you yet. I wanted to be the other me just a little longer. Until I could be sure you'd understand.'

'You thought I wouldn't?' I sat back, devastated.

Amandine rubbed at the soft traces of anguish that creased her forehead. 'Listen, I've never told anyone this, Baptiste, but those first days after her birth changed how I saw myself. I was so tired. So lost. I had no one to help me. Even my own mother said that I had made my own bed and I should lie in it. I've never forgiven her for her spite. But worst of all, the love didn't come like I'd been told it would. From the way people had described it I'd expected a perfect love to blossom within me even as they cut the cord. As though having a baby would transform me into the patient, selfless woman I had never been as a girl. But when they handed her to me, nothing had changed. I wanted to love my daughter so much, but I just couldn't find it in me.' Amandine gazed out at the towpath, the broad trunks of trees emerging from drifts of dead leaves. 'I blamed her for what was happening to me, because I had no one else to blame. I resented her. How my life would have been different if she had never been born.'

'I think you're being too hard on yourself,' I said. 'You resented the situation, not your child.'

'Either way.' She twisted the silver ring around on her thumb. 'I suppose you can figure out how the story goes.'

'You had her adopted?'

Amandine looked up at me and rubbed her forehead. 'What? Baptiste? What are you talking about? Why would you think that?' She stopped and checked herself. 'No. Of course I didn't. Just because it was hard I didn't give up. Just because I imagine losing people I love doesn't mean I would actually abandon them. Yes, I imagined her being taken from me. As I held her and rocked her and fed her I pictured the most terrible things – kidnapping, car crash, cot death – anything so that I would feel that crushing pain of loss, the surging of my need to protect her. I'm not proud of it. But it made me feel love, if love means spending your waking hours being terrified of losing what is most precious to you.'

'So that is how you love people?'

'We all find our ways.' Amandine pulled her chair closer, leaning in until her fingertips found my skin once more. 'Which brings us back to the question, Baptiste, where do we go from here?'

The first frosts took us by surprise as we slept. Seduced by months of mild weather, January had already given us mimosa and sweet-scented apple blossom, but then the cold sprang down from the mountains, bearing in on the city like a tide, and when it finally smothered the city everything stopped.

Bitter weeks lay ahead of us. It was all they could do to keep the main streets and roads passable. Everywhere else the snow was left to drift thickly over deserted streets and pavements. Blankets of quiet lay like relief over the city and her outskirts.

The flow of water slowed and then stopped. The canal froze around our boats and crackled against their flanks at midday. The wide sprawling Garonne river set hard in places. Every winter when the village duck pond first iced over my father used to tell me of the time the Garonne froze solid right through Toulouse. Maybe it was the same year some time in the early seventies – I can't have been that old – when a child drowned on that icy pond. That year our house was as cold as the church, and smelled of tallow and musty blankets brought up from the cellar. I remember the day they found him under the ice, my mother drew me the first hot bath after what seemed an age without warm water, and stood watching as I sank my cold skin under the steam as though it were a miracle. The village children were kept away from the pond for a few weeks after that – not that I needed any persuading – but when spring came around life got back to normal. The water had been forgiven.

Everyone along the canal did their bit. Despite Etienne's protests I insisted that I was perfectly capable of clearing my part of the towpath, going out every morning in my old skiing salopettes to shake the nearby branches free of snow and clear the path up to the *Yvonnick*. From there Sabine and the kids cleared up to the *Florence* and Etienne and René cleared between there and the *Rouge-Gorge*. We all did our part clearing the path out towards the car park and the council took it from there.

I hung my salopettes in the shower, drenched and smelling of snow until the evening, when I lit the stove. With demand surging and deliveries unreliable, my stock of wood was waning rapidly. To fend off the cold I moved around as much as possible, bundling up in hats, scarves and gloves. It made playing the piano tricky again just as my hands were improving, but for a while everything seemed manageable and strangely serene, as though I had been given the retreat I needed to think things over.

Amandine had put me on the spot. I hadn't expected her to take my illness so lightly. I hadn't expected that now I'd explained how she could no longer be my client she would still want to pursue something more personal between us. Made reckless by the wine, I had given her the impression that it was possible. I hadn't said yes exactly, but I hadn't said no either. I had asked for some time. Amandine had acquiesced, and so the question remained open. I had agonised over it almost constantly in the days since. If she was going to come into it with open eyes, what was there to stop us? And yet … and yet she had been my client and I hadn't fulfilled the contract. No money had changed hands, but she had invested a lot of time in our sessions. I had let her down. And even putting ethics aside, how could you go into a love affair with a clean conscience knowing that inevitably you're going to hurt the other person? The longer I waited before contacting Amandine, the more uncertain and nervous I became. My heart and mind battled it out in the cold. I knew Amandine would have had time to rethink as well. Perhaps she had already reached the logical conclusion that there was no happy future for us.

I went out to clear the snow at first light as usual. The night had been so cold that my clothes hadn't dried properly from the day before and it was a miserable job. Every breath burned my lungs and after a few minutes the bone-dry winter air had wormed its way in through the fabric of my gloves, causing a stabbing pain in my fingers as the joints began to seize. Back on board in the chilly bathroom, where the windowpanes had turned to ice, I turned the tap to hot, waiting for the water to run through so I could fill the sink and bring some warmth slowly back into my throbbing hands. But no water came, nor the hollow gasping in the pipes which would have meant a water cut. I looked down at the tap in confusion. I couldn't see what was wrong.

I must have stood shivering in that bathroom for minutes, trying to figure it out while my fingers and toes burned with cold. Eventually I had the sense to take off my wet clothes and put on some dry ones, still trembling the whole time and rubbing my hands together in desperation. They said things like this would happen, but not so soon, not so abruptly. What was I going to do? Finally the reality of my future came into focus, everything I had glossed over in the shocked days since the riots. It wasn't the forgetting of taps and teapots and piano keys that I feared most of course, it wasn't the inevitable humiliation, it was the isolation. The realisation that the day would come when the faces of people I love meant nothing to me any more. I was to steadily grow more and more alone and nothing could stop that from happening. I let the despair wash over me, crouching on the floor and letting anguished sobs wrack my body.

If it had been a few weeks earlier I would never have got so upset over a tap. We all forget things. Ridiculous things slip our minds all the time. But when memory is a symptom of the menace lurking within you then every misplaced pencil, every word just on the tip of your tongue, every little thing that in the past would have been put down to absent-mindedness becomes suspect. This is the way it would be from now on. Is this part of it?, I would think. Is this it?

You have to pull yourself together, I told myself. Work it out. The tap. Silver. The plastic disc, half red, half blue. Left for hot, right for cold. Up for on, down for off. Don't forget to leave it running. Don't forget to let it drip.

I got to my feet and inspected the sink. It was bone dry. But I always left the taps slightly open in winter, just enough for a dribble of water to flow through. If I didn't and the temperature dropped far below freezing at night the overground pipes would fill solid with ice and in the morning there would be no water. I'd been doing it for ten years or more. It was as much a habit as brushing my teeth. My teeth. I ran my tongue over my teeth. Had I brushed them the night before?

No. I remembered now. I had been upset. It was the golden hour, just before sunset, and Candice was bathed in its warm light. I had been at the piano trying to persuade fingers like rusty levers to generate a degree of joy in a Bach concerto when there had been a commotion outside on the canal. Voices. At any other time I would have assumed a passing boat, but that was impossible since the water was frozen solid. I had lifted my head just in time to see someone ride a bike past the window. Whoever it was was well wrapped up, a red hat pulled tight over their ears and a grey scarf covering their mouth, but their muffled cries of delight were unmistakable.

If my piano had faced the towpath, of course there would have been nothing so extraordinary in this. But my piano faces the canal. I looked back into the room. Piano. Couch. Writing desk. Log stove. Books. Amandine's chair. Everything was normal. And outside my window, people continued to glide across my view, perhaps a dozen or so, gliding and sliding and laughing. They were close to the boat. All around it. They were in the wrong place. Uninvited. Crowding me. Hemming me in. Their scarves were striped, students probably, and their boots heavy and urban. Black boots. A sharp lump rose in my throat, cold sweats on my skin, claustrophobia in my chest. Why were they here? This was my home. I should be safe here.

I closed my eyes and began to play again, Satie, for calm, but I couldn't shut them out. When I peered out from the window again some of them were dancing. Taking photos of each other on their phones in front of the boat. One of them looked in at me, 'Don't stop, mister!'

They were just kids, I told myself. Out there playing, capering around on the ice, they had thrown off any pretence that they were anything else. The thought didn't even cross their mind that the ice might be too thin. I closed the piano lid and retreated to my bedroom, where I drew the curtains, huddled under the covers and waited for them to leave. I had fallen asleep listening to their laughter as the sun had set. I had woken at first light to clear the path. I had not brushed my teeth, or left the taps on. The pipes were frozen.

Where was my phone? My father would have something comforting to say, I thought, and my mother something wise. At least they would if I had told them the truth. I had only had the briefest of phone calls with them since I got out of

247

hospital, and I hadn't seen them at all, fobbing them off with a vague story of being under the weather. I didn't know how to face them looking as I did, or what I would say. I didn't want to lie, but how do you tell your parents you're dying? No one ever tells you how to do these things.

What was I thinking? I couldn't let this happen to me, becoming so wrapped up in my own problems that I wasn't even considering my parents. When was the last time I had called them? How were they managing in this weather? I rubbed my fingers together gently until they eased up sufficiently for me to dial their number. My mother answered.

'You're up early,' she said. 'How lovely to hear from you. Yes, completely snowed in, but Maud's son, the tall one, he's a lovely boy, he's been around to dig us out and brought in some dry wood. No of course you can't make it, none of the trains are running, Marie-Thérèse told us. Are you feeling any better?'

In the background I could hear church bells. 'You're staying indoors, aren't you?' I said. 'Keeping warm? Father too?'

'Yes, yes, of course,' my mother told me, 'I made a big pot of soup yesterday with potatoes and lentils and bacon. It'll keep us going all week. Don't worry about us. We're just fine. I wish I could bring some over for you, I bet you're not eating properly. And you must be freezing on that boat.'

'Yes. No. I'm fine, honestly. I was just worried. Are you sure you don't need anything? Promise to call me if you do?'

'Son, we stocked up in advance. We knew the cold snap was coming; we have a radio, you know. In any case it's nowhere near as bad as nineteen fifty-six, is it?'

'I wasn't born in fifty-six, Maman.'

There was a short, confused silence. 'I'm not senile, you know,' she said, 'I was talking to your father. I said it's not as bad as fifty-six is it, darling?' There was a faint voice offline. 'The weather, darling! The cold!' Another pause. 'No, he agrees, nothing like as bad as fifty-six. Don't you worry, we'll see you after the thaw. You take care of yourself.'

Swayed by my mother's urgings I relented and lit a fire. I made tea with what was left in the kettle, using the biggest mug I had, and warmed myself by the stove, my hands clutched around the hot drink, lost in introspection.

For days Jordi's place had been packed, hot and damp and full of elbows. Locals who usually drank in town were trading city centre variety for cheap and decent proximity.

It was pleasant enough meeting more of my neighbours, but this new sense of community had fallen at a bad time. I didn't want to be sociable, I wanted to talk to Sophie, who was tantalisingly out of reach. I ached with disappointment every time I arrived to find the place crowded yet again and Sophie swamped.

This night though, I arrived early enough to find her skulking around the draughts by the doorway. She grabbed me by the arm. 'At last! I've been waiting for you. I was going to call you if you didn't turn up soon.' Her hair was tied with bright ribbons and she was looking pleased with herself. 'Where were you last night?' she demanded. 'I have news!'

'Me too.' I kissed her quickly and hastened past her towards the fire. 'Come and sit down for a minute.'

'Baptiste!' she said, following at my heels and snapping her dishcloth at me. 'Wait!'

Rich meaty smells drifted over from the kitchen. 'What's on the menu? I'm ravenous.'

'No, Baptiste, listen!'

'Cassoulet?' I suggested. 'If it were me I would have done cassoulet. Or perhaps confit duck? Is it the duck?'

Sophie took a seat, perching on the edge of the chair to make it clear she didn't intend to stay long. 'Baptiste, will you shut up for a minute?'

'Chasseur then?'

'No, for goodness' sake, it's a pot-au-feu, but listen—'

'Pot-au-feu? No wonder the place is half empty.'

'Baptiste, don't be insufferable, we've only just opened.'

'I don't know what you—'

'I've got a job on the TGV as a barista.' She beamed at me, waiting for her friend to be pleased for her. But I need you here, I thought, especially now.

'Is that really what you want?' I said.

She looked as if she were weighing me up. 'As I said to my mother, and as I told Jordi, I can't stay here for the rest of my life. I've seen what that does to people. I'm going to take an apartment in Paris.'

'Paris?'

'Of course, Paris. And there are strikes planned for April or May. I can't wait.'

250

'You're taking a job so you can strike?'

She raised her voice in warning: 'Can you at least try to be happy for me?'

'No, it's great,' I said. 'I don't mean that the way it came out. I'll miss you.'

Her eyes flickered. 'I'll miss you too,' she said, 'but this is my chance to affect my future and the future of my children.' She threw her shoulders back. 'They say this could be our generation's May sixty-eight,' she said. 'We could change the country's direction completely.'

Pascale came over, setting a small plate of dried sausage and cornichons and a basket of bread on the table. 'It's nice to see you looking better, Baptiste,' she said, her arm on my shoulder as she bent to kiss my cheek. 'Haven't you got him a drink yet, Sophie?'

When it had become clear that managing the bar and the till alone was too much to ask of one person during the snows, Jordi had asked Pascale to pitch in with the serving of the food. Initially she had been reluctant and perfunctory, but it soon became clear that she was starting to enjoy herself, striking up conversations with the customers and even entertaining a little flirtation in situations where Sophie would have brushed it off with a scowl or a sharp wave of her finger. Rumours started that she had taken a fancy to one of the customers, fuelled by her growing attention to her appearance – every day her dark grey hair would be piled on her head slightly higher, her eyes slightly smokier, her scent following her around the room – but I suspected she was just enjoying spending more time around her husband.

'Thank you. It's my fault, I've been keeping Sophie talking, we haven't had the chance to catch up in a while.'

Jordi appeared, leaning against the kitchen door jamb, his belly restrained by his white apron, his pink face barely visible through the rough red cloud of hair. 'Has she told you?' he said, shaking his head.

'About the job?' I said. 'Yes.'

'What an idiot.'

'I'm sitting just here.' Sophie rolled her eyes.

'Leaving a perfectly good job to go and spend your days serving sad sandwiches to strangers and your nights holed up in a shoebox in Paris, just to make a point.'

'Not to make a point. To make things change,' Sophie said.

'Nothing will change, the fuss will be over by the summer.'

'Not if we stand our ground. Haven't you seen how angry people are?'

Jordi shrugged. 'We'll see. I notice there are no riots while it's cold outside. In the end people in rich, peacetime countries have a limited appetite for railing against the establishment. We have other things to think about. We're too lazy. It won't be long until we're back to the bog-standard strikes.' Seeming satisfied with his standpoint he turned back to the kitchen. 'Oh, and Pascale, you're looking radiant tonight.' Pascale preened, the colour rising in her cheeks. 'Now get a shake on, Sophie, you're not on strike yet. Pour the man some wine. Pot-au-feu, Baptiste?'

Sophie smoothed her apron over her hips and over the soft curve of her stomach as she stood and swayed off around the bar like a dancer. Something had got into her. Optimism came off her in waves. I was happy for her, of course. Her life stretched before her, horizons full of promise. As she pushed through the cascade of coloured beads into the kitchen she looked back at me over her shoulder.

'Hey, why are you smiling?'

'Because you look so happy.'

Sophie grinned. 'Life's just got pretty scary, but I have a lot to look forward to.'

By the time she returned I had warmed up and shifted my things over to the counter. The bar was filling up and I needed as much of Sophie's time as I could snatch, now more than ever.

She set twin short, squat glasses on the counter in front of me, and a carafe of tap water, still cloudy, the bubbles settling and thinning. A half-full bottle of wine followed. 'I didn't even ask you,' she said, 'are you feeling any better?'

'Pretty much mended.'

'Good. Help yourself,' she said.

The cork came out with a stiff pop.

Sophie raised her glass of violet syrup to my glass of red. 'Let's drink to the future then,' she said.

'What does your boyfriend think about you going away?' I asked.

'Didier's not my boyfriend.' Sophie frowned but didn't look up.

'He sometimes behaves as if he is,' I said.

'No, he doesn't. Not any more.' Having scribbled my tab on the paper place mat, her pen now hovered uncertainly above the corner where the kingfisher should go. 'Baptiste,' she said, setting the pen down on the counter, 'do you want to talk about it?'

Words fluttered as though caged in my mind. I didn't know which ones to set free. I didn't know where to start. 'Do you have friends in Paris?' I said. I tried for a smile but it felt weak even to me.

'We've talked enough about me,' she said. 'You said at the door you have news. I want to hear about you.'

I would have to tell her eventually, but not then. I couldn't overshadow her excitement with bad news. 'Oh, it's nothing really,' I said.

'Baptiste, out with it.'

The words chose themselves in the end. 'Etienne was right,' I said. 'I've fallen in love.' I took a drink of water. The words had felt dry on my tongue.

Sophie threw her hands up in delight. 'At last!' She came out from behind the bar and wrapped her arms around me in a strong, swift embrace. 'The timing couldn't be more perfect. I'm going away and you're in love.'

I put my head in my hands. 'It's not perfect. I didn't want to be in love. And now I am, I do' – I swirled the wine around in the other glass, watching as it spun close to the brim and the legs descended in oily arches – 'but it's impossible. For the first time in my life I'm really miserable.'

Sophie bit her bottom lip, her dark eyes glistening. 'Nothing is impossible. The only thing standing in your way is you.'

'You don't understand.'

'I do understand.' She looked up at me squarely. 'And there's no way I'm indulging that kind of negative thinking. What are you doing in here now if you're in love? You need to be making up for lost time. Why aren't you getting on with actually being in love?'

'Because it's complicated.'

'For God's sake, Baptiste,' she said. 'Of course it's complicated. What were you expecting, fairy tales? An ideal of love that doesn't exist?'

There was a trickle of condensation pooled on the bar by the carafe of water. I ran my fingers through it and closed my eyes, trying to fix the feeling in my mind. The cool water on my fingertip, the slight friction of the varnished bar, the fire against my back, the tannin in my mouth, and Sophie still there at my side, her hand on my arm. The hope she had for love.

Afterwards, you told me, everything looked different, although in the early days very little changed. I noticed you talking to yourself more often, speaking out your actions under your breath as you did them as though you had a baby on your hip, showing her the world, telling her its names. 'I am watering the plants, I am making the tea, I am calling my parents, I am cleaning my boat. This is Candice. She is my boat. Red. Green. Blue.' In another life you would have made a good father. But as things deteriorated you began to feel more ethereal, more afraid. Your world became sinister and unpredictable. People, who you had always understood easily, were now indecipherable. We knew things about you that you didn't. All times are different, but perhaps the hardest for you was those middle years. Part of you wanted to touch nothing, to have no consequence, and you began to draw away from people. You began to draw away from me.

Then the nightmares came. Once they started it seemed as though it was almost every night. Once you startled so violently in bed that I had to wake you to calm you. You had been dreaming that Candice had rotted through the hull and you were falling through, down into the water. You couldn't remember how to swim. The piano sank too, tilting at forty-five degrees, the lid flying open and music spilling out of it. 'Like a shoal of dark fishes,' you said, 'or a drowning man's last breath.' I realised then that the thing we were both most scared of was the thing that you needed most: you needed to forget that you were forgetting. Eventually you did.

While you still knew what was happening to you, while you still knew who I was, at the end of every night you used to say goodbye, in case when you woke you had forgotten. 'Don't forget,' you would say, 'that whatever tomorrow brings, I love you.' Your words fell into my waiting heart where I kept them safe until the morning, praying that tomorrow would not be the day when I was glad to have had them.

When it came it wasn't as I expected. On the day it happened you woke as usual, kissed me as usual, took a coffee out on to the towpath and sat barefoot amongst the tree roots to drink it. You seemed more relaxed than you had in a while, and I bathed in the respite. It was a weekend and we spent the day at your parents' cottage. I suppose it was because we were there that I failed to notice how you were no longer talking to yourself. Your mother felt the peacefulness in you too, and I could see it feeding her hope that you would get better, despite everything we had told her. We had a lovely day. But that night, back home in bed after you had turned out the light, you curled around my back, your arms tight around me as they always were, and all you said was goodnight.

My parents' cottage was weighed down by an unrecognisable stillness. I had walked in to find my father sitting in a wicker chair in the conservatory, like a sickly house plant that had been given water and set in the sun to see if it might effect a recovery. When I greeted him the only response was the rattling breath of the dozing man.

I retreated silently. My father was wearing the wrong clothes, a pressed shirt and a tweed jacket, and the house didn't smell like Sunday at all. The cooking aromas were sulphurous and sour. I followed my nose through into the kitchen where my mother was stirring a pot.

'Oh!' she exclaimed as I embraced her. 'You took me by surprise.' She wiped her fingers on her apron and reached for my hands to clasp them in her own as she did every time we met, no matter that her hands were half the size. The bruising was so faint now as to be barely noticeable.

I bent to kiss her. 'There's a strange air to the cottage today,' I said. 'Why is Papa asleep in the conservatory?'

'He's tired.'

I look over at the bubbling pot on the stove. 'And what are you cooking?'

'Fish stew.'

'Fish?' Not one Sunday in my entire life had we eaten fish.

My mother laid the wooden spoon on its ceramic rest and gathered herself. 'Your father was taken ill this week. We had to take him to hospital. We didn't want to worry you, because, well, there's nothing to worry about. But yes, he's tired now, and low.'

'The hospital?' I took a step back towards the kitchen door. 'Why didn't you tell me? What's wrong with him?' I felt as though I were sinking.

'He's OK, it's just a downside of living so long. We're falling to bits. Now apparently your father's diabetic, which should be easy enough to manage but he's taken it hard. He hasn't been out to the chapel in three days and only two of those were doctor's orders.'

'Perhaps he's had a shock, decided to take things a bit easier?'

She shook her head. 'No. Before the snow came he was getting so close to finishing it. You should have seen how excited he was, like a boy. Perhaps he overdid it, I don't know.' She looked at me hopefully. 'I was wondering if you'd have time to help him finish? Maud's son did offer, but I thought if he'd let anyone help it would be you.'

'I'd be happy to, but you know how that's gone in the past.'

'Just try and talk to him. Maybe it will be different now.' She paused, then turned back to the stove, slicing lemons in two and squeezing their juice into the stew, straining it through her fingers. As she discarded the pips she said softly, 'I'm not ready to lose him.' She rubbed her eye with the back of her hand, seasoning the food with her tears. I stood behind her and put my arms over her shoulders in a hug made awkward by more than our difference in height. 'Right well, let me get on now,' she said. 'Lunch won't make itself.' Later my father would push the fish stew around his plate miserably and remark that it was too salty.

Feeling disoriented and seeking an escape from the oppressive silence of downstairs, I retreated up to my room, still lively with ghosts and good memories. Everything was the same there as it had always been and I found a moment's comfort in the familiar walls that came together at angles slightly off ninety degrees, the particular softness of the mattress, the way the light drifted in from behind the thin, faded curtains. Then I looked again at the window, remembering the conversation with my mother in the garden at Christmas and felt the breath sucked out of my lungs.

I opened the windows, letting cool air blow in across my face, and looked down into the garden below. There was no new growth yet, the plants all a dark winter green, and frosted in the shade of the wall. I held on to the windowsill and pressed my face against the bars, seeing myself as a child reaching for the shutters, picturing the tulips below, remembering the hard line of the windowsill against my hipbones, trying to summon the sensation of falling. I still could not recall the fall, but I could clearly remember my mother's certainty that it had never happened and felt the truth, sharp as a knife at my throat.

'Baptiste, why are you letting the cold air in?' I jumped, startled to suddenly find my mother at my side. 'Are you OK? You look pale,' she said, following my gaze down into the lavender beds.

'I'm fine.' Was there anything I could hope to salvage of a memory I had replayed so many times, constantly evoked by the scar on my leg? 'Are you sure we never had tulips there, Maman? They are so clear in my mind.'

'You and your tulips,' she laughed. 'I haven't a clue where you got that idea from. At least the garden will be coming back to life soon. That'll cheer us all up.' It was going to take more than that, I thought. She turned and gave me a measured look. 'How are you getting on with your friend? Amandine, isn't it?'

'I called her,' I said. I had finally plucked up the courage. 'I'm going to take her to dinner next week. She's chosen a restaurant just across from where she lives.'

My mother raised an eyebrow. 'Well, that's lovely. Your father will be pleased to hear that too. I'll admit we've been worried about you, being single for so long. Especially after what you told me that time in the garden, that you weren't even sure you wanted someone. I'm so pleased you changed your mind.'

'It's early days,' I said.

'When women get to that age they don't mess around with just anyone. They're choosy. Does she want children?'

'She has a daughter.'

'Oh. Well, lovely. How old is she?'

'I don't know. I mean, I suppose she must be a teenager. Amandine said she had her when she was young, but I haven't asked Amandine her age either.'

'And what's her name?'

'I didn't think to ask.'

'Baptiste, you need to show an interest! And the father?' I shook my head. 'That must have been hard for her. A ready-made family. Well, I can't wait to meet them.'

I laughed at her enthusiasm. 'I'm not sure I'm ready to be a father just yet.'

'Oh love,' my mother said, 'none of us are ever ready to be parents, we just get on with it.'

Later, as we were eating lunch at the table, my mother exclaimed out of the blue, 'We had tulips on the wallpaper in the sitting room! I'd completely forgotten about that. Do you remember, Gaspard, how we had to change it when we gave Baptiste the piano? We hadn't noticed how much it had faded until we saw that big patch of flowers, still bright after all those years.'

'What are you talking about, Bernadette?'

'The wallpaper with the tulips.'

The photograph at the foot of the stairs, me on tiptoes on the piano lid, leaning into the box. My mother's regret. Could it be? I tried to bring back anything but the image in the photograph but had nothing.

My father grunted, his humour spoiled by the fish. 'We should have just left it. You'll be bringing the piano back here when we die, won't you, Baptiste?'

'Do we have to talk about dying at the table?' My mother's expression had grown weary.

'I know we've discussed it before,' my father went on, 'but it's different now. You have a girlfriend, your mother tells me. When you settle down you'll want a garden for your own children, surely?'

'Your father's right,' my mother said. 'And you'd have to consider Amandine's point of view too. Will she want to live on a boat? Wouldn't she prefer a nice cottage in the countryside?'

I wasn't sure Amandine would like either, I thought. Then I caught myself. I had been pulled into the practical details of my parents' fantasy. 'You're talking as though I've already set a wedding date,' I said. 'And we haven't had our first date yet.'

'We're just thinking about your future,' said my mother. 'That's what all parents do when they get to our age. Your children's future is what counts.'

The bannister up to Amandine's apartment curved up the wide, lazy staircase and was reflected in the warm pink marble of the steps. Light slanted across the tiled corridor from behind the coffee-coloured door, left ajar for me. I knocked anyway. I watched through the slender gap as she approached, her face composed and yet also on edge, two opposing ideas merged into one expression. Her eyes were like lagoons. I held out a hand, which she ignored, stepping close in to kiss me. Not on the mouth, but almost. All I would have had to do was angle my face to catch her lips with mine. Before she pulled back I felt her inhale as though she had been hoping I would. She withdrew a step. 'Come in.'

Her apartment was warm as spring and smelled of lilies, although there were no flowers in sight, and something else, something that reminded me of home. I struggled to place it, then struggled again to not let it matter that

I couldn't. On an oak bureau in the hall was a framed black and white photograph, half in shadow, half in light: Amandine clutching an infant to her breast. She was standing by a small, perfectly manicured tree in a city park, the rooftops of Paris unmistakable in the background, a weary smile on her face. I wondered who could be behind the camera. A friend, perhaps? I stepped in closer. In monochrome, Amandine looked all wrong. I could not know the colour of her shoes, or of the summer dress that hung loose on her girlish figure. Her eyes could have been any colour at all. I stood for a moment, trying to remember something, until I felt a hand on my arm. 'Come on, let me show you around.'

It was the kind of apartment that other people would have described as stunning: high-ceilinged and bright, the decor tasteful and coherent. The living room was dominated by a large ornamental fireplace. On the hearth, an African elephant threw back its head to peer up at where the chimney should have been. Before its raised front foot was a shabby oriental rug that looked as though it had been brought back from travels rather than acquired at the Galeries Lafayette. Morocco, I thought. Two expensive-looking armchairs were positioned either side of the fireplace. I wanted to sink into one, pull Amandine down on to my lap and kiss her, but it was too soon to give in to desire. I didn't want to be presumptuous. We had all evening ahead of us in which to establish if that kind of behaviour was something she'd be amenable to.

The living room was open to the kitchen and between the two, by a large arched window, was a small table, round, polished and perfect. That's what the smell was: beeswax. I sighed with relief. Diffuse orange streetlight filtered through sheer white curtains, laced with the shadows of the ornate ironwork swirls and curves beyond. Heavy cream curtains were tied back with leaf-green silk rope. It was all so elegant. But there was a certain emptiness to the place, a lack of life, in stark contrast to the shabby warmth of Candice.

The kitchen was just the same. Spotless. I've always thought you can tell a lot about people from their kitchens. My galley kitchen, small and spare. My parents' kitchen, ruled over by my mother, permanently hot and floury. Jordi's vast range at the bar, his steel boat tossed on the waves, and Sabine's kitchen on the *Yvonnick*, messy and stuck about with fading children's drawings. Then there was Amandine's kitchen. Empty. Bereft.

That was it. There was no sign of a child. No toys, but then it was likely her daughter was too old for toys. No babysitter either. Perhaps she was old enough to not need one. But no mess at all. None of the adolescent detritus found heaped up on work surfaces and propped against walls in the *Yvonnick*. It didn't look at all as though any child could live here. My heart sank with the implication. I had forgotten to ask so many questions. Had I even thought to ask the most important of all?

'The bathroom's over there,' Amandine continued, 'and those are the bedrooms.' Two doors, both ajar. She motioned at the first door casually. 'She'll be back later if you'd like to say hello. And mine is the one at the back.' She pushed the dove-grey sleeves of her sweater up to her elbows and caught my eye, held it a little too long. I shivered in the warmth. Amandine grabbed her coat. 'Shall we go?'

Just across the road at the Restaurant du St Sernin the maître d' greeted Amandine affectionately as he took our coats. 'Table for two this evening, Madame Rousseau?'

He led us through towards the back of the half-empty restaurant, weaving through tables dotted about the room. 'This way, sir.' The tablecloths were the sunny yellow of the ducks in children's drawings. Tall white candles stood on every table and there were fresh flowers in the corners of the room. We were seated at a table in a half-corner, the angle cut off by a fireplace with an ornate surround. There was a clock on the mantelpiece, and ivy draping from each edge.

'These look very fancy,' I said, offering Amandine the plate of elaborate appetisers. 'They seem to know you very well here.'

'I dine here most nights,' she said. 'It's my local, if you like.'

I pictured myself sitting at the bar at Jordi's place, eating his hearty food and chatting to Sophie, while at the same time a few miles upstream Amandine would be sitting here alone drinking from long-stemmed wine glasses and being called 'madam'. 'Madam' this and 'sir' that. Amandine was in her element and I didn't fit into this place at all, just as I didn't fit with her classy apartment. I tugged at the sleeves of the only smart jacket I owned – suitable for weddings, funerals and first dates. The sleeves had never been quite long enough to cover my cuffs correctly. How could I have ever thought I would fit with Amandine Rousseau?

As though reading my mind, Amandine smiled kindly at me. 'Take your jacket off,' she said. 'It's fine.'

I glanced over the menu. The côte de boeuf immediately caught my eye. Served with marrowbones, caramelised onions, sea salt and dauphinois potatoes it made my mouth water just reading the description, but it was only served for two people and the meat alone was 500g. It was not a sophisticated choice.

'What do you recommend?' I asked.

'I usually have one of the salads,' she said. 'The one with the scallops is delicious –' she looked at me shrewdly – 'but if you wanted the beef, for example …'

'No, no,' I said hurriedly. 'The scallops sounds great, I'll go for that.'

'Right.'

After we had ordered, our clichéd first-date conversation faltered at every turn. Amandine seemed tense and expectant but I had no idea what she was expecting. She had been my client for six months and what did I really know about her at all?

The clock on the mantelpiece had an intrusive 'hick' that marked the long pauses between us like a metronome, giving a hypnotic rhythm to the silence. Amandine's expressions came and went, passing through minute variations that would have escaped the notice of someone who wasn't observing her as intensely as I was. I was searching for clues, watching as her face conducted its tiny battles and wondering if I could just ask. Finally I cracked. 'What are you thinking about?'

Amandine sat back, taking a sip of wine but keeping her eyes on the tablecloth. 'I was wondering,' she said, 'would you prefer to live in the city centre, or would you want to move back out to a village?'

'I don't imagine moving at all,' I said, thinking of what my parents had said, feeling panic rise in my chest.

'But in the future' – she was choosing her words carefully – 'living on a boat might not be very practical for you.'

'I don't know about practical,' I said, 'but they'll have a fight on their hands if they try to take me off Candice. I can't imagine being happy anywhere else.'

Amandine leaned back, staring into the profound well of her wine glass. 'Good,' she said quietly.

'Why do you ask?'

'Because I'm trying to figure out what you really want. Now I know at least one thing you'll fight for.'

'Don't mistake contentment for a lack of passion,' I said. 'We all need different things to make us happy. Sometimes it's good to be satisfied with what life gives you.'

Amandine folded her arms. Her eyes glittered. 'Haven't you ever just wanted to say to hell with it? To bite off more than you could chew?' From the corner of my eye I saw the waiter approaching to top up our wine. I held up my hand and he retreated discreetly. Amandine took a deep breath. 'Do you know what,' she said tersely, 'I really hoped you'd choose the beef. You're not a scallop salad kind of person, and I've had enough salad to last me a lifetime. If you'd chosen the beef we could have shared it.'

My confusion deepened. One minute she was alluding to moving house and the next she was angry with what I chose for dinner. I apologised. 'You should have said. I did ask what you wanted.'

'It can't always be about what I want. You have to be hungry too. To not hesitate to ask for what you want.' She clasped her fingers together, a tight knot in front of her on the table. 'Maybe I should have been more outspoken. Maybe I should have said something. Well, I'm saying it now.'

'Perhaps we can change our order.'

She shook her head. 'That's not the point, Baptiste.'

'What is the point?'

'The point is I think we both wanted it. Yet we both settled for the fish.'

Ah. Everything became clear. Heat prickled on my face. Something like vertigo. I reached for a drink. Sharp bursts of apple stung the skin behind my teeth. My hands were shaking, feeling too large, too fumbling on the glass. I was aware that Amandine was watching me closely. She smoothed a lock of hair off her forehead and back behind her ear. The small diamond in her earlobe twinkled in the candlelight.

'Do I need to say any more?'

'No.' I reached for her hand tentatively. She gave it to me with a sigh and the world contracted to the warmth of her skin, the pulse in her wrist.

'Are you managing to play the piano again?' Her voice had softened again. It was the kindest thing she could have asked.

'A little,' I said. 'More and more.'

'Good.'

I only released my hold on her when our meals arrived under silver domes. When the waiter lifted them to reveal the food we both looked down at the bright fresh salads, the soft white flesh of the scallops, the crescents of coral. It looked delicious, but we both knew the other was imagining a rare rib of beef and buttery potatoes. We laughed in chorus as the nonplussed waiter said, 'Enjoy your meal,' and hurried away.

Later, back out in the cold, Amandine paused on the grass outside St Sernin and stood looking up at the apse. It seemed like an odd thing to do, to stand there in the cold looking at a church you live right next door to. I waited at her side, kicking at the last of the snow, hunched up and dirty in icy clumps at our feet. That's all there was left now, even down by the canal. All but the compacted snow had melted and in its wake snowdrops and crocuses were pushing up through the cold earth. We were on the cusp of spring. Amandine said nothing, just waited, until eventually I understood that I was expected to put my arm around her shoulder. I realised later that this was the moment, the opportunity before we reached the steps of her apartment building, when I could definitively turn the evening into something more than dinner, and that the onus was on me to do that.

By the time I had understood what I was supposed to do it already seemed too late. If I put my arm around her now after so long it would seem reluctant. Instead I pushed my hands down into my pockets and stared up at the church too, as though in thought. When it became clear I wasn't going to touch her, she turned her whole body towards me, forcing me to look her squarely in the eyes.

'Baptiste?' My name condensed into clouds around her face. My heart became all of me, just the blood in my veins. It was incredible that she couldn't see me exploding right in front of her. All the feelings I had for her, all the fear at the prospect of hurting her, all the regret at what I had to tell her.

I shrugged miserably into my jacket. 'I only ever wanted to make you happy, Amandine,' I said.

'Then do it.'

'You know I can't. I'm sorry. I don't want to make this worse than it is.'

'You're going to accept defeat just like that?'

'You deserve someone you can rely on. Who'll be there for you. What's the point … ?'

Amandine folded her arms. 'Don't tell me what I deserve.'

'Please don't be angry with me.'

'Goodbye then.' The words were breathed, soft as air yet sharp as needles. She turned and strode across the grass.

For a moment I just watched her go. A shiver of déjà vu ran over my skin. That was happening more and more. They say that when you fall in love you feel as though you've known the other person your whole life. Was that what it was? I could almost feel the curl of the question mark around my throat, its tail reaching down through my ribs and punching me in the gut with its final jot.

I caught up with her on the steps as she let herself in, reaching out for her hand. But Amandine shrugged away from my touch. She turned, sadly. 'Baptiste, I can't keep pushing this. It's gone on way too long. I've had enough. What I deserve is someone who loves me so much that they would fight to have me, whatever the circumstances. I'm the one who should be reticent about this relationship, not you. What have you got to lose?'

'Everything,' I said. But the door had already swung closed behind her, the lock clicking into place. The steps back down to the pavement felt like a precipice.

I trod the long, slushy roads back over to the port, the smoky smell of Toulouse still on my clothes. A stiff melancholy had settled over me and I thought I could walk it off, but I had just given myself more time to think before I could sleep, and the more I thought the more miserable I became. By the time I was approaching the canal I had had enough of my own company and just wanted to get home to bed.

As I tramped past the solid bulk of the apartment blocks two men hunched down into hooded coats approached from around a corner. I froze, stepping back under a streetlight and waiting for them to pass. As they got closer they slowed down, heads turned my way. The blood pounded in my veins. My lungs tightened. I shifted my weight from foot to foot, telling myself to calm down, to be rational. 'Nutter,' one of them said under his breath as they went by, giving me a wide berth.

I was still trembling when I got back to Candice, silent and sulky in the pitch-black night, water lapping against her flanks. For the first time in years it didn't feel like coming home. I could have still been in the city now, I thought, in Amandine's pristine apartment. In her bed. We could have been making love to each other, hushing and shushing so as not to be heard by her daughter. All over the city, couples would be climbing into beds big enough for two. Beds where they had made children together. Beds where they had not. Beds where arguments explode and are resolved, a turned shoulder slowly becoming two humans curled together, holding each other until the irritation dissipates. There is a solidarity in that kind of long-grown love that somehow keeps things moving, I know. Something I never had. Sometimes things are just not meant to be.

Although I was exhausted I knew I wouldn't sleep unless I spent a few minutes at the piano to calm down. Even though the cold had stiffened up my hands and it was certain to hurt, I needed the intimacy, the release. With my heart still pounding and adrenaline racing through my veins I sat down and took out a score, but when I opened it all I saw were flocks of little black notes, migrating like starlings across the page.

There was a wet girl with a hungry dog. The rain brought her in. It had been pouring solidly for two days, the clouds so low for so long it seemed they had become snagged on the branches and the telegraph poles. A constant stream of water flushed the roads, sluicing the winter dirt of Toulouse into the gutters, readying it for spring. Inside the bar the damp air from rain-soaked coats and shoes clung to one side of the window-panes, the rain rapping like fingernails against the other. That night the place felt unfamiliar and disorienting; I always sat to the right of the entrance, whether at the counter or at a table, but there was a match on the TV that night and it seemed as though everyone had moved over to watch, even though no one could hear it over the buzz of voices. There wasn't even standing room on the right side of the room. I pictured Jordi coming out worried that the whole bar would capsize, telling people to move over and balance the place out. The new perspective from my table against the wall on the opposite side of the bar made the place look as though I were dreaming it – recognisable, but just uncanny enough to put me on edge.

I ate my dinner slowly, hoping that Sophie would have time later for a chat although she had been offhand with me earlier. With Paris on her horizon she was pulling away from me, and I could feel the void opening up inside me where she had been. Perhaps it was her way of softening the blow. I picked at the food in front of me; I didn't really have the appetite for it. The hollow ache in my stomach was not something Jordi's cooking could fill. I lifted forkfuls of couscous and let the grains scatter back down on to my plate. I challenged myself to see how precisely I could skewer morsels of sausage on the tines of my fork. I watched how the sauce fell first in curtains and then in teardrops off the carrots. I recall the lamb being too salty, but the chickpeas were good – soft, fatty and satisfying. Then in she came.

She was a young woman of about twenty, bustling into the bar as though looking more for shelter than a drink. I hadn't seen her before. She was slim, almost too thin, her dark dreadlocks tied through with orange cord, dripping on to the floorboards. She had a scrappy little dog on a frayed rope lead and as she sized up the place, looking longingly through the crowd of sports fans to the blazing fire, she didn't notice how it shook itself dry on the doormat. The woman slipped around to the counter on my side of the bar and waited to be served. I watched her, glad to have an interesting distraction, the way she stood leaning on one hip, the thin coat she wore that was soaked through; my tendency to size people up was still very much alive. I had just tilted my wine glass towards my lips when, 'Sophie Rousseau!' the girl exclaimed. 'I don't believe it!'

I struggled to draw breath as months of confusion crystallised into perfect clarity. For me it was as though there was an avalanche in the room, yet Sophie was calm, continuing with service as though nothing was wrong. She embraced her friend across the bar, handed her a towel, poured her a drink. I fixed on her face as though I were seeing it for the first time: the up-curve of her lips, the strange tilt of her eyes. The skin was the wrong colour but there was no doubt. A surge of astonished energy filled me and I jumped to my feet, knocking my bowl to the floor. The dog on the rope strained in my direction towards the food scattered around my feet. Sophie and her friend turned and stared.

Five minutes later, the mess dealt with, Sophie sauntered back over with a fresh plate of food and a bottle to top up my wine.

'Try not to give your dinner to the dog this time, Baptiste.'

'It's you,' I said quietly.

She looked at me hard. 'What's got into you?'

'I know who you are. You can stop playing games now.' Why hadn't I seen this? How could I have missed it?

Sophie looked at me gravely, pulling up the chair opposite and taking a seat. 'Are you OK?' she said.

There was a ringing in my ears. 'You look just like your mother.'

'Baptiste?'

I glanced up. The bar was still busy, and her friend was watching us intently from by the bar. I wouldn't have her for long. 'You're the one who sent her to see me, Sophie.'

'Yes. But you screwed it up all by yourself.'

'How is she?'

'She's wretched, thanks for asking. I've been trying to stay out of it, none of my business and all that, but frankly I'm pretty pissed off with you.'

Sophie leaned forward, her hypnotic eyes like a secret that had been hidden in plain sight. 'How could you lead her on that way for so long, especially if you were in love with someone else?'

'Someone else?'

'Your client.'

'Sophie, I was in love with your mother. With Amandine. She was the client.'

'My mother?' Sophie faltered. 'My mother was never a client.'

For long minutes you said nothing, just sat there on the edge of the bed, staring at your hands as if trying to place them. Your fingernails have grown long and you refuse to let me cut them. Above us rain hammered on the deck. To the south thunder grumbled. The dense air beyond the windows was sullen and grey and on the windowpanes condensation glittered and slid.

When I reached cautiously for your hand you took it without question, then frowned and looked slowly around the room as though trying to get your bearings. Your eyes skimmed the walls where I had hung a few framed photographs and some of Sophie's drawings. Most of the drawings were smaller than the palm of my hand; Sophie could get right to the heart of something in just a few strokes. The one that used to be your favourite was the smallest of all – a tiny, impertinent-looking kingfisher – but you no longer see anything but art in those sketches. They could just as well have been picked up from junk shops. It's the same with the photos. They are mostly places, boats in harbours, meadows, horses, a dragonfly hovering above the canal. I keep photographs of people to a minimum; it frightens you to see yourself pictured with people you don't know in places you don't remember. I keep just one photo of you on display: a small driftwood frame by the piano, where you and I, or you and Amandine, smile hopefully out from the past.

'We all start off as raindrops,' you said finally, 'but we all end up in the sea.' You had fixed on a sunset photograph I'd hung of the oyster beds down on the Mediterranean coast. I closed my eyes. I like it when you talk this way. You could always find a perfect analogy to make life sound more beautiful than it is.

I thought back to that very first time I came to Candice. I'd picked up a splinter from the handrail along the gangplank and you took it out, saying something about splinters that was at once unremarkable and yet terribly profound. Your hand was so large around mine, your eyes kind and enquiring, and an astonishing sadness had rushed in at me from nowhere, a sadness I didn't even know I had that knocked me sideways, hard. I must have felt the beginnings of it even before that, because I had lied to you about being pressed for time and then felt bad afterwards for getting our relationship off on such a dishonest footing. If only I had realised just how distorted the truth was. Perhaps I liked believing that I had met a man genuinely interested in what made me happy; it made a change from being the one everyone turns to for help. When I was with you I could surrender the controls, even just for an hour. I liked, too, that you were clearly attracted to me and yet did nothing about it. Yes, you would say odd things to me sometimes, always trying to figure out what made me tick, but I took it as a game. A drawn-out flirtation. It was fun, at least to begin with. Unwittingly I had played along with the fallacy. When Sophie told me what happened at the bar that night it explained a lot. My perspective of you shifted again, as though I had been looking at that optical illusion, a goblet before, now two faces in silhouette.

I had been silent for too long and you too had drifted away into your thoughts. You yawned, stretching your arms wide. I leaned in hoping for an embrace, but you didn't notice me and got to your feet, still wearing creases in your brow.

'Baptiste?' I said, but you were already moving away.

I followed you down the corridor, hanging back in the entrance to the sitting room, where you had gone directly to the piano and were standing, perplexed. After a few moments your fingers reached out and you raised the lid with a clatter. The keys shuddered, letting out a soft complaint that echoed within the box. Your hands used to caress those keys, your fingers spread wide across them, the architect of a melody. Some part of you still knows how it used to be, but now information is missing. Connections weaken and snap, weaken and snap. Your frown deepening still further, you crossed to the galley and rummaged in the pot of spoons and spatulas on the counter and returned holding an old, scratched wooden spoon with which you began to strike the keys. Knowing you would soon realise something was wrong and feel foolish, I feigned distraction, turning away from you and busying myself with the stove where the logs were burning low.

I used to love how you could read me, how I couldn't hide a thing from you and nevertheless you wanted me without reserve. Not any more. You are still so attuned to me: the words I choose, my expressions, every visible truth. But now when I feel like this I must do all I can to protect you from it, and since I cannot hide my emotions I have to free myself of them. I empty myself of the pity, empty myself of the feelings of injustice, empty myself of the sadness. I stoke the fire, make the tea, water the plants, breathe in, breathe out, breathe in, breathe out, until I am calm, until my self is poured away and there is nothing but space to let you in. Some days it works better than others.

The noise must have stopped, but I hadn't noticed. Everything was flowing out of me, just embers cooling slowly to grey. Then your hand was hard on my shoulder. I gasped, my heart racing as I turned my face to yours. The years look well on you, but the beard that you have abandoned to its own wild devices leeches the light from your face. In the shadows your eyes were dark and determined and in your other hand you brandished the little driftwood frame, our smiling faces against the twin blues of the sky and the water just beyond.

I forced myself to look at the photo, trying to pretend that face I knew so well was a stranger, but tears were springing to my eyes and I wriggled out from your grasp, which though still gentle was strong and insistent. 'I think I'll just draw the curtains,' I said. You let me go.

When I had composed myself again and turned back to you, you were sitting on the piano stool, but facing into the room, your eyes flickering between my own and those in the photograph. I lowered my gaze. The droplets of water that had pooled on the windowsill were now soaking the hem of the curtains.

'I can still picture her face, you know,' you said. 'I still remember all the important things.'

Etienne and I were sitting out on the deck in shorts under
the hot blue skies, soaking up the light. The rainclouds were
finally exhausted. The towpath and the banks were steaming,
a white haze rising off the saturated earth. I was suffering the
kind of nagging, empty hunger brought on by insomnia and
too much of Etienne's ferocious coffee.

'You look atrocious,' he said.

I didn't know how long I had trodden the towpath after
I rushed out of Jordi's or how far I had walked in the rain. I
only knew I felt as though I'd spent the entire night on my
feet. Foxes had slipped into the trees before me like otters into
water. I had disturbed a barn owl perched on a low branch
with a mouse in its talons and later a gravid hare had loped
across the path, turning her wise, unworried face towards me
as she went. In their company the night had come to seem
just like day and I had walked on and on, further and further

from home, trying to clear my head, searching for answers. If Amandine had never been a client then all her frustrations with me became clear. But how could a misunderstanding like that have gone on so long, and why had she never mentioned Sophie? I strained to remember as much as I could about the day we met, the particular yellow of the September light and the first fall of leaves on the deck. Only one winter had passed since that day yet it seemed a lifetime ago. I had heard her arrival, hesitant footsteps on the towpath. I had greeted her at the door as I did all my clients and said the things I always say to try and put them at ease. I had noticed her shoes, as green as a springtime coat, and she had chosen the Louis XV. We had discussed Candice, always a good talking point to break the silence, just easy chitchat while I made coffee. 'So,' Amandine had said, 'I can see why you're so fond of her. You're kindred spirits.' I had taken my eyes off hers just for a moment. I hadn't been concentrating. Fooled by the small talk, I had missed it. 'So.' She hadn't been talking about Candice at all. I steadied myself against the nearest tree, pressing my forehead against the rough, wet bark, dazed and disoriented. Where did it all start? What was the last true thing I remembered? The dementia reached its tendrils further and further into my past.

Back on Candice I towelled off and dragged myself to my lonely bed, but sleep wouldn't come. My mind, ironically, wouldn't rest. On the contrary, the cacophony in my head was louder than ever, half-formed thoughts and unanswerable questions swimming in the dark spaces behind my closed eyes.

I tossed and turned and tried tricks to relax and clear my mind, all to no avail. I padded along the dark hallway and played the piano until my head nodded so low it was barely above the keys. I wrote in my notepad as I would for a client, searching for clues and hidden truths, fooling my mind into believing it was resolved once it was down in ink on the paper and then returned to bed, where I lay wide awake once more.

I knew it was a lost cause when the birdsong began before daybreak. Perhaps I would sleep later. I washed and dressed and paced the room, suffused with nervous energy. I made a 4 a.m. breakfast and took it up on deck to watch the sun rise. It was there I finally understood that the past could be the past, and that now I knew its secrets a fresh revelation had presented itself: I had another chance to make things right with Amandine Rousseau.

That was six hours ago, but we were still far from a reasonable hour for lunch so I was sucking the salt from sunflower seeds and cracking them in my teeth. Etienne smoked a cigarette, leaning back, squinting out beyond the boat's edge and letting the smoke glide from between barely parted lips. He had arrived early yet was distinctly more taciturn than usual.

'Want to tell me about it?' I said.

'Can't a man finish his cigarette in peace?'

We both gazed out at the blank canvas of water, ostensibly sitting in silence but each with his own internal pandemonium. Mine was so loud that it wasn't until they were right alongside Candice that I registered a passing boat of cheerful weekenders. Like seeing the first martins back over the water, pleasure boats were a sure sign of spring. We smiled and called out our hellos before letting the outer silence settle over us once more.

'That's the back of winter broken anyway,' Etienne said eventually.

I nodded, stretching out my legs. 'Yep.'

'Well,' he said, stubbing out his cigarette, 'since we've got the weather out of the way I'll go first, shall I? I'm splitting up with René.'

A dull resignation washed over me. I should have been more shocked than I was, but what reason did I have to expect anything to escape the sinkhole that was swallowing my life? There are times when inconceivable news can nevertheless seem inevitable. I looked up at the trees, bursting with optimism and renewal, bright green buds and blossom. My life had fallen out of step with the seasons.

It took a solitary gull calling out a reproach as it swooped down over the water to bring me back to my senses. What had come over me? This was about Etienne, not about me. I turned to face him. 'I'm so sorry,' I said.

'Don't be.' Etienne reached for a handful of sunflower seeds. 'I'm relieved. It's been on the cards for some time. It feels good to have finally made a decision.'

I saw Etienne at least once a week and I hadn't seen this coming at all. What kind of a friend had I been lately? 'And René?'

'He took it hard at first but he's coming round to it. He knows it's the right thing for both of us, but he's worried how the family will take it, especially the younger ones, the nieces and nephews.'

'I have to say I'm surprised. I thought you were the perfect couple.'

'No such thing.' Etienne popped a sunflower seed in his mouth, crunching it whole.

'Is there someone else?'

'No.'

'Then why?'

Etienne sighed. 'Baptiste, what did I tell you about love when you asked? That it changes. René and I have grown together and our affection for each other will always be a part of our lives, but it doesn't fill us up any longer. We want different things now. We'll be better facing the world as friends than staying tied to each other just for the sake of it. We're making space for something more while we still have the chance. Life is too short for stasis.'

But stasis was what many people spent their lives looking for, I thought. 'And what about the *Florence*? Who will keep the boat?'

'We'll sell her. Split the money, buy apartments.'

My heart sank. Etienne looked at my face and laughed. 'You know, it's just a house to us. We're not obsessed like you are with Candice.'

'It's not the boat really,' I said, 'it just seems like everything is breaking apart right now. Everyone is leaving.'

'Don't be melodramatic,' he said. 'I'm not moving to China.'

Etienne closed his eyes, his face raised to the sun and scratched idly at the stubble on his throat. He insisted that we'd stay in touch, you know. How could we not? Neighbours always say that when they move away, but even with the best intentions in the world a few miles can put a disproportionate distance between friends. You're never 'just passing' any more. Everything has to be arranged. Life slips into the cracks and before you know it you've not seen each other in months. Years. It's a shame Amandine never had a chance to meet Etienne. She would have liked him.

The scent of the daffodils from the pots along the edge of the deck came in waves. The gull had wheeled around and was flying back towards us. I tracked its low path over the canal, the sun hitting it in just such a way that it cast both a shadow and a reflection on the water. Three birds, all existing in their own way, sharing a single heartbeat. As it approached Candice the bird banked sharply and soared away, the tricks of the light vanishing with it.

'I'm sorry.' Etienne spoke without opening his eyes. 'I should have said something to you sooner, I know. I've just been hoping that something would work out between you and this client of yours. I didn't want to scare you off romance any more than you already are.'

'Very considerate of you,' I said, 'and in fact on that note I have something to tell you too. I need your help.'

'Oh?' He opened his eyes and looked over at me, the light bright on his face.

I didn't really know where to start. 'What would you like first, the bad news or the dilemma?'

Etienne balanced a flimsy cigarette paper and his pouch of sweet-smelling tobacco on his knees and started to roll. 'Bad news first.'

My head swam. How many times was I going to have to hand out this unwelcome information? Would I find ways to cushion the blow for people, to mitigate their discomfort? How was Etienne going to take it? 'Well,' I said, 'against my better judgement I took your advice and asked Amandine out on a date.'

Etienne wet the edge of his cigarette paper. 'Fantastic! How did it go?'

I laughed. 'Oh, I completely screwed it up.'

'And that's the bad news?'

'No.'

'Go on.'

'It's a long story. But the important thing is that I've finally admitted to myself that I'm in love with her. And it turns out she's in love with me. I don't know how, but we fit. We belong together.'

'And that's the bad news?'

'Obviously not.'

'So what's the bad news?'

'Last night I discovered that she was never actually my client at all.'

'What? How?'

'Sophie told me.'

'Sophie from the bar? What would she know about it?'

'Amandine's her mother.'

Etienne blew air through his teeth then stopped short, looking as though something had just clicked into place for him. 'Hang on, the one she was talking about setting you up with last summer?' Another stone dropped in my belly, the ripples shuddering through me. Was it going to feel like this every time now, the jolt of every false reality? 'So why would you have ever thought she was a client if she wasn't? What did Sophie say exactly?'

'I didn't give her the chance to say much at all. I had to get out of there. The thing is it all makes sense. And that is the bad news.'

'What?' Etienne looked confused.

'I have dementia.'

Etienne froze, the match in his hand burning dangerously close to his fingers. 'You? But you're …'

'Too young, yes I know.'

'So how?'

'It happens.'

'But you don't seem …'

'I am.' Etienne lit his cigarette, both of us temporarily transfixed by the lick of the flames and the first bright glow of the paper before it settled. 'I'm fine at the moment, just a few symptoms that you'd hardly notice – well, except for wandering off into the middle of a riot – but it's only going to get worse.'

'But over years, right?'

'It could be, or it could take just a few months, the doctor says there's no real way of knowing. So it might not be long before I've forgotten Amandine even exists.'

Etienne rubbed his brow. 'I'm sorry,' he said. 'Is there anything we can do?'

I shrugged. 'Maybe just point me in the direction of Candice if you see me wandering about on the towpath looking lost. That is, while you're still around.' I smiled weakly at him, but we both knew it wasn't funny.

'Cheap shot.'

'Sorry.' I watched Etienne wrestling between sympathy and pragmatism, trying to weigh up what would work best.

'Let's not waste time dwelling on it,' I said. 'I still need your help with the dilemma.'

He relaxed and inhaled. 'OK, let's go.'

'The question is, what do I do about Amandine?' Her name made nausea swim in my gut. Bubbles popping in my chest.

'You're in love with each other. Where's the predicament?'

'Imagine if it were René who were ill, would you still leave?'

He thought for a moment. 'No,' he said. 'Of course I'd owe it to him to stay. I couldn't leave him alone to cope with an illness like that. Although … I don't know. Even when he just has a touch of flu I get terribly impatient. I don't have the best bedside manner.'

'And what if it were the other way round, if it were you? If René were staying not because he wanted to, but because he felt he owed it to you, would you let him stay?'

'No, of course not. I want him to be happy. How can I imagine my lover, my best friend becoming my nurse? It's humiliating.'

'Exactly. So there's the dilemma. In both scenarios you are considering what's best for the other person. The one you love. And I am considering what's best for Amandine.'

Etienne leaned forward impatiently. 'Have you talked to her about it? What did she say?'

'We haven't gone into great detail, but she's made it clear she still wants me, despite whatever love we have coming with an expiry date.'

'It always does.'

I could see what he was trying to do, of course. Etienne cared for me, he wanted what was best for me, but if he was going to help me he had to see things plainly for what they were. 'Fine, but this illness is going to make me unlovable. I'm going to be hard work. Eventually even people I've known for much longer than Amandine will drop away.'

'We won't. Not the people who really care for you.'

I could see it in his eyes though. It had been there since the moment I told him. He knew it was true. He had already become a little afraid of me himself, of the shifting weights of give and take, of the new implications of our friendship. 'They will, and I wouldn't want them to stick around, hurting themselves on my broken edges.'

'We'll still love you, Baptiste. You're not alone. You'll never be alone.' Etienne stood. 'Have you got any wine?'

'Wine?'

'Yes, wine. We need wine. You're still allowed wine, right?'

'No one has told me otherwise. Are we drowning our sorrows?'

'What kind of talk is that? You're in love, we're going to celebrate. You're lucky I'm not calling all the neighbours over. And then we are going to sort everything out. Wait there.'

Etienne came back out into the sunshine with the half-full bottle of red left over from my heart-to-heart with Amandine, and poured two glasses. 'Here's to the rest of your life,' he said firmly. I looked him in the eye and met his glass with my own. It was too early to drink, but what the hell. The wine was tannic on my tongue, its warmth spreading fast in my legs, my shoulders, my heart. 'So, what's the plan?' he said.

'I have two plans,' I said. 'Plan A and Plan B. And both of them start with Sophie persuading Amandine to move up to Paris with her.'

'Sophie's going to Paris?'

'She's got a job on the trains so she can strike.'

Etienne raised an eyebrow. 'I see. And both your plans to seduce Amandine start with her going to Paris and you staying here? I can see why you've asked for my help on this.'

'Wait,' I said, lifting a hand at a passing pair of joggers and waiting for the crunch of their footsteps to recede. 'Let me explain.'

I had not got far into outlining the first option when Etienne frowned and lifted a halting finger. 'Stop,' he said.

'Plan A is shit. You need to follow your own advice more. What's Plan B?'

It was hot on the deck, the wine was going to my head and I was swimming in adrenaline and insomnia. I took another pinch of sunflower seeds and explained the alternative. Etienne's smile grew broader as he listened.

When I had finished he raised his glass with a flourish. 'I'm proud of you,' he said. 'Here's to plan B.'

When I walked through the door you were standing in a thin shaft of sunlight at the wheel, like a lizard trying to get heat into your blood. You stayed there, watching me silently as I came in and put my bag down on the table. The boat was cold. You had let the fire go out, and outside on the deck your plants huddled miserably together, the geranium leaves already starting to sag, leaves fallen from the lemon tree. You must have taken them all out that morning before you went to bed.

It's true that we'd had some beautiful bright days. I had been sure that any time now the crocuses would flower up along the banks. I had been watching them hopefully all week, the bright shoots, the swelling buds. But there was nothing yet. It wasn't time. I looked out at the sad little garden on the deck. 'They're struggling,' I said. 'I think the weather has turned again. Perhaps winter is going to drag on a while longer. Should we bring them in?'

You looked at them confused and then, as though vindicated: 'You see? I can't even take care of a few little plants. I'm not fit to take care of anyone. That's what she would have become if she'd stayed. I would have withered her.'

Is that what happens to those who love the sick, I wondered. The carers who have to stare disease in the face and pick up its pieces, do they become withered? How could anyone be expected to flourish when providing such tragic ministrations? I looked at the squat, bushy tub of rosemary, standing defiantly bright and sturdy amongst its suffering neighbours. 'I suppose it depends on the plant,' I said. 'Some are pretty robust no matter what kind of a gardener you are.'

'By the time you find out if they are or not it's too late. If a plant dies you learn from it. You can replace it and try again the following year. You can't treat people like plants.' You inched into the melting sliver of warm light. 'How could I ask her to take the risk? You don't do that to someone you love.'

People do, though, all the time. None of us know how long love will last, how long life will last, which of us will suffer illness and which of us remain healthy. Who will be the carer and who the patient. We all hope there will be someone there to take care of us. We build families and societies around ourselves so that we will not be left alone. Most of us fall in love when we are young and healthy and can't imagine half the things life will show us. We are playing a blind hand. It is only much later we find out what love really is and by that time, hypothetically, it's already too late to fold.

But that's not how it was for you. I tried to look at it from your perspective. If you had let Amandine love you then the choice would have been hers: stay with you for better or for worse, knowing that the worst was already guaranteed and that soon she would pay for a few years of love with the weight of your care. Or else she could stay only until you became a burden, then leave you behind and face her guilt. That's not a choice I would offer someone I loved either. I see why you pushed her away. You loved her. You didn't want her to face a decision with no right answer.

And so Amandine's story splits from yours. Once you have made the decision for her she is gone, and you are alone once more. You will never allow yourself to love again. And Amandine, when she has got over the separation, will go back to life as it was before she met you. Perhaps she has found someone else. Even if you speculate about these things, you never mention it. You have never offered an explanation as to where she went.

I shivered. Beyond your slim ray of sunlight it was freezing up there. I moved closer, reaching out a hand to touch you and then, sensing your unease, withdrew it again. You were raw just then, your reticence to let anyone love you exposed, your fear of hurting anyone who would try right up on the surface. I had to tread softly. I don't know how you reconcile feeling that way with sharing your bed with me. I suppose you have told yourself that what we have isn't love. Or perhaps you don't think about it at all. We never talk about what there is between us, and I try to hide it when it hurts. It does hurt, of course it does, but I've learned that the pain won't destroy me. Life didn't give this pain to me, I chose it, and it's better than the alternative.

'You simply can't treat people like plants,' you said again.

'No,' I said. 'Well, I'll bring them in while it's still light. And I think I'll light us a fire. It feels like there'll be a frost tonight.'

'Can we sit outside?' Sophie asked, planting a kiss on each cheek. 'It's such a beautiful day.'

'Later,' I said. She put her hands on her hips with a petulant scowl. 'Thanks for coming, Sophie.' I put my arm around her shoulder. 'At least come and have a proper look around Candice while I make some tea. I wasn't in any state to be a good host last time.' I needed to get her inside the boat, it was my one chance to see her in my home before she left, to leave an impression of her passing that would echo in her absence. Jordi's place resounded with her of course, but I couldn't see myself spending as much time at the bar when she was gone. It just wouldn't be the same without her.

She shrugged me off and sauntered in through the sun-strung wheelhouse, slipping off her rainbow-striped espadrilles and backing down the steps. Would that be the image of her that would linger when she was gone?

I was doing this more and more lately, trying to force a memory to be made. Trying to pick my favourites as though I were going on a journey and could only take a small bag of them. In the past I had paid little attention to the souvenirs chosen for me: the memory of bats flitting into my bedroom, the shape of my father in a field of sunflowers, my mother crouched in her garden pulling out the weeds, the strange snapshot of a small group of strangers seeking shelter from an explosion, the rainbow line-up of syrups along a high shelf of a bar – liquorice, almond and peach, mint, grenadine, violet and lemon. Even in that one small room on Candice there were so many ghosts of people I would never see again. I could see a pinched-faced man standing with his back to the towpath, staring across the room and out into the water as he did for the first few minutes of every session; one woman sunk deep into the couch like a cat; the grey eyes of a tall, sad man who sat in the Voltaire chair one day and wept for an hour, his tears disappearing into the turquoise and green velvet as though into an ocean.

I was learning too that certain echoes grow louder in the face of loss. You don't notice them when they are still reflections of the present, only when things are sliding into past tense. The slide had begun for me. It felt inexorable. Even the path I walked to the bar now resonated with the footsteps of ghosts: the Baptiste who was happy, the one who was well, the one who had never fallen in love. Etienne, who would soon be gone too, had transformed into a ghost of himself even as he was still sitting there in the flesh. The nicotine stain on the ball of his thumb, the bite of the coffee he made, these were the things he would leave me with. At least for now. And then there was Amandine. Everything sang of her. The place she had stood on the towpath when I kissed her, the corner of the wheelhouse where she always left her shoes, the violin with her fingerprints on it. She occupied so many of the spaces in my mind, but I didn't trust any of it to last.

'Have a seat,' I said to Sophie as I sliced lemon for the tea. I can still smell the sharpness of the fruit and feel the hairs lifting on my arms as I watched her look around the room and settle upon the Louis XV. 'No,' I said, a little abruptly, 'not that one.' I couldn't let her overwrite that memory. She threw me a surprised look, then drew out the piano stool, pulling her legs underneath her so she perched upon it cross-legged like a child. She tilted her head to one side, wisps of dark hair falling over her face. 'Is this OK?'

'Yes, sorry, it's just that, that particular chair is …'

'Is?'

'Special.'

Sophie looked at me, weighing up whether to tease me, and decided against. 'OK,' she said simply. 'Now are you going to stop staring at me and sit down?'

'Sorry.' The teapot and cups rattled on the tray. 'It's just that I …' I faltered, and tried to grin it off, but Sophie wasn't having it.

'What is it?'

How to explain the tightening in my chest and the sudden sensation that I had swallowed a bag of pebbles? 'It's you,' I said, although that wasn't strictly true, it was the way I saw

Amandine in her. 'Well, no, it's your mother. It's the madness of what I'm about to do.'

'I can't wait to hear all about it. I have to say I'm here despite rather than because of your cryptic phone call.'

'Amandine doesn't know you're here?'

'Of course not. So what's the plan?'

'Hold on a minute.' I needed to regain my composure.

Sophie pursed her lips and glanced around the cabin. 'Is this where you do your, you know, therapy thing?'

I weighed her up. Why was she not curious about what I had said in the bar? It could mean only one thing. 'Your mother told you about my dementia, right?'

She nodded. 'After I got home. I was worried about you, you looked so shocked. I couldn't understand what was going on. I did try to call you later but there was no answer.'

'Probably forgot to charge my phone,' I said.

She looked at me hesitantly, then burst out laughing. I smiled back at her and poured the tea, but as I did the spout of the teapot jolted against the lip of my cup, tipping it over. Tea pooled on the wooden lid of the chest, shimmying in several directions, undecided which way to flow. Was this something too? Was I becoming more clumsy or was I just noticing it more? Sophie jumped to her feet and grabbed a teacloth from the galley. I held my hand out for it and she handed it over with an uncertain expression. 'I'm sorry, Baptiste.'

'It's not your fault.' The hot tea soaked up through the cloth on to my fingers.

'I mean about Mum. I wasn't a great matchmaker, was I?'

'Was it your first attempt?'

'I suppose it was.'

'You can tell.' I grinned at her, a meagre revenge.

'Hey! Someone needed to take you two in hand. And I was right, you're perfect for each other.'

There was a pause. I looked at Sophie. She looked at me. Beyond the open window a pair of mallards were involved in some kind of dispute. A mistle thrush called from a branch overhead. In my hand, my teacup rattled against its saucer until I put it shakily back down on the chest.

Sophie shook her head, sudden tears welling in her eyes. She rubbed them angrily with her knuckles and took a deep breath. 'Shit.'

Don't let it be this, I thought. Not the sadness. I hadn't expected her to cry. I looked away as she gathered herself together.

'Are you OK?'

Sophie frowned. 'I'm feeling a little seasick,' she said, looking longingly out at the sunlit canal. 'Can we go outside now?'

'Let's just finish our tea,' I said, blowing air across the top of my cup, 'and I'll answer your question about the plan, if you're still willing to help me?'

Sophie scooped the half-slice of lemon from her tea and sucked at the pulp. 'Tell me what you want me to do.'

I took a deep breath, laden with the scents of spring blowing in through the open window. Etienne had worried that I would lose my nerve at this point. He told me that if I didn't think I had the courage to do this, he would do it for me. 'First

I just need to check one thing,' I said. 'As far as you know, is your mother still in love with me?'

Sophie rolled her eyes. 'Just how easy do you think it is to fall in and out of love? Don't you know her at all? You're the first man she's loved in years.'

'But I let her down. Do you think she would ever consider giving me another chance?'

'I honestly don't know. She might take some convincing.'

'Then here's what you have to do,' I said. 'First, you have to persuade her to take some time off work and go to Paris with you. Tell her a month away will do her good. And then after that, who knows, maybe she'll like it. Maybe she'll want to stay.'

Sophie looked exasperated. 'In Paris?' she said with incredulity. She folded her hands over her stomach. 'For someone who wants to make her happy it's about the worst idea I've ever heard, although, funnily enough, it's something she's already considering. But I can't see how you think that's going to help anything.'

Amandine was already thinking of going to Paris? My heart leaped. 'Sophie, trust me. Before you say anything else, hear me out.'

She shifted, stretching her legs out from under her, sliding the soles of her feet along the varnished boards. 'Go on then,' she said.

After I had explained it all, Sophie sat silent for a while, resting her face in her hands, elbows on her knees. Anxiety pulled me to my feet, but when she finally looked back up at me her dark eyes glittered. 'I don't know if this is what's best for her,' she said, 'but it's worth a try.'

'I'd never do anything to hurt her,' I said. 'I just want her to see her options.'

'Yes.' Sophie swallowed the last of her tea. 'Well, I'll have no trouble persuading her. She's so frustrated with you right now that she'll jump at the chance of getting away for a while. And neither of us has been to Paris for so long. There's so much we can do together when I'm not working. We can visit the museums and galleries, she can help me set up our new apartment, maybe even visit my grandparents.' She smiled wryly.

'And you'll insist she comes to see me one last time before you go? Saturday?'

'Yes, Baptiste.'

'And you'll bring me what I asked for?'

'And anything else I think of.'

Gratitude swelled within me. 'I'll miss you, Sophie,' I said. 'I know you have to go to Paris, it's the right decision for you. Come back and visit some time though, won't you?'

Sophie stood and put her arms around me, resting her head against my chest. 'I'll miss you too. Probably. And I think you're making the right decision too.' She poked me in the ribs. 'Now can we please go out on deck and enjoy the weather a little?'

This was how I would remember her, I thought: standing in the middle of the room, tiny within my arms, the sun streaming through the windows, her head against my heart. I bit my lip, and held my breath like a long shutter release.

When Sophie came to me that night after you fled from the bar I was already in bed. She lay down alongside me. 'Are you asleep?'

The truth was I never slept until I heard her key in the lock, listened for her moving around in the apartment, the rhythm of her feet on the parquet, the bathroom extractor fan whirring for a couple of minutes while she brushed her teeth, the soft click of her bedroom door.

'No,' I said. 'I'm just thinking.'

'I have to ask you something,' Sophie whispered.

I rolled over to face her. 'What is it, So?' I had been wondering when she was going to say something. Waiting so I could be there for her, in whatever way she needed me.

She propped her head up on an elbow and looked at me anxiously. 'Did having me make you unhappy, Mum?'

Out of nowhere, tears stung my eyes. How could I possibly explain to Sophie how it had been for me, now of all times?

There is a reason why those who extol the ecstasies of motherhood never give us the full picture: there's no way to adequately describe either the overwhelming despair and exhaustion, or the joy so profound it taps into a well of strength you never knew you had. And how could I ever admit to my child that there was a time I didn't love her?

When the love did come – because I made it come – it swallowed me whole, consuming me to the point that I was sure there was no room left in my heart. They say your heart stretches to fit, but it doesn't always. I couldn't even find the will to care for the house plants that my parents had given me a year earlier when they moved me into my first apartment. They all died. I had run out of capacity to care for anything but her. She asked me for kittens and puppies when she was growing up but the thought of something else to love and care for was overwhelming and I always said no.

I left Paris with Sophie as soon as I could. If I was going to be raising her alone then I would be alone in a city where nobody knew me. I took the train, buckling under the weight of a single suitcase, a crying, struggling child in a flimsy pushchair and the irritated glances from the other passengers. Once in Toulouse I worked in the daytime while Sophie, now a toddler, was at nursery, and I studied after I had put her to bed. At the end of every day I crawled into my own bed, too tired even to cry about how hard it was. I was young though, and I told myself that things could only get better for us. We were going to do just fine.

One morning, not that long after we had arrived in the city, I was driving to work after dropping Sophie off at the nursery. The low winter sun was behind me, reflecting in my rear-view mirror, so I was driving slowly, but that was fine, I was in no hurry, I had the radio on and the window cracked open to let the cold city air blow through. Sophie had been in such a good mood that morning. She had come into my bed before it was even light, sunny and chatty, and we had cuddled while she told me about her dreams and what she wanted for breakfast. It was always bread and chocolate. I could never stop her drawing on the walls of the rented apartment, so I had bought a white oilcloth for the breakfast table and she was allowed to draw on that while we ate. As I drove I was thinking about the picture she had done of me that morning, a round head/body combination with a big lipstick smile and my arms and legs stuck out at jaunty angles, when a van came haring around the corner ahead and, dazzled by sun, veered over on to my side of the road and hit my car head on.

The bones were crushed in both my feet but I didn't have the option of wearing casts for two months and using a wheel-chair. The hospital were very accommodating; they put the most badly broken foot in a cast and I had crutches. I had no choice but to walk on the other foot, on the broken bones. Every step I took hurt. Of course I couldn't carry Sophie to bed, but that first night she had been too young to understand. She didn't want to walk to bed when I had always carried her down the corridor, wrapped in a blanket, already singing a lullaby. And why should she? She screamed and tantrummed and cried her eyes out and nothing I could say would console her. I went to bed resentful and angry, soaked in her tears and plenty of my own for good measure. I couldn't sleep for the pain. It could have been her, I told myself as I prayed for oblivion to take me. She could have been in the car. She might not have survived. After that everything came back into perspective. It didn't make it any easier, I've never felt so lonely, but we all walk on broken bones when we have to.

'No, Sophie, you have never made me unhappy,' I said, truthfully. 'I am thankful for you every day. What brought this on?'

'It must have been hard for you though,' she insisted, 'raising me on your own?'

I rested my hand gently on her hip, willing her to open up. 'You can tell me anything, So,' I said. 'I'm here for you.'

Sophie shifted her weight slightly on the bed. She hesitated. 'Well,' she said, 'and don't be angry, Baptiste was in the bar tonight and he said the strangest thing.'

I felt my stomach turn. I had thought I'd put you behind me and yet only a few days before I had found a parcel from you in my letterbox. Inside was a tiny horse carved out of what looked like driftwood. The note with it had said, *It may never tell me who I am, but it will always remind you who you are.* I had been both touched and infuriated by the enormity of the gesture. Another reason that getting away from here for a while was appealing more and more. Then we would both have to let go. I took a shaky breath. 'What about?' I said.

'He seemed to think you had been seeing him professionally, as a client. I told him you weren't of course, but why would he even think that?'

With only the streetlights beyond the curtains lighting the room I could barely see the outline of Sophie's face, but I could tell by the way she held her breath that no matter how much we had discussed my relationship with Baptiste there was still a fragment of doubt in her mind. Had I withheld a secret from her? The pang of sadness I felt that she would doubt me even in her confusion was offset by the pleasurable reassurance of her continuing need to count on me absolutely.

'I'm sorry, So,' I said. 'It wasn't really my place to tell you this. I'm sorry you had to find out this way before he told you himself. Baptiste has dementia.'

'Baptiste?' I felt her tense under my touch. 'No, that can't be right. He seems completely normal. And he's too young. Are you sure?'

I slid my arm around her back. 'We're sure.'

'Oh,' she said softly. 'Right.' Sophie sighed, and shifted as though to get up.

'Hang on,' I said, unable to wait any longer, 'I have to tell you something too.'

'What?'

'I'm proud of you, So. I think Paris will be good for you. And if you want me to come with you, I will. If you want help with that baby, I'm here for you.'

Sophie froze. 'How do you …'

'I'm not blind.'

'Oh, Mum.' She turned her back to me, curled herself up into my embrace. 'Didier doesn't want it,' she whispered.

I stroked her hair, still tied up with ribbons, still like a child. 'Do you want it?'

'Absolutely.'

'Even without Didier?'

'I can do this on my own.'

'You're going to be great,' I told her. 'And you won't be on your own. We're all going to be just fine.'

There is a time now at the end of each day when I am reaching my limits, when I long for your waking hours to be over so finally I can watch you sleep. When that happens I am at my happiest. You are calmed, all the stress fallen from your muscles. Then I lay my face against your shoulder, breathing you in, missing you ferociously and hollow with love.

I have sat here and looked at that last sentence for a long time. The love you hear of in books and films is seductive and euphoric, not an emotion that hollows you out. It is beautiful and poetic, not brutal and messy. I don't recognise that kind of love. Either they know something I don't, or they're not giving us the full picture. When I told you on the first day I met you that I was looking for love, you didn't understand. You thought I wanted saving, a happy ending. But what I wanted was to love and be loved the only way I know how.

If you go into love with your eyes wide open, ready to embrace everything love is and will be, you will never be disappointed. Even when you are watching his hands spread wide over the piano keys, when you can see the ecstasy in his eyes, when the smell of his skin feels like home and you know that this is the person you want to spend your life with, you can't let it blind you. A life is a long and complicated matter. Later there will be sadness. Later, one way or another, there will be grief. If you embrace the beginning you must also remember love rarely has a neat and satisfactory resolution.

There is a certain kind of breeze that is neither warm nor cool, so that when you stand in it the only sensation is the weight of the sky shifting across your skin. On the day Amandine came to say goodbye, the breeze that blew in through Candice's open door was just like that. My spirits were lifted by the long-awaited unfolding in the air. Poppies now lined the banks, buds were cracking open, the morning was thick with birdsong and bees. A new beginning.

I had done as much as I could, I told myself. I had gone over the things I wanted to say to her again and again. All I could do now was wait, so I sat at the piano, incapable of playing, incapable of finding music that fit this mood. My body was more alive than I could ever remember. My skin burned and prickled, my mouth tasted sour. My stomach clenched and twisted and my heartbeat knocked as though I were hollow. It's strange how our bodies can make love and fear feel almost the same.

The previous night, Sophie and I had said our goodbyes. She had turned on the television in the bar to show us that things in Paris were calm, told me not to worry. There were demonstrators on the streets again but it looked peaceful and there seemed to be an unspoken collusion between the protesters and police. The police were baking in their riot gear, all standing back in the shade. The protestors had stripped down to T-shirts, anonymity forgotten as they tied their scarves around their waists and tucked bandanas into their pockets. They were hanging around in disorganised straggles, leaning on their placards. Every now and then the camera would shift to a pavement café where lunchtime customers sat under parasols, watching the marches pass and drinking coffees and cold beers.

The early warmth of that spring was working its magic on everyone. Winter has such weight: the heavy clothes, the rich, meaty food that lies dark and dense in your stomach, the mass of your own body working against you as you try to carry it without falling on icy streets, and at night the weight of the bedclothes pushing you down deep into your bed as you sleep. With spring all of this is lifted away. People shed winter like a cocoon and emerge hopeful into the air, baring their skin to the light. When I used to think of spring I thought of my mother, the heat of a train, the strikes that kept her from reaching her destination. Then, when I moved to Candice there was a shift. Spring became the first flowers, the balmy air, the fresh juicy colours transforming the markets. Now it is different again. Spring is a piece of seaweed blowing across the sand, a cormorant wheeling above.

I was waiting for Amandine in the wheelhouse. As she stepped across the gangplank a boat sped past and Candice swayed in its wake. Amandine put her arm out to steady herself, and I caught it. She was wearing perfume that smelled of summer grass, of salt water and of something in my mother's garden that I couldn't put my finger on. I wanted to lean in to the scent, but sensing her tension I released her and stepped back. 'Thank you for coming,' I said.

'That's OK. It's important to leave things on good terms. We owe each other that at least.' Her eyes were too focused, as though she too had been memorising her lines. All ready to tell me the words I knew were coming.

'Come down,' I said.

As she backed downstairs, Amandine paused and lifted her face with a puzzled expression. 'Candice smells different today,' she said.

'Different how?'

'There's an oily smell that catches in your throat,' she said. 'Can't you smell it? Have you been cleaning out the stove?'

She was right; away from the windows there was a distinct odour of diesel. 'Oh that, yes. Sorry about the smell. I had some maintenance to do. I'll go now and check that I closed everything off properly. Would you mind awfully organising the tea, and then we can take it back up into the fresh air?'

'No problem.'

I only had a few minutes. Back out on the towpath my hands shook as I released the rope from the mooring. I had been fine when I practised these actions, but now it had come to it they seemed momentous.

In my haste, as I returned downstairs I stumbled on the bottom step, twisting my ankle. Amandine, relaxed and at home in the galley, turned to see me swearing under my breath. She had set the tea to brew and was putting cups on to a tray. 'Are you really OK with this, Baptiste?' she said quietly. 'I'm not here to start a fight, you know. I thought it was a good idea to come when Sophie suggested it but I don't want to upset you.'

I straightened up, pushing my shoulders down and took the tray from her. 'Come back upstairs, I've got a surprise for you.' A flicker of confusion crossed her face. 'Come on,' I said, 'quickly. Trust me.'

In the wheelhouse I put the tray down on the table and went to stand at the helm, motioning for her to join me. As I tried to compose myself I looked down at our bare feet, together side by side, painted in stripes of bright and dull where the sunlight cast shadows over the boards. Next to hers my feet seemed so big, dark and ungainly. Doubt filled me once again. Just say it, I told myself, but the words seemed stuck in my throat.

'Before you show me your secret,' Amandine said, looking downstream, 'there's something I have to get off my chest.'

I rested my hands lightly on the wheel. 'Go ahead.'

As she looked up at me, Amandine's direct gaze seemed to be scouring my own, searching for my true reaction to what she was about to say. 'I'm going away, Baptiste. You know Sophie is moving to Paris, right? Well, she's invited me to join her for a while.' She sighed. 'I've really enjoyed spending time with you, I have, even though it didn't work out. And I am sorry it didn't. So anyway, I think it will do me good to get away.'

'I see,' I said. 'How long are you going for?'

'I don't know yet. It depends on a lot of things. For now I've taken extended leave from the surgery –' she paused, weighing me up with a frown – 'but it's possible I might not come back at all.'

I nodded, but said nothing. Amandine frowned and went on, 'I could easily find work there. Cities always need doctors. And they do say Parisians are romantic.'

She was waiting for a reaction. Shock. Regret. Jealousy. 'That's a big change,' I said.

'You changed me, Baptiste. You were the one who asked me what I wanted. I'm glad you did. I should have asked myself that question a long time ago. And now I know … there's no going back. I have to move on.'

'We both do,' I said.

Amandine had finally lost her sangfroid. She spun her whole body towards me in confrontation, her eyes dark with frustration. 'You see, this is where you are supposed to tell me that I should stay here. That you want me to stay.' Her voice grew louder. 'I want you to want me to stay.'

'Amandine,' I said. 'Stay.'

The word stretched between us like a bridge. She looked defeated, turned away so she didn't have to look at me. 'I wasn't joking,' she said.

'Neither was I.'

Down on the canal, a string of garrulous tawny mallards shepherded by an emerald-headed drake swept downstream hugging the bank. We waited for them to pass. The corridor of blue sky still visible through the increasingly verdant plane trees stretched forwards and away, like a promise we could sail right into.

'What was your surprise?' Amandine said stoically.

'I thought you might like to listen to Candice's heartbeat,' I said. Amandine shook her head. She wasn't in the mood for puzzles. 'Look. I've been thinking about the things you've said, thinking more than you can imagine, thinking about why I never move,' I said. 'And you're right. You've changed me too. So I've made a decision. I'm taking Candice down to the sea.'

'Oh.' Amandine turned back to face the canal, her chest rising and falling. 'Such timing. Better late than never, I suppose.'

'Come with me.'

With a turn of the key, Candice's engine rumbled into life, just as smoothly as when I had tested it for the final time that morning. Did you know that ninety per cent of what we see is just memories? Rather than constantly registering our environment, we let our brains focus on what has changed and the rest is filled in by what we saw last time we really looked. As the boat hummed beneath our feet I saw Amandine's equilibrium falter. Things, she realised, were not as they had been before. She took in the missing gangplank, the barely perceptible shifting of Candice on the water.

'Is this a joke?'

'Still no.'

I turned the wheel slowly and began to navigate out of the moorings and on to the canal. The water became more than scenery and the land became the other place. Even the other boats moored along the towpath, when viewed from that perspective, looked as though I had dreamed them wrong. We passed the *Yvonnick* and the *Rouge-Gorge* and the *Florence* where Etienne and René stood on the deck waving wildly. '*Au revoir, La Candice!*'

Amandine looked at them in surprise and raised her hand warily. As she lowered it she looked at her watch. 'Where are we going?' she said.

'Where do you want to go?' We were passing the other boats I knew well from my runs. It was strange to see them from the canal side. First the green boat with the car parked on the deck. The red boat with the pagoda, complete with wind-chimes and dream-catchers. The boat that must have been full of children, where there was always a line full of flapping laundry strung from the wheelhouse to the prow. The banana yellow boat, painted with red and green swirls, gaudy with flags and bunting. The sad, empty boat that had been for sale for years and always made me wonder what its story was.

Amandine leaned in to me, allowing me to breathe in her mysterious scent. She rested her hand on mine. 'Don't play games with me, Baptiste. I don't think you know how much it hurts.'

'It's not a game. It's an adventure. It can be as big or as small as you want it to be. And if you don't want it at all, now's the time to tell me. Once we're through the lock there'll be no turning back.'

'If I don't want what? You're not making any sense. What time will we be back?'

The sensation of steering Candice out on to the canal felt like flying, like holding her by the hips and guiding her forward in front of me. After so long moored in the same spot, I had the unshakable impression that I would never tire of this feeling. 'If you don't want me. If you don't want this. If you don't want to come away with me, right now, today.'

'Baptiste, are you going mad?' She flushed slightly. 'I'm sorry, I don't mean it like that. But is this really you? I've just told you I'm going to Paris.'

'No you're not.'

'No.' Amandine's eyes glittered. 'You can't just make a decision and get everyone to change their plans around you.'

'I'm sorry,' I said. 'I know this must all be a bit of a shock. But I did say it was a surprise.' I grinned weakly, but Amandine was still floundering. 'Sophie knows all about it, you can call her. She packed you a suitcase; you'll find it in the spare bedroom at the end of the corridor. I'm sorry I haven't had time to show you around yet, but when we stop for lunch I can give you the tour.'

'We're going to the sea? You're taking me now? Right now?'

'Picture it,' I told her. 'Long, lazy spring days travelling down the canal. We can stop and start wherever we choose, but I thought we could head for the Camargue. They say it's beautiful at this time of year and not too hot. We can get there in a week or so. You'll see the wild horses. We can moor up by the coast, taste the sea in the oysters and samphire, and the earth in the wine. We can stay as long as we feel like it and come back when we're ready. I'm in love with you, Amandine. Come and do this with me. Stay.'

I will never forget the look in Amandine's eyes. Finally I could see right into her. 'Well, if you put it like that,' she said.

Keeping one hand on the wheel and my eyes on the horizon, I put the flat of my hand on her back and turned her gently towards me. I pulled her as close as I dared, the smell of her skin now overpowering me. Amandine pressed her hips against me, leaning back slightly. 'Now,' she whispered, and I slid my hand through her fine hair and bent towards her until our lips touched. As easily as that, the landscape began to slip past.

That night we sat out on deck for hours, talking about every-thing but the weight of expectation between us. The stars in the clear skies were already fading when we finally went to bed.

Of course, in the stories you told me you never spoke to me about sex with Amandine. While I was still Amandine there was nothing to tell, we were still making the story, and when I became Chouette it was a private matter between you and her. I hope that these memories were amongst the tenacious ones though. I hope they're there for you so, like me, you can still remember our bliss, still re-live those precious moments when you are left alone with your thoughts.

I was surprised to find that unlike the rest of Candice your bedroom was cramped, dominated by the bed that filled it. You went through the door first and pulled me down on to the fresh sheets without a word, wrapping yourself around me in a way that was so inevitable I couldn't imagine how I'd gone so long without it. But that night everything was new and waiting to be discovered. Waiting to be tasted for the first time. We lay there, curled together in the deep-sea light of the first breaths of dawn, complicit in our inaction. We both knew what was going to happen. We were as still as if sleeping, but each acutely aware of the other's heartbeat, the rise and fall of their breath, the slightest movement, the momentum building silently between us.

When the moment came, drowsiness had already settled on me like a fog, pulling me deeper into the bed. You brushed my hair back from my face with your thumb. A second later I felt your unshaven kiss press upon the skin you had exposed. I could finally let out my trembling breath. At last we were here.

I waited a few moments before responding. Your fingertips brushed across my chest and your kiss dropped lower, to my throat. I had never wanted to kiss a man so much in my life. And when my mouth found yours, the release was almost unbearable.

We kissed, and we kissed again, peeling away the clothes that had become a barrier between our skins, getting closer and closer until our breathing had synchronised and I couldn't distinguish your desire from my own and the only thing to do was to fit ourselves together. Once we had we barely moved. It was as though we were making something fragile. Perhaps in a way we were. My every nerve was alight. Your hands were on my face and between my shoulder blades, pulling us deeper. I felt you trembling, on the edge, and rose to meet you. Then came the moment when we abandoned ourselves, leaving thought behind, becoming our bodies. And you whispered in my ear, 'Amandine.'

When I think back on that journey, it is impossible to remember it without recalling the hours that we devoted to making love. Mornings, midday, evenings, we would reach for each other, delighted with ourselves, drenched with desire. When we lay together you were like a thirsty man drinking from a pool. You buried your face in me, bathed in me, ran your hands through me, my name in your mouth. When we slept you lay curled against my back, your long arms folded around me, the bones of your hands hard against my cheek and your fingers knotted in my hair. Your intensity took me by surprise. Once you had decided, at last, that you wanted me, your desire was so fierce it was as if you were trying to absorb me through your skin. And yet every day as we stood at the wheel you tried to let me go.

You told me that I should leave you while things were still good. That was the deal. That was your plan. That way, you said, we would have all of the highs, but I would be released before things got too bad. When I resisted that idea you reminded me that if I didn't leave I would lose you anyway. You would be gone, you said, and I would find another man in your place. Perhaps a ghost from your past, perhaps a stranger, but that either way I wouldn't recognise him.

'I can get to know your ghosts,' I said. 'You can tell me about your life. Then I'll recognise you, whoever you are.'

'Maybe,' you said. 'But there's still no escaping the fact that even if you recognise him, he might not recognise you. He won't love you. I couldn't bear that to happen.'

I knew you were right. There was every likelihood you'd forget me; the dementia would make you confused and out of confusion would come mistrust. And later you would need the kind of care that relies on trust. 'We don't have to think about that now,' I told you. 'Let's cross that bridge when we come to it.'

But you were adamant. 'No. Promise me you will leave when the time comes,' you said. 'There can be no happy ending for us.'

That's where we were divided. You had already begun to think about the end because you had it in your sights. But I was happy to let the future come at its own pace. I told you long ago that what I really wanted was to feel alive. I wanted love and everything love is. You put that within my reach. With every day I spent with you I felt gravity returning. When I first met you I was air. Now I was water, now I was earth.

I had never been looking for the happy ending you find in books. That's not the kind I believe in. They are simplistic constructs that make it easier for us to bear the long continuum of our stories. But no one ever ends at the ending. After the lovers kiss and the last page is turned, their lives barrel on messily towards the grave and maintaining some kind of happy ending is an ongoing battle. If you don't keep that in mind, happiness will slip through your fingers like water.

In that sense you might say it was a blessing to know how little time we might have, for it made us truly alive. Everything good became magnified: every embrace was a gift, every morning you woke and said my name my heart sang, every kiss was like a reunion, a second chance. I took those exquisite days and salted them away. They have sustained me through the days and weeks when I wished more than anything that I had taken your advice and cut my losses.

I had been ready to go to Paris, the idea had appealed. A chance to give Sophie something I had wanted for myself, stepping into an unknown future rather than choosing one that I already knew bore pain and responsibility. But it would have been a mistake. Sophie didn't need me there, she only needed to know I'd be there if she asked, but you needed me and I needed you. There are still days when I question my decision, but when I have rested, when the family have rallied round as they always do, I always come back to the same conclusion. I do not regret choosing you at all.

In the end I told you that you must be the one to decide. I promised you that when that day came, when you thought it was time, I'd go. All you had to do was say. And until then we would rejoice in the present.

Time stretched and compressed in strange ways. It could have been days we were away, it could have been months. Whole, perfect minutes stay with me, sense-rich and vibrant, yet entire days seem to have vanished. The sun was glorious – I don't recall a single rainy day – and newly emerged butterflies filled the sky like wind-blown blossom. The mornings were heralded by distant cockerel calls and the glockenspiel chimes of cows. White light reflected off the water giving bank-side grasses stars for blooms and dappling the underside of bridges as we slipped beneath.

'The light is different on the water,' Amandine said one afternoon as we stood side by side at the wheel. I agreed, but I couldn't explain how. 'There's no need to,' she said. 'We both feel it. If something speaks to your heart, why try to pin it down with a description?'

I hadn't expected to find the travelling so soothing. Our pace through the water was so sedate that cyclists on the towpath regularly overtook us, much to Amandine's delight. We let this serenity guide us and soon sank into a deep, peaceful rhythm, sank into each other. Every day a little. Never too much. Never too far.

Every evening, as the twilight plane trees transformed into sentinels against the violet skies, we found a place to moor and stepped off the boat, walking out together to feel the new, different earth under our feet. To smell the place, listen to its sounds, breathe in the subtle differences, to try and know it even for a while. You'd be surprised how much changes in just a few kilometres. When we returned to Candice we would sit up on deck and listen to the cicadas in stereo, the amorous frogs and the chatter of late-night mallards, drink a glass of wine and eat a simple supper. Neither of us was a great cook, but we managed with what we found in the villages we passed – cheese, asparagus, artichokes, fresh bread and eggs.

At night it took me a while to get used to having Amandine with me. I had been accustomed for so long to the weightlessness around me when I slept, the way the covers fell over the shape of me, and now, even if we were not touching, if she had rolled away from the heat of me, my skin could sense her. Her presence invaded my dreams, my mind inventing scenarios to explain where I must be. I was working, or on the streets, or in the bar. Amandine said I talked a lot in my sleep those first few days, asking strange questions and murmuring to myself, and it was only after a while she realised she wasn't expected to answer. When I woke and got my bearings the first thing I would do was pull her closer, so that everything made sense again. Amandine filled a space in my bed that hadn't existed before, but would be forever desolate when she left.

That wasn't the only change I found unsettling. Nothing was familiar any more and it bothered me more than I thought it would. I came to understand that Candice was only part of my home. The towpath was home too. The trees where owls made their clandestine nests, the way the light and shade fell through the leaves on to the deck in the afternoons, the time the ducks took their noisy breakfast. I had known my surroundings so intimately that I hadn't had to think about it at all, and now every tree was new, every face, every cloud. Many times I woke hazily and had no idea where I was. Whenever I asked Amandine she always replied that it didn't matter. She felt it too, the ambiguity of having left our moorings, but she was so contented it just washed over her. 'We're right here,' she'd say.

We both liked to rise early, while the morning mist still lay over the water like an exhalation. We found our routine; I made the coffee and laid the table while Amandine warmed bread and croissants, then we would open the windows and let in the air, sweet with the fresh scent of dew and the sharp tang of cut grass that drifted over from the canal-side cottages. While we were moored I felt at least partly connected to that world, the world of houses and bakeries and offices and roads, of postmen and politicians. But as soon as we set off again and the bank released its hold on us our lives became perpendicular. It gave me the same feeling I got when I was on a moving train and saw the faces of people in cars waiting at a level crossing.

Beyond the confines of the Toulouse tourist circuit it was clear everyone on the canal felt this otherness too, creating an instant bond between us. Every time we passed a boat travelling upstream there would come a cheerful call, 'Bonjour, Candice!' We quickly learned to look out for the names of boats as they approached so we could reciprocate. 'Bonjour, Beatrice!' we'd reply. Or, 'Bonjour, La Coquette.' There was so much in those simple greetings, an acknowledgement of community, a shared joy. By contrast those on the land still saw us as otherworldly. People would park their cars on the roads that ran parallel to the canal or stop on bridges that crossed it, leaning out of their windows to take our photograph. On the move, Candice had become even more of a curiosity.

There were lots of cars, I remember, lots of families. Perhaps it was the Easter holidays. They looked hot up there in their vehicles stuffed full of belongings and crisps and squabbling, the radio bleeding out of their windows. When the children waved to us from the back seats we always waved back. Amandine never tired of their fascination, and at a distance I didn't mind it either. I was quite used to it. But when walkers and cyclists on the towpath photographed us it felt somehow more intimate, more intrusive. Some would smile, say hello and ask if we wouldn't mind them taking a photo, but many others just snapped away, viewing us through the screens of their phones as though we were on television. As though we couldn't see them back.

One day when we had found a particularly beautiful spot to pause for tea, we were sitting on deck watching a robust yellow and black dragonfly hunting the delicate petrol blue damselflies across the water when a young couple walked by hand in hand. The first thing they did when they stopped by the boat was to turn their backs to us. I thought it strange until I realised the woman had her arm extended, taking their photograph with Candice in the background. 'They haven't noticed us,' Amandine whispered, with a grin.

'Let's say hello,' I whispered back. I cleared my throat loudly and they both spun around with startled expressions.

'Sorry,' I said. 'I didn't mean to alarm you.'

'Oh gosh, I'm so sorry!' the young woman said. 'I didn't see you there.'

'It's no problem.' Amandine smiled kindly. 'People do it all the time. But would you mind taking our photo too?'

My heart sank. I have hated posing for the camera ever since I realised how much significance a photograph can give to a random fraction of a second. After a long battle with my escalating reluctance, my mother gave up asking me to be in photos years ago. Of course it's all changed now. You can take a hundred snaps and pick and choose and edit. Still, I was reticent at first but after having been persuaded by Amandine I was greatly relieved afterwards when she showed me the picture they'd sent to her phone. There we were, the two of us shoulder to shoulder, framed in blue, the hint of a mischievous grin still playing on my lips and Amandine looking right at the camera, smiling and radiant. Everything about it looked perfect. I couldn't quite believe it was me in the photo. Was that how we appeared to other people?

The woman with the camera had asked Amandine afterwards if we lived on the boat all the time. For the sake of simplicity Amandine had said we did. 'That's amazing, you're so lucky,' the woman said. 'I wish I could do that.'

I wondered if we offered, the woman with the camera, the people in the cars, would they really want to exchange places with us, for a day, for a week, for ever? Those people looking down at us from the bridges on the outskirts of towns and cities, all they could see was the long corridor of calm, a rare stretch of empty air in their cluttered world. It must have looked idyllic. But what they couldn't see below their feet was the graffiti scrawled under the bridge, the mattresses and bin bags alongside the dandelions. Looking back on their holiday snaps they would never see the homeless man hidden from sight. We try to keep our shame hidden, the things we don't want tourists to see. But even they can't help but notice the trees.

All along the Canal du Midi are the tall iconic plane trees that have strengthened the banks and given shade to the passing boats for generations. They are dying one by one and there's no cure. Once a tree is infected it can still look healthy and strong on the surface for years, ripe with fresh green leaves in spring and the balls of seeds that hang on threads like baubles, but it will be shrivelling from the inside. Eventually, if you're observant, you might notice clusters of small branches where the new growth is stained and curling at the edges as though dipped in caramel, the first signs that the disease has taken another one. It's an epidemic and no one knows how to stop it.

The further we travelled the more evident the disease became. Many trees were already stripped bare, their branches bent haggard and hopeless. Some were taken by ivy, giving the appearance of living on, yet others remained inexplicably rejected and barren. In other places there was nothing but a stump, or turned-over earth where a tree should have been. A missing note in a song.

I looked back down at our smiling faces on the screen and realised I was spoiling the idea of what was just a beautiful photograph.

I pulled Amandine close. 'Thank you for insisting,' I said. 'I love it.'

'I bet your parents would too,' Amandine said. 'We could send it to your father's phone.'

'Let's wait,' I said. 'When we get back to Toulouse I'll take you to meet them.'

Your mother and I took to each other straight away. She set you to peeling potatoes and took me out into the garden, vigorous with growth and vibrant with the scent of sun-warmed fruit and flowers. 'Do you know much about gardening?' she asked.

'I'm terrible with plants,' I told her.

She laid a soft-skinned hand over mine. 'I'll teach you.'

'That's kind, but I don't have a garden. I never have.'

'And your mother?' I shook my head. 'Everyone should have a garden, no matter how small.'

'That's what Baptiste says.'

Your mother smiled. 'He's been alone for so long, gardening is good for his soul. A garden teaches you to work with what you have, the space, the soil, the light. No one gets it right first time, but you work at it. Some things fail, some things flourish and things happen beyond your control – bad winters, pests and droughts – but the rewards are so satisfying, and eventually you know your garden so intimately it's as though it is the only possible garden you could have sown.' She looked back at the cottage pointedly. 'Well then,' she said. Was I imagining it, or was she trying to tell me something?

You still hadn't told your parents. As long as you could hide it, you had decided to spare them the upset. If they had noticed a change in you, and as a mother I would be surprised if they hadn't, they had chosen to leave it unsaid.

'Baptiste tells me we have something in common,' your mother said as she walked me slowly around the garden. 'You're a doctor, aren't you? That's good.' She paused long enough for her next question to sound like a non-sequitur. 'He's looking well, don't you think?' Without waiting for a reply she lifted a handful of soil and raised it to my face. 'And look at the colour of that,' she said. 'I was a midwife myself. Of course, it's not the same thing exactly.'

'Baptiste told me. It's as hard a job as mine, if not harder.'

She nodded. 'See how the sun floods the garden now?' she said, bending slowly to pluck out a sticky length of trailing weed, 'but look, there under the apple tree there's still plenty of shade for the little flowers that don't like the heat. As the sun gets lower in the sky at the end of August, that shade will swell across the garden and those little things spread like wildfire.' When she spoke her face was creased into the well-worn smile we reserve for those dearest to us. I could see your warmth in her and it made my heart ache.

'What's that?' I asked, pointing at a tall, rangy tree with just the earliest signs of fruit.

'It's a persimmon,' she said. 'Looks like nothing now but just wait until Christmas, it will have no leaves at all but its fruit will hang like golden baubles.' She reached for my hand. 'Under the persimmon tree, that's our spot. When we die that's where we'd like our remains to go, but only if Baptiste decides to keep the cottage. Not if he sells it to strangers. When the time comes you'll know what's best for you both, but if you did keep the cottage, could you remember that for me?'

That weekend was the first and last time I saw your father, although you don't remember it that way. You don't remember the call the following day from your mother, or the way we all sweated through the funeral that blistering summer afternoon. You don't remember the way his ashes sat in an urn on the mantelpiece for years, as though in limbo.

'I knew it was coming,' your mother told me as we milled around with neighbours and distant family in the cool of the house. She was calm in the way that some wives are at funerals, busying herself with others, passing canapés, tissues and condolences. She claimed to have seen it in his face, the afternoon just days earlier when he had pulled up outside the house in his old blue truck with all his tools stacked on the flatbed. He had brought everything back. He was finished. 'When you've been with someone this long,' she said, 'you know.' She took hold of my wrist then looked me in the eye. 'I'm glad he got to see you and Baptiste together. I'm glad he saw his son in good health as well as good spirits. He died knowing everything would be all right.' A chill ran over my skin. She knew. I nodded, and she drew me in for an embrace. 'Bless you both,' she said.

You hadn't seen it at all. On the way home, still astonished by his revelation, you had remarked on how, compared to recently, your father had looked like a new man. There was colour in his face, his hair was combed, he had shaved and was wearing two thirds of a Sunday suit, his chest puffed out. 'Papa, you look extraordinarily well,' you had told him. 'The fish must be doing you good.'

'Pah!' your father had exclaimed. 'I've had enough of fish. Can't stand the stuff. What's the point of eating it just so you can live another day to eat more fish?' He strolled into the kitchen to see what was cooking but returned with nothing but a kissed cheek and a boyish grin. 'My wife says it is not ready yet and could I kindly get out from under her feet,' he told me, with a shrug. 'But there's plenty of it, thank goodness. I'm famished.'

'What is she making?' you asked.

'Quail I think, and some kind of an onion sauce. We had better take a robust red wine with it, it looks good and rich.' He put his hand on my elbow. 'Come and help me choose something, Amandine.'

Lunch tasted as delicious as it smelled. We ate in companionable silence, but for the soft scrape of knives and forks against the plates, all the while twin smiles playing on your parents' lips. From my chair at the table I could see out into the hallway, where photo frames fluttered up the wall just as you had described them: you as a baby, a toddler, a boy and a young man. Different layers of you, somebody else's memories, captured and pinned to the paper, safe under glass.

You laid your cutlery on your plate. 'Are you not going to the chapel today, Papa?'

'I wondered when you would ask,' your father said with a foxy smile. 'I thought today we could go together. I have something to show you.' And so we drove out together into the wide expanse of golden sunflowers, the Citroën bumping over the rutted track and red dust billowing through the windows.

'We still need to tidy up this track a little, to make it kinder on people's cars.'

'Would you like some help?'

'Don't worry, son, there's a nice young man from the village going to do it, I only have to pay materials. People have been so helpful, it's a miracle really.'

You weren't sure what he was talking about, but I could see that you didn't want to question him, unsure if you had forgotten something, wary of giving your secret away. Up ahead I could already see something else of a miracle. Rising up out of the sunflowers was a roof. No dome, no steeple, a simple slate roof, grey against the clear open sky. In the clearing were log benches and a path through the sunflowers to the forest beyond.

Your father's hands shook as he took the keys out of the ignition. 'Come on then, let's see what you both think.'

There was a tidy paved area around the building. Each wall met the pitched roof and the roof met itself at the apex, sealed, finished, a small chimney rising highest of all.

'A chimney on a chapel?' you said at last.

'It's not a chapel.'

'But ...'

'What would the village want with another chapel out here anyway? What would God want with another chapel? I don't know what I was thinking, silly old man that I am. Did I think I could please God, thank him, keep you safe just by giving him another empty pile of stones?'

You smiled, confounded. 'Well, Papa, it's the thought that counts.'

A smile rippled over his leathery face. 'Maybe, yes.'

'What sparked it off, this change of heart?'

'All that damned fish,' he said with a guffaw. 'What a price to pay.'

'Seriously?'

Your father laughed. 'Oh, son, I'm tired. I'm not going to live for ever, am I? Your poor mother living like a widow in that cottage while I'm out here for hours helping nobody but myself. I needed to wake up, and I suppose being ill like that ... well, I realised that if I didn't finish it, nobody would, and all my efforts of the last forty years would benefit no one. Not me, for I would regret it with my dying breath. Not your mother or you, who have had to suffer my absences and my pig-headedness. Not the village, who will have nothing on their hands but a half-finished ruin. And not God, who quite frankly has enough trouble filling the churches he already has.' He shook his head. 'I'm going to take care of your mother like the husband I should have been, and if there is a God, then I think that will please him just as much.'

'May we go inside?' I asked.

'Ah yes,' he said, pleased, 'that's the best thing.'

There was no door on the cottage, and we walked straight in, the cool air a balm on our hot skin. There were more benches, an old leather sofa like the one on Candice – you told me later it had come from your father's study – shelves full of books and stacks of paper and pencils. In the corner a wood stove was surrounded by a fireguard, and a few small logs cut neatly in a pile next to it, incongruous with the birdsong beyond the window and the yellow light falling through the door. It was a perfect, cosy nook in the middle of a field of sunflowers.

'I don't understand, what is it?' you asked, taking a seat on one of the benches and looking at the wooden walls, the wooden ceiling, already bearing a few children's drawings, pinned up with tacks.

'It's a library,' your father answered, 'a refuge, a calm place. It's anything that people want it to be, really.'

'Who is it for?'

'It's for anybody who wants to come here. I was thinking particularly of the children in the city. I'm hoping word will get around.'

'There's not even a door though,' you said. 'Aren't you worried that people will come here to sleep, you know, homeless people or teenagers? Aren't you worried about it getting damaged, or the books stolen?'

Your father smiled. His hand shook on his stick, but he remained standing. 'The door is coming, but there won't be a lock. A locked door is the fastest way to make people resentful. If you leave doors open, trust walks in, don't you think?' His face was anxious, waiting for your approval.

'Yes, Papa. You're right. This is wonderful. Wonderful.'

He smiled broadly and sat down as though all the weight had been lifted from him. 'There is one last thing, Baptiste. You should know that I spent most of your inheritance on this.' Your eyes flickered. 'I'm sorry about that but you've always insisted we benefit from that money ourselves rather than leave it to you. This way I hope it will make many more people happy, and' – he turned to me with a wink – 'you'll still get the cottage.'

I loved that cottage. I could easily have lived there one day. Everything about the place was filled with love. The kitchen where your mother poured her heart into the meals she prepared. The way your parents looked at each other. The way they spoke to each other with so much kindness. The garden that your mother tended so attentively. You learned so much from her, I don't think she ever knew how wise she was. For a long time, even after you began to neglect your own body, you continued to care for your garden on deck, down on your knees, bending over the pots of geraniums and lavender, picking through them with gentle fingers, watching over the marigolds and the multi-coloured succulents, the lemon tree and all those herbs. Something in your mother's insistence was strong enough to fight the decline. Just as with your piano, it seemed to keep you focused, keep you you. Then one year not so long ago you simply stopped, and everything started to die.

Your mother had grown very frail by that time and I didn't want to bother her. It was hard for her to see you struggling. I tried to manage it myself, but with my help the violets wilted in the hot August sun and I soaked the poor jasmine until her flowers all turned brown and shrivelled. In the end I gave in and called her. 'It's really time you learned to garden, Amandine,' she said. She insisted that I brought her out to Candice so she could show me properly, and when we turned up at the cottage she filled the car boot with cuttings and bulbs and everything that could be potted up. She had given up on us ever moving to the cottage and had decided she'd bring her garden to us. She spent hours with me that day, leaving me with sheaves of notes and instructions in spidery handwriting, and soon afterwards the deck of Candice was transformed, the most beautiful I have ever seen it.

I thanked her with all my heart. 'You're a mother,' was all she said. 'You understand.'

I held her for a moment. 'I'm so sorry,' I said. On board the boat and out of context you had not recognised your mother at all. You were polite with her, calling her Madame, but annoyed with me. If her heart was breaking she didn't let it show. It had stopped her for the briefest of instants, her hand flying to her throat as though she were winded. Then it passed as quickly as it had come and she managed a smile and got on with the gardening, her old fingers slowly working the earth, caressing the little seedlings. Later as we drove her home in my car, your mother nodding off in the back, you turned to me and said, 'Don't hire her again.' Her eyes were closed and her hearing was failing, and I prayed that she hadn't heard.

You still don't remember that she came. The last memory you have of your mother is of her sitting in her chair in the kitchen, asleep. Her eyes were closed, you said, and the fire had gone out. And your father must have been at the chapel because the house was quite silent.

I wish now I could tell her how she left her echoes all around you. Sometimes now when you sit out on deck, breathing in the scents and casting your eyes over the colours, you believe that you are back home.

We were sitting on the deck under a canopy of stars, swatting away mosquitoes and supposedly sharing a bottle of wine, although neither of us was drinking. You had been silent for several minutes, your fingertip following the scar down from your knee. 'Fell out of my bedroom window,' you murmured under your breath. 'Shutters. Bats.' But something was bothering you.

We had spent the last hour naked on your bed, carefully tracing every scar, every crooked toe, the whorls and curves of our fingerprints, mapping out the unique bodies that held our hearts. I had told you the story of my broken feet and you had told me your story of your broken leg.

Later, your mother would tell me another story. The story of the boy in one of the photographs on the wall, standing on tiptoes on the piano lid, bracing himself against the wall, reaching down into the open box. It is evident from the photo that you have lost your balance and are about to fall. 'Can you believe I took that photo?' your mother said. 'I still regret it to this day.'

You turned to me. 'When I broke my leg,' you said, 'do you know what surprised me most?'

'The ground?'

You laughed and put your other arm over my shoulders, kissing the top of my head. 'Well, yes,' you said, 'but also the realisation that my body wasn't me. That parts of me could break and yet I still stayed the same. That the real me was somehow separate to the flesh and bone I carried myself around in.' You leaned back and looked up at the salted sky. 'That's what I thought I had learned. I thought it for a long time, but I was wrong.'

'What do you mean?'

'The flesh is me, there's nothing more to it than that. Just this body, just these billions of cells. That's who I am. That is who you are. We are made of nothing but elements and the stories they hold: the stories we have told ourselves and the stories we have been told.' You reached for my hand. 'I'm made of nothing but remembered feelings and they are the most fragile thing of all. Once you realise that, everything becomes clear.'

I couldn't look at you. Every day we found new ways to philosophise, but when it came to it, no matter how many beautiful metaphors you made, in the end we had no answers. Keeping my eyes instead on the dark space above us, the stars and planets that appeared to shift across the sky as though we were fixed and everything revolved around us. Perhaps that's how we rationalise it so as not to be overwhelmed by our insignificance.

I felt at that moment like my eyes were at the waist of a vast hourglass, the infinite universe expanding out and away from me in one direction and, in the other, the explosion of galaxies in my mind. Every grain of sand could be a star. Every grain a memory. This is why we hold stories so dearly, I thought. And this is why we cling to gods.

I'm an introvert at heart, so at times I found the instantaneous switch into such an intense relationship exhausting. Sometimes when we were on the move I liked to find my own space, taking myself away around the side of the boat to the prow where I could soak up the peace of our languorous drift through this secret tunnel, closing my eyes to feel the sun on my face. Nothing in my ears but the chirrups and callings and chatter of the birds and the rumble of the engine under my bare feet. When I felt rejuvenated again I would return to your side at the wheel as you guided Candice around the meandering canal.

I had quickly noticed that navigating the boat silenced your inner dialogue. You were at your calmest then, absorbed in the task. You would stand there with your hands light on the wheel and your eyes fixed on the middle distance. When I was in the mood for company I would stand at your side following your gaze, the space between us a breath of air where desire built.

One day we were standing like this, saying nothing, when you turned to me. 'Take the wheel,' you said. 'It's your turn.'

'I don't know how.'

You guided me into place. 'Take it. We all start off not knowing how.'

I lay my fingers around the handles, the varnish worn from them. I wondered then where Candice had been, and with whom, before she was yours. You put your hands lightly over mine. 'Feel it?' I nodded. 'Don't look at the wheel. Look at the water ahead of you. She won't turn like a car or a bike, she needs time, so you need to anticipate for her, OK? Try it.'

I turned the wheel left a little, pointing the prow into the canal. Nothing seemed to happen. 'More?' I said.

'Patience.' Beyond the trees I saw farmers were ploughing deep furrows in the rich soil, readying to sow their sunflowers. And then slowly she began to turn; she was more responsive than I had thought, we were turning too far. Instinctively I began to turn right again and you tightened your fingers over mine, slowing the turn. 'Steady on,' you said, 'not so fast. It's all about making tiny adjustments and keeping your eyes on the horizon. If something is right in front of you it's already too late, so you always need to be thinking about correcting your course for a bend or another boat as soon as you see it. You have to visualise your path along the water.'

'It all makes sense now,' I said.

'What does?'

'When you're here at the wheel, apart from when you're playing the piano it's the only time you're fully present, completely in the moment.'

'Not the only time,' you whispered. I felt your breath on the back of my neck. Not a kiss, but enough to make the hairs stand on end. 'Keep concentrating,' you said. 'Return the wheel before she has finished the manoeuvre or you'll go too far.' There was something dreamlike about looking out at the water, feeling Candice respond under my touch. 'Good. You're on your own,' you said gently, lifting your hands from mine.

'Not yet.' The boat began to veer towards the bank. 'Take the wheel back, I'm going to crash.'

'No you're not.' You adjusted our course again. 'You're going to be fine.' You stepped forwards, leaning over me until I could feel your heart pressed against the curve of my back. 'I'm going to fetch you my old notebook,' you said, your voice soft and sad. 'If you want to get to know my ghosts, we'd better start now.'

I could say something trite like, 'Those days on the canal were some of the happiest in my life', but if I am honest even perfect memories like these are tinged with a haunting sadness. When we look back on things we tend to magnify the strongest emotion; it makes it simpler if we can distil time down to just a single essence. For me it was the bitter-sweet taste of a last meal.

After a few days on board it was clear that Amandine was falling in love with Candice, and I began to feel optimistic that our lives could converge for however long we had. One morning when I emerged from the shower I found her out on the prow, ducking under the flapping towels on the laundry line, dusting away the cobwebs caught up with dandelion seeds and poplar fluff and the fractured scraps of brittle oak leaves. She looked up at me, pointing at some rust spots on the prow.

'She could use a lick of paint.'

'It's been a hard winter.'

'Let's spruce her up again when we get back home.'

She had her eyes on the horizon, I thought. She was steering me. She steered me through the rise and fall of the birds over the fields, where a piping of mortarless stone wall ran along the crests of the distant hills. Through the clutches of spruce and silver birch huddled in stands of low yellow light and the distant wind turbines standing proud on the smooth curve of the horizon, and on and on to glades of pine, their scent syrupy in the baking afternoon air. We were nearing the coast.

I knew where we had to go, but even I was surprised when we eased along the spur canal and out through close-knit trees into a wide open sky and into the path of a great expanse of river busy with boats, its surface rippled by thousands of tiny waves.

'Where are we?' Amandine called from up on deck.

'It's the Hérault. We have to go across.' I smiled up at her, but inside I felt nauseous. Candice, just the right size for the quiet, shallow canal, suddenly felt so small on this flow. I could sense the depth of it beneath us. It didn't feel safe. 'Come down if you want,' I said, and she came.

That night I dreamed we took Candice down to the sea, but instead of sailing into harbour we pushed out past the oyster beds, past the rocky outcrops and out again into the choppy waters, then further into the heart of the Mediterranean, where we hit a storm so wild that the boat was tossed about like a child's dinghy. The dream broke as we capsized and were sinking into the blackness. The water was cold but I was happy for the end of it. I woke to find Amandine had taken all the bedclothes.

I curled back around her and rested my arm over the valley of her waist. For a moment I thought I was still dreaming, I could feel Candice shifting in the swell, then I realised it was the rise and fall of Amandine's breath. That was when I understood what Amandine had meant when she told me, 'We're here.' The changes around me didn't matter at all. It wasn't important where we ended up. Wherever I was with her I was home. I rested my lips in the nape of her neck and exhaled.

The next morning everything was different. The light shifted, neither one thing nor another. The clouds were new; cirrus clouds high above, scudding broadly, slowly across our course. The unfamiliar sky stretched out, smoothing down the tall thick-set trees to the low silk trees and alders, pampas grass and the occasional pine. The thick red earth of the banks, still saturated from the April rainfall, was peppered with burrows like Emmental cheese. Black-headed gulls skimmed across the water and martins dived for insects. Only two locks remained before the sea.

Along the canal side we passed clusters of small shabby boats, coastal gypsies moored on the towpath going about their lives. We waved and called in the way we had become accustomed, but they didn't respond, they barely seemed to notice us. Then I realised I was on the outside looking in. We were just tourists to them.

In the calm of the next lock we descended to sea level at last. 'Only one more lock before the Mediterranean,' I told Amandine as I guided Candice back out into the canal. I saw the thrill run over her. She was thinking of the Camargue, as excited as a girl by the prospect of the wild, galloping horses, their hooves pounding through the salt water, flashes of white against the blue just as she had seen in photos all her life. I felt her excitement as if it were my own. I couldn't wait to see her face when we finally saw them. Soon after, we bisected a long stretch of grassy fields where well-muscled horses grazed, half hidden by swathes of bamboo, the copper sunlight bright on their coats, shimmering like asphalt. Their heads were bowed in the heat, their long manes draping to the earth.

'Are we close?' she asked.

'Still a way yet,' I said. 'But we'll be at the sea by noon.'

Amandine would often sit alone up on deck, or up front on the prow while I piloted, but for that last stretch of canal we stayed together, side by side at the helm, taking turns to navigate the limpid waters, passing ochre houses with tiny windows, half taken by climbing roses and bordered by marshmallow-coloured flowers on the oleanders. Down in the reeds and bulrushes nearby a fisherman cast his lines into the brackish water trapped between the two locks.

It was the faint salt smell of seaweed and – beyond the low bridge – the tall masts of sailing boats that announced the *étang*. The trees curling over the top of us evoked a passageway and I felt a swell of anxiety as I saw the light ahead, growing brighter, the blue white light of the open water. Amandine, standing beside me at the wheel, put her hand over mine. Then the trees parted and the sunlight glittered off the blue salt-water lakes, throwing Candice's shadow back behind us, only the light ahead. I had been told we could expect flocks of flamingos and herons down there, but at the moment we arrived only a single heron stood, silent and still in the centre of the *étang*, looking off into the distance. The cry could have come from the bird or from my own throat. I am still not sure.

It was your birthday. Sophie was sitting on the floorboards at your feet, her sketchpad open beside her, the last image of Candice navigating through a tunnel of plane trees reflected in the water, with the canal stretching forwards into the distance. There have been no new stories to write down lately, but she will always draw for you, whatever you want to tell. Time flows through you now, evolving, iterative, degenerative, but always beginning with the story of your birth and always ending with the sea. Beyond that your stories are seamlessly stitched from the true, the uncertain and the imagined.

You leaned over to watch. Her illustrations still capture your attention, you gaze into them as though they had depth. On paper – a picture of Candice at her mooring, red banners flying outside the Capitol, sketched skaters on the frozen canal, a field of ripe sunflowers – and on her skin. On her right arm she has added to the vine. Now there are tiny, perfect bunches of grapes on there, and reflected in their surface, if you know where to look, you can find the even tinier silhouettes of a kingfisher, a little owl, and the sun itself. I went mad with her when she tattooed that first vine on her arm as a teenager but I think it played a role in bringing her home from Paris, plus she's made a good business of it now; people seek out her designs.

The trains did suit her for a while, but in the end motherhood suited her more. She came back to Toulouse more determined than ever to change the future, but with her own point of view about how that should be done. When I see her with Lucas now I'm so proud of her. He slipped into her life as if he was always meant to be there. Easy when they're together, easy when they're apart. They have a garden full of rabbits and guinea pigs, bird tables and flowers, the love spills over and everyone is welcome. Your mother would have been overjoyed to see the cottage that way, safe in their hands.

Sophie had been the first at the door, grinning and wishing you a happy birthday.

'Oh?' you said. For a moment there was a chasm of incomprehension, an emptiness of tongues. I was about to step in, but Sophie spoke first.

'We didn't wake you?'

'No, no.' You turned to me, and your face was composed but uncertain, as though you were five again and wanted to reach for my hand. 'Chouette, I was already up and about, wasn't I?'

I smiled at you, but just a little. 'Yes, of course. You've been up since nine or ten.'

You smiled back, reassured, turning sideways to let people through and opening your arms to our friends and family. 'Come in, come in,' you said, in that charming way you always have with visitors, but your face was wary as they filed over the walkway and down the steps. 'Ah, look at the boy!' Your hand reached out for him as he passed, but Sophie caught it gently. Lucas was slumped over her shoulder, much too big to be carried these days, but Sophie loves it and is stronger than she looks. 'Hold on, Baptiste,' she whispered. 'Don't wake him, he's tired. He'll come to eventually and say hello. Let him sleep for now.'

I took your hand from hers and whispered, 'Baptiste, do you remember why everyone is here?'

'Have they come for Candice?' Your hand trembled in mine. No one else noticed and I pretended not to.

'No, Baptiste.' 'They' are the people who know what's best for you. They came here and shook their heads at the boat, poked their fingers into our bathroom cabinets and regarded the stairs with suspicion, told you that you should move out to your parents' cottage. That was the logical solution. When you told them that your bedroom there wasn't big enough for the two of us they reminded you gently that your parents were dead. I saw the mixture of sorrow, disbelief and anger building in you like a held breath, stepped back as it exploded into the room, watched as they took this as confirmation of their prognosis. Can they not understand how cruel it is to make you live the loss of your parents over and over? Even Lucas understands that.

Lucas has your old room at the cottage. Every time we visit he grabs you by the hand and leads you upstairs to show you that the bats are still there, then he takes you down to the persimmon tree to show you how high he can now swing on the branches. Sophie tells me that later, when we've left, he goes back to the tree and chats to your mother about your visit. Your mother loved Lucas.

'No, Baptiste,' I said again. 'It's a party, remember?'

'Ah yes, are there going to be sweets?'

'There's cake. I didn't think you were too fond of sweets.' I paused. 'Would you like sweets?'

'No,' you said. 'My parents wouldn't like it. When are they coming?'

'Your mother's cakes always beat mine hands down,' I said, 'but it's your favourite.'

Downstairs everyone had already made themselves at home, the Louis XV the only seat left empty. I sat on the floor by Sophie, who put her arm around my waist. In her other arm Lucas woke, wearing a slight frown and rubbing away the bleary stirrings of his eyelids, disrupted by the noise. He looked around at us, seeming to sense that we were all on edge. He has always been a sensitive child. You were the only one still standing.

'Hi, Grandpa,' he said.

'Hi, Lucas,' you replied, and I bit my lip.

Lucas stood and crossed to give you a hug. At seven he could pass for ten or eleven. Tall and reedy, with puppyish hands too big for his young body and a Moorish look about his dark features, he could easily be your blood grandson. He wasn't at all moved by your recognition of him. As far as he is concerned, some days you know him and some days you don't. Either way he is happy to potter about Candice, getting on with tending your plants – a passion your mother passed on to him before she died – or playing the piano if you let him. He has already learned the pieces that please you best depending on your mood. He accepts your illness as a fact of life, loving you in that detached way that children can when they have not yet learned to grieve – either for those who die, or those who leave us while they are still alive.

'Hey,' he said, spotting the cake from the corner of his eye, 'birthday cake!'

'Is it someone's birthday?' you said. Grief fluttered around the room, followed by an adjustment, as though a bat had entered through a window, flit about seeking a long echo, and left. Sophie got to her feet and cut you a slice. 'It's your birthday, old man,' she said, winking at you. 'Happy birthday.'

'You're a funny girl,' you said, winking back as though the two of you were complicit in some kind of a joke.

Sophie still instinctively knows how to talk to you where most people don't. They don't know quite how to approach you any more. Everyone tries to be kind but it rarely works well. Some talk to you as though you were an infant. Others tiptoe around you as if you were so brittle they could break you with their very existence. The worst is when someone uses nothing but past tense, as though you were already gone, like an obituary.

The lemon in the cake reminded you of something, set you off talking and we sat around for a while listening to your stories, Sophie sketching in her notepad, until you lost patience and got to your feet. 'Who would like some breakfast?' you asked. From the cupboards you brought jam, mustard, tins of asparagus spears, crackers. You laid them on the table and the others all joined in, adding the bread, croissants and juice that they'd brought. Jordi knocked up an omelette and Sophie made coffee. The table was too small for so many of us, so we ate our midnight breakfast in shifts, coming and going from the wheelhouse while you sat at the end, pushing the food around your plate, refusing a drink, accepting our attentions with a blithe smile, your fingers reaching out to keep contact with the wheel.

Lucas found the idea of breakfast exciting but bizarre. 'I'm not hungry, Grandpa,' he said. 'Please can I play the piano?'

'Be my guest.'

As the sound of his neat rendition of Bach reached your ears you closed your eyes for a moment, rubbing them with your knuckles. There are freckles on your eyelids that I had never noticed before. Have they always been there or are they arriving with age? There's so much about you I've yet to learn.

While Sabine tidied away, Etienne and René washed the dishes together, playing up to their role in the charade with tender little touches and loving glances so authentic that even I was almost fooled by their artifice. When everyone left you leaned back against your chair, looking contemplative. 'I think I might go out for a walk,' you said.

'Baptiste, it's late.'

'I've only been up an hour or two.' You crossed to the window and recoiled at the blackness beyond, the only light the hazy glow of a waxing moon under cloud. I waited to see if you needed an explanation. I could see that expression on your face. You knew there must be something you'd forgotten. You were searching, searching. You rubbed condensation from the windowpane, to see if that helped. 'I've got a baby owl up on the deck,' you said. 'Come on, I'll show you.'

By the time we were outside, wrapped in blankets, thankfully you had forgotten about the owl. I sat beside you as you gazed out into the night, our bare toes meeting on the roughness of the deck. The blossom is thick on the acacia trees now, its scent honeying the air and filling my heart. 'Can you smell that?' I said. Your eyes followed the shadowy curves of the trees down to their roots and over to the water, where white petals waltzed across the moonlit surface. 'It must be nearly my birthday,' you said. 'It must be May.'

'Yes,' I said.

'I was born on a train, you know?'

You stretched out the fingers of your right hand and moved them softly on my thigh as though you were playing the piano, your breath deepening. You looked tired but calm. I waited to hear your story, wondering how it would have changed this time.

You must have played an entire concerto before your fingers came to rest. When they did, as though there had been no pause in the conversation at all, you said, 'Yes, on a train.' You became animated, using the full span of your arms as you recounted the rattle of the train, the woman's fear, the blood spilling on the carriage floor and the midwife sucking the fluid from your lungs with her own mouth. Your descriptions were so confident and vivid, the irony was not lost on me. And then you told me how the woman had been wearing green springtime shoes.

For a moment I was caught off guard. 'A coat,' I corrected you without thinking. 'A green springtime coat?'

Your eyes flickered. 'She had green shoes,' you said. 'I remember it clearly.'

You looked at me hard as I tried to keep my composure, and then your face crumpled. You covered your head with your hands. 'Chouette?' It was a question, but I had no useful answer. Instead I just sat there, listening to my own breath, the way it mixed with the slosh of the water, the waking call of the starlings, the frogs on the banks and the thrum of the cicadas.

You regarded me miserably. 'Chouette,' you said, 'I can see you're unhappy. Don't stay if you're unhappy. I couldn't bear to watch her stop loving me.' I looked up sharply and saw confusion flit across your eyes. There are echoes within you, I'm sure. Something that tells you you knew something significant about me, although you have no words to describe it and no reason to explain it. You frowned. 'I've told you this before. I can't make you happy,' you said.

'Baptiste,' I said, resting my foot on yours, 'you can.'

Dawn was breaking. Beyond the trees the world had rested and was setting in motion for another day, the rhythm already defined, the hours planned out. I had a sense of being in the wrong place or time. Disjointed, as though I had forgotten something important. I wondered if this is how you feel now. You yawned. 'Come on,' I said, 'let's go to bed.'

As we passed the piano you stopped, your gaze drawn to the open piano lid, to the score that Lucas had left there. It's years since you played from a score, but you seemed to be reading the music. Do you still hear music when you see the notes, I wondered. Or is it nothing more than ink on the page? Quavers and semi-quavers, rising and falling like the sea.

The wind carried us down to the sea. It seemed to me that it had been many years since I last saw that water, and I couldn't remember why I had left it so long.

The sea I saw as a man was not the same sea I saw as a boy, although it had not changed. I had remembered it in the sound of breaking waves and their wash upon the shore, the colour blue, the reflection of light, the salted crests of white foam and the cry of the gulls, the scoop of it filling buckets and the way I could entice it slithering down freshly dug channels into paddling pools and castle moats. As a man I was drawn not to any of this, but to the shift in colour where the darker waters began out beyond the shore, the border between safety and wilderness.

I don't remember how long we stayed by the coast. I remember how the wind blew across so many grains of sand, and the horizon was as wide as a smile. How, at dusk, the grey silhouette of gulls passed overhead in the dimming light, the bamboo and pampas grass and proud bulrushes dulling into erratic shadows. There were nights where I laid awake for hours while Amandine slept, my fingers tracing the marks on her belly where the sea had washed over her, the moon pushing and pulling and dragging her skin into the shape of the waves, leaving its mark. The salt was on her skin, warm and damp. I would taste it as she slept. Wake her with my lips.

In Amandine I found more bliss and more sadness than I had ever known. This is what happens when you let happiness slip out of your grasp and attach itself to something beyond your control, something so intoxicating that you ache to keep it although you know you cannot. We choose to bargain with pain because what alternative is there but regret? Under that soft, salt-water sun every day dawned bright with intoxicating desire, but heavy with fear. All I could do was to plunge in and swim, smiling and accepting that the tide could carry me away any time it pleased.

There was more than one day when we simply sat in silence for hours, staring out across the unfathomable deep, the clouds casting vast shadows of teal and royal blue across the turquoise shallows until night fell and we raised our eyes to a shifting sky studded with stars. When talking makes no difference at all, it's better to welcome silence. Words give our tiny tragedies more importance than they merit. If you feel overwhelmed one day you should try it: nothing but the sea, the sky and the silence. If you are like me, eventually you will feel your self shrink away. There where my safe waters tumbled off the edge of the world I became perfectly small again, perfectly light, still in love, but with the scale of the universe restored. And all the while she held my hand.

When the time came to find our moorings again we steered ourselves away from the sea as though it had been a dream. Back through the grazing horses, with wildness in their eyes and their tangled horsehair whipped by wind. Away from the scudding cirrus clouds and the tall grasses. Away from the brackish locks and the sulphur-scented air, and back through alleys of poplars and whitewashed blue-shuttered cottages sheltered by the soft rise and fall of the land. Back upstream we went, to the familiar safety of the weary shallows, pursuing the end of the story like salmon do. And then Amandine was gone.

Not a day goes by when I don't miss her.

Months later, in the middle of a bitterly cold December night, I woke with a start and a heaviness in my stomach like a sunken stone, knowing I had made the worst mistake of my life. You were already with me by then, filling the gap she left, and I lay there in the dark, edging away from you as though creating twenty centimetres of space between us would repair the damage done. As though not touching you now could change anything. Eventually you shivered and shifted under the covers until there you were again warm and naked against me. I lay a hopeless hand on your shoulder and waited for daylight, bereft.

By dawn I knew that calling her was inevitable. I knew it would hurt you, and did it anyway. Even though nothing came of it in the end, the intent itself must sting and for what it's worth I am sorry. Perhaps you remember that day; you left at the usual time for work, but you had to come home early. Immediately your footsteps had faded I had grabbed the phone. I tried several times, thinking I had misdialled, but there was no mistake, the digital voice on the line was insistent: Amandine's number was no longer in use. It didn't make sense. In those few grey hours before dawn I had imagined any number of scenarios, I had played discussions in my head, with Amandine, with you ... but I hadn't imagined that she would simply not be there. I began to imagine the worst. I thought of calling the police, ringing around hospitals, but even I could see they wouldn't take me seriously. A person can't be declared missing based on the irrational fears of one man who hadn't tried to contact her once in ... how long must it have been? When I had calmed myself I realised there was most likely a more rational explanation. She'd switched to a different phone company perhaps. Of course, that must be it.

High on adrenaline and hope I practically ran over to her apartment in the centre of Toulouse. The metro would have got me there faster, but I always found the walk along the towpath helped me organise my thoughts, and by the time I arrived I would be ready to express myself without faltering. The streets of Toulouse were almost empty. On the Allées Jean Jaurès, just the shadows of a few homeless souls sleeping in doorways, hunkered down in sleeping bags against the cold, with their scrawny dogs curled by their sides. The pavements of the Boulevard de Strasbourg were busier, and the road just starting to back up with tetchy drivers, the heels of their hands quick on the horns. As I turned down past the library I felt a shiver of relief, yet at the same time nerves swelled in my stomach like waves. Just seeing the vast rise of the church in the square once more and the marble steps up to Amandine's building sent thrills racing across my skin. By the time I came to a stop, breathless, by the stuccoed entrance to her apartment I was feverish with excitement and knew exactly what I was going to say.

I could recite that speech to you now, exactly as I had planned it. I tumbled those words like pebbles as I made my way to her house until they were polished so bright as to be irrefutable. I still have them, set aside and waiting for their moment in the light. How is it that some things are forgotten so easily while others wait around with purpose, optimistic in the face of experience?

I never did have the chance to tell Amandine how I felt. It was a stranger who answered the buzzer that day. She wouldn't let me in, but she came downstairs, hurriedly dressed. Amandine was gone, she said. She left months ago. She must have sensed my confusion, because for someone disturbed at such an hour she was remarkably sympathetic. She was young and polite and looked me in the eye. But, she said, she couldn't tell me where I could find Amandine Rousseau. She stood with me on the steps while I explained what had happened. How I had made the worst mistake of my life. I felt the cold then. A wild wind whipped around St Sernin and howled past us into the lobby. I should have brought a coat. The woman put her warm hand on my arm, she could see I was upset and cold, but she still didn't invite me inside. Then a taxi arrived to bring me home.

I must have called you, because you were there when I got back, waiting with money in the car park by the canal. I had left in a hurry with empty pockets. I stared down at the asphalt as you paid the driver. I was embarrassed, yet you were as kind as ever. As we walked back over to Candice together you took my hand in yours, and I remember how it trembled. You didn't ask any questions, just pulled out the piano stool for me and went to make some tea. Sometimes I wonder what I'd do without you.

Perhaps Amandine went to Paris after all. Still, it wasn't like her to just disappear. Had I hurt her more than I'd thought? I did the best I could. I'd hoped we could be friends, but I suppose that wasn't enough for her. Or maybe it was too much. Sometimes it's easier to sever ties completely than to live in the shadow of what might have been. I hope wherever she is that she found what she was looking for.

When I think of her now, as I often do, I am so grateful that at least we had that time together. I can still picture her on Candice on that journey. We are standing together at the helm. She is close, so close beside me that I can feel the air between us shift with the rise and fall of her breath. The canal is dark, but there's light at the end. The air is hot, but a pale wind blows through her hair, long and dark around her bare shoulders. She smells of cinnamon, fresh-cut grass and horses. I can hear the insistent rocking of her heartbeat, feel the strength of it resonating. And above it her voice is a hymn, calling back to me like a distant violin, white noise like static.

Acknowledgements

Because of a misunderstanding, Paul Simon's Penguins provided inadvertent inspiration for the opening and closing paragraphs of this novel.

The wonderful Eas Mor library on the Isle of Arran provided inspiration for later in the story as did 'Au Comptoir' in Toulouse. For taking the time to share with me their experiences of life on board l'Yvonnick, thanks to Chloé and Dominique Gérald, and for your welcome on board the Péniche Beatrice, merci Michel et Jean François.

The beautiful sketches of Baptiste's kingfisher and Chouette's barn owl at the opening of each chapter are the work of James McCallum and are just as Sophie would have drawn them.

In these pages I have only hinted at the struggles we face and the choices we have to make when someone we love has dementia. For a more explicit account of what it really means to live with Alzheimer's disease, I recommend Andrea Gillies' terrific and eye-opening memoir, *Keeper*.

Most important of all, the shrewd editorial insights and meticulous eye of Helen Garnons-Williams have been instrumental in shaping the way this story was told. Thank you, Helen. Working with you has been both a pleasure and privilege.

Many Thanks and One Apology

Thank you to my agent, Annette Green, for your continued support.

Janet Mckenzie and Tracey Upchurch – thank you for reading a draft in edits and kindly telling me what I needed to hear to keep me sane.

Sarah Salway's writing group – thank you for taking the time to consider the title of this novel, and for all your ideas. I hope you approve of the title that emerged.

Claudia Watts, for teaching us the importance of the colour of a kingfisher's beak.

For suggestions on details within the story, thanks to the Twitter and Facebook hive mind:

@AlysStuart, @AJ_Wils, Andrea Hernández,
@BathStoryAward, @bcurranYA, @bjwalsh, @BookMagpie,
@bookshaped, Catherine Breheny, Claire Tinsley,
@ConfusedMuse, @DandelionGirl01, Danielle O'Keefe,
Evie Dudley, @Frizbe, @GillHoffs, Heather Todd, @helennsta
@jamesgwriter, @joannechocolat, @jendelamere, Kalman Reti,
Kirsty Simpson, @LissaKEvans, Liz Wray, @LouiseTondeur,
@MargotMcCuaig, Matt Wray, Nora Anderson,
@PercivalAlison, @PeteDomican, @RachaelDunlop, Richard
Leach, @RosieBBooks, Sam Loynes, @SarahBallWriter,
@Sea_Penguin5, Sue Haigh, @SullyJulia, @SwallowDares,

@thebooktrailer, @TracyShephard, @VanessaGebbie and @writeanne.

Special mentions to Rosemarie Sayer, who placed the wooden horse in Baptiste's mother's violin case, and @DillyTante who uncovered Sophie's real name.

My heartfelt, pre-emptive thanks go now to the team at Bloomsbury who take things from here, as well as the many booksellers and librarians, who in their turn help to put this book into the hands of readers.

Finally, for Charlie, Amélie, Beatrix and everyone else who has had to put up with Baptiste's and Amandine's moods and preoccupations throughout all this, as if my own were not enough: sorry about that.

A NOTE ON THE AUTHOR

CLAIRE KING's debut novel, *The Night Rainbow*, was published by Bloomsbury in 2013. She is also the author of numerous prize-winning short stories. After fourteen years in southern France, Claire has recently returned to the UK and now lives with her family by a canal in Gloucestershire.

claire-king.com
@ckingwriter